Can a runaway English bride find love with a haunted Irish rebel?

Paris Burke, Dublin's most charismatic barrister, has enough on his mind without the worries of looking after his two youngest sisters. The aftermath of a failed rebellion weighs on his conscience, so when the young English gentlewoman with an unwavering gaze arrives, he asks far too few questions before hiring her on as governess. But her quick wit and mysterious past prove an unexpected temptation.

Rosamund Gorse knows she should not have let Mr. Burke think her the candidate from the employment bureau. But after her midnight escape from a brother bent on marrying her off to a scoundrel, honesty is a luxury she can no longer afford. With his clever mind and persuasive skill, Paris could soon have her spilling her secrets freely just to lift the sorrow from his face. And if words won't work, perhaps kisses would be better?

Hiding under her brother's nose, Rosamund knows she shouldn't take risks. If Paris learns the truth, she might lose her freedom for good. But if she can learn to trust him with her heart, she might discover just the champion she desires…

The Lady's Deception

A Rogues & Rebels Novel

Susanna Craig

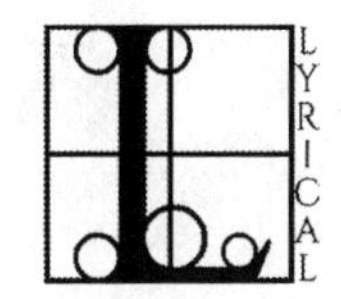

LYRICAL PRESS
Kensington Publishing Corp.
www.kensingtonbooks.com

To the extent that the image or images on the cover of this book depict a person or persons, such person or persons are merely models, and are not intended to portray any character or characters featured in the book.

LYRICAL PRESS BOOKS are published by

Kensington Publishing Corp.
119 West 40th Street
New York, NY 10018

First Electronic Edition: November 2019
eISBN-13: 978-1-5161-0404-8
eISBN-10: 1-5161-0404-8

First Print Edition: November 2019
ISBN-13: 978-1-5161-0405-5
ISBN-10: 1-5161-0405-6

Printed in the United States of America

To the teachers

who inspire us, challenge us, and sacrifice for us.

And to my students,

who push me to be the best teacher I can be.

Acknowledgments

Many thanks to those who make my life, and this book in particular, better, especially Jill Marsal, Esi Sogah, the Kensington team, the lovely ladies of The Drawing Room group, librarian extraordinaire Trenia Napier, Anne, Amy, my mom, my amazing husband, my wildly creative daughter, and of course, my readers.

Chapter 1

The ghost was the last straw.

Lord Dashfort's two children, still grieving the loss of their mother, had been most unwelcoming. An orphan herself, Rosamund had tried to be understanding. She'd ignored the items that had disappeared from her trunk. Shrugged away a grimace when salt had been substituted for sugar in her tea. Swallowed her shriek of surprise when she'd found the half-dozen muddy toads in her bed—accompanied by an equally muddy set of child-sized footprints leading to and from her bedchamber.

But the spectral figure of a child drifting across the south lawn of Kilready Castle went well beyond the realm of an ordinary prank.

Within hours of her arrival at Kilready, Rosamund had begun to hear bits and pieces of the tragic story, whispered through the castle corridors in a brogue almost unintelligible to her English ear: servants' tales of the tragic loss of Lord Dashfort's first son, brought into the world too soon. As soon as she'd been able to travel, Lady Dashfort had left for London, declaring she meant never to return to her husband's Irish estate. The grief-stricken earl had followed her. The servants swore he'd been driven away by the ghostly sounds of babbling in an empty nursery. In the years that had followed, the legend had grown with the lost child. Unexplained footsteps in an abandoned schoolroom, books knocked askew by an unknown hand. And now the shadowy form of a boy who walked the castle grounds on moonlit nights.

Rosamund had been accused of imagining things so often, she was inclined to doubt the proof of her own eyes. But she felt certain she was not imagining this. Not that she believed in ghosts. No, her first reaction to the sight was more disappointment than fear. She liked children. She might have bonded with Alexander and Eugenia over their shared experience of loss. Instead, the two of them had plotted and planned to give her a fright.

In the evenings, after she'd readied for bed, Rosamund often sat by the large window in her chamber, studying the choppy water of the Irish Sea. Now and again, she fancied she caught a glimpse of the neighboring island and wondered how things got on at home. The children had obviously discovered her habit.

As if expecting to find her at the window, a boy who could only be Alexander paused in his progress and looked up, his pointed face unearthly pale. An effect of the moonlight, which bathed everything it touched in pearly luminescence. Still, she shivered and clutched her shawl closer—afraid not of a specter, but of the steep cliff that lay just beyond the scrub into which the boy was now disappearing. How easily he might lose his footing and tumble into the sea. With a soft yelp of alarm, she leaped to her feet and hurried out of her room.

The stairwell, aglow with that same strange light, sent another chill through her. She refused to allow her eyes to dart into corners or to examine the oddly-shaped shadows that stretched up the walls. Her hurried footsteps whispered across the flagstones, and in a few moments she was standing on the threshold of the nursery.

Two child-sized lumps filled two child-sized beds, and in the corner their nurse nodded over some sewing. Sparing nothing more than a frown for the woman's inattention, Rosamund stepped to the bed on the left-hand side of the room.

"Eugenia." A whisper, but only just, and harsh with fear. "Eugenia." A shake this time, and at last the lump stirred. "What can you and your brother have been thinking? Where is he now?"

"Xander?" Eugenia mumbled in a fair imitation of drowsiness. Tousled brown curls made an appearance from beneath the bedclothes, followed by a pair of eyes puffy with sleep. Still, Rosamund was not convinced of either the girl's ignorance of her brother's whereabouts or her innocence in this scheme. Though she was only just seven, she was unquestionably the leader of the pair, considerably more hardened than her soft hair and lisping voice suggested. Alexander—diffident, quiet, and hardly taller than his sister—was far too squeamish to catch toads. She could only guess what coercions had been required to convince him to take a midnight stroll across the lawn.

"What is it, Miss Gorse? Is Xenia ill?"

The sound of Alexander's muffled voice, coming from the neighboring bed, nearly sent Rosamund to the floor.

After a few ineffectual swats, the boy managed to paw the blankets away from his face and sat up, his blond hair sticking out at all angles and his rumpled nightshirt clinging to his slight frame. Unless he had developed the powers of flight, he could not have made it to the nursery ahead of her, changed into his nightclothes, and climbed into bed. Yet there he sat.

Rosamund could not keep herself from reaching out to reassure herself he was not a specter, excusing the action by brushing the hair from his pale, pinched brow.

If Alexander was in the nursery, who—or what—had she seen on the lawn?

Had she perhaps dreamed the whole thing, dozed for a moment and fallen into a nightmare fueled by the ghoulish gossip of the castle's servants? Her brother was always chiding her flights of fancy.

Or had the boy been a villager, bent on poaching or stealing? There seemed to be any number of desperate people in the vicinity of Kilready, and midnight was an hour for mischief. Perhaps she ought to tell someone what she'd seen. But who would believe her? And if by chance someone did, well… Justice would not be served by sending a poor child either to the noose or to New South Wales.

"Why, Miss Gorse."

Lord Dashfort's voice made her jerk as if struck. She turned to find him standing in the doorway of the nursery, her shawl gathered in his hands. Reflexively, she felt for it around her shoulders. When had it slipped away?

"How kind of you to come up to wish the children good night," he said, his eyes traveling over her lightly-clad form.

"What's this? What's this?" The nurse bustled toward them, shaking off sleep more quickly than the children. "Who's feelin' poorly?"

"No one," Rosamund said. "No one. I came because—" With a little shake, she broke off. How could she possibly explain why she'd come? What she'd seen? Or thought she had…

"Why are *you* here, Father?" Alexander demanded.

Lord Dashfort's chuckle did not disguise his annoyance. "You must be half asleep, my boy. Don't I always come and wish you and your sister good night?"

The surprised faces of both the nurse and the children persuaded Rosamund that the answer was *no*.

Nevertheless, Lord Dashfort approached. In a strikingly awkward economy of affection, the earl patted his son on the head with his free hand, at the same time leaning toward his daughter for a kiss. Eugenia squirmed away, her eyes still fixed on Rosamund. "Are *you* quite well, Miss Gorse?" she said. "You look as if you'd seen a ghost."

"I daresay she's simply cold." Lord Dashfort straightened and turned, unfolding Rosamund's shawl as he spoke. Under pretense of assisting her with it, his arm came around her shoulders and did not leave. "Come, Miss Gorse. Let me escort you back to your chamber. It's easy enough to lose one's way in this old pile, especially after dark." He paid little heed to his children's murmured "good nights" or the nurse's curtsy as he steered Rosamund from the room.

Several times as they walked along, she shrugged, trying and failing to dislodge his arm. "Why, you're shivering, my dear Miss Gorse. I hope you haven't taken a chill."

"I'm fine," Rosamund insisted. Or rather, tried to insist. Even to her own ears, her voice lacked all conviction.

"And Eugenia was right. You are pale. Though," he added wryly, "one wishes she had chosen some other simile."

"Yes." Rosamund hesitated. "Although, in truth, I did see *something*—"

"Have my children been repeating the servants' ridiculous stories to you?" His accompanying sigh was deep, and his shoulders must have sunk with it. His arm grew heavier still. "Clearly, they need a steadying hand, the influence of a sensible woman." He paused and gazed down at her. "Poor motherless things..."

They had reached the corridor in which her chamber was located. "I wish you good luck in finding such a woman, my lord. I do believe this place could turn the soberest mind." Her words appeared to take him aback, giving her another opportunity to make a bid for freedom. "I will say good night."

His grip on her shoulders tightened. "So soon?"

"It's very late."

His other arm came around her, caging her between his body and the wall. Her shawl was no barrier to the chill of the stones against her back. Instinctively, her hand rose to his chest and she tried to push him away.

"Come now, Miss Gorse. Surely you will not deny your future husband a good night kiss?"

He had stopped beneath an unlit sconce, casting his expression in shadow. But he must be teasing her. *Future husband?* Much as she might long for a family, marriage to Lord Dashfort was the furthest thing from her mind. Why, the earl was her brother's old school chum, more than twice her age. Worse yet, he—

In the near darkness, his hot, moist mouth grazed her cheek, bringing with it the stench of brandy and mushroom ragout and making her stomach churn. Twisting sharply, she winced as the rough stone snagged her shawl and dug into her skin. "Lord Dashfort, unhand me this instant!"

He relented, but not because of her words. Farther down the corridor, a discreet, masculine cough had broken the stillness.

"Charles," she gasped, slipping away from a stunned Lord Dashfort and hurrying toward her brother.

Her brother regarded her coolly, arms crossed over his chest. "You should be in bed, Rosie."

Arrested in her flight, she rocked back on her heels, thinking of Alexander and Eugenia's pet names for one another. She was only ever *Rosie* when Charles was unhappy with her. Which was most of the time.

"Yes, Charles." With a backward glance at Lord Dashfort, she slipped into her room.

Hardly had the door closed behind her when Charles spoke.

"I am appalled, Dashfort."

For just a moment, foolish hope sparked within her. Of course her brother would defend her honor. Only...only instead of reprimanding Lord Dashfort's shocking conduct, Charles sounded...bored?

"Setterby." Lord Dashfort's voice was little more than a growl. If she didn't know better, she would have thought that the earl and her brother were enemies, rather than friends. "It was your suggestion that I begin to accustom her to the idea of our marriage."

"Yes," said Charles, and the tiny flicker of hope in her breast sputtered. The earl had not been teasing her, after all. No wonder he'd been so inordinately attentive to her during their visit. No wonder the children had been on their worst behavior. They resented their father's plan to remarry. They were doing all they could to prevent their mother's place from being usurped.

How naïve she'd been.

"But I have no intention of allowing you to anticipate the wedding *night*," continued her brother, chiding.

It was not difficult to imagine herself trapped in the unwelcome embrace of an old—well, almost old—man with foul breath and clammy hands and one wife already in the grave. Her shudder rattled the door against which she leaned.

Undisturbed by the sound, her brother continued speaking. "At least, not until I have the money in hand..."

The chill in his voice snuffed the last embers of hope. *Money?* Had she gone back in time when she'd crossed beneath the portcullis of Kilready Castle? Returned to some feudal age? It seemed Charles had done more than arrange what he imagined to be an advantageous match on behalf of his sister. It sounded for all the world as if her brother were trying to *sell* her!

Of course, he *was* forever bemoaning the state of the family finances. But how on earth had he persuaded anyone to pay for the privilege of wedding her?

And what might the earl expect of her in exchange?

She quelled another shudder. Her brother did not like to be gainsaid, as she well knew. But this time she was going to have to put her foot down.

"We agreed on Lady Day," Lord Dashfort was quick to remind him, forgetting to whisper. "I've spoken to Quin, my agent. The new rents will be more than enough to meet your price."

"If your tenants come up to scratch," Charles sneered.

"They haven't much choice, have they?" Lord Dashfort's voice was an odd mixture of anger, desperation, and…guilt?

"From what I've seen, they haven't much of anything. Except, that is, for the wily Mr. Quin."

"He's none of your concern," snapped the earl. "You'll have your money on Monday, Setterby. And on Tuesday—"

"On Tuesday, Rosamund will be yours to deal with." A low laugh. "However you see fit."

Despite herself, she hissed in a sharp breath at his dismissive words. Everyone knew that the first Lady Dashfort had died under suspicious circumstances. She might be Charles's mere half-sister, but didn't he care at all for what became of her? Since their father's will had named him her guardian, she had come to expect Charles's indifference. But this?

Slowly she backed away from the door. The door with no lock to protect her. And if she didn't act quickly, she might find herself a prisoner at Kilready Castle, with or without a lock.

Before the echo of Lord Dashfort's footsteps had entirely faded away, she turned and walked to the armoire. With one finger, she riffled through the dresses hanging there: elegant silks, soft woolens. Time and again Charles had told her he only wanted what was best for her. Like this visit to an old friend in Ireland.

Too far from home for her to resist what he had planned?

Quickly, she removed her nightgown, and slipped into the only dress she owned that did not require a corset or a maid's assistance. She had been under her brother's protection for most of her life. Or thought she had. Now, however, she was going to have to find a way to escape it.

Once clad in an airy confection of muslin in the newest style, far more suited to a ballroom than the outing she was about to undertake, she closed the inlaid door of the wardrobe with a snap. The weight of a bag of fine dresses would only hinder her getaway.

But where would she go? A sympathetic clergyman might be persuaded to take her in. Then again, perhaps it was only in novels that such gentlemen provided sanctuary to unfortunate women. She needed someone bold—or reckless—enough to challenge her brother over the matter of his guardianship. After all, she was nearly one and twenty, almost of an age to take responsibility for herself…though she hadn't the slightest idea how to begin.

So, a lawyer? But she had nothing to offer such a man as compensation for his services. Charles controlled the family purse strings.

Well, she would have to find a way to do without money. If she could make her way to Dublin, surely *someone* would help her.

In a fit of resolve, she strode to the window. The full moon had risen higher, casting a glow almost as bright as daylight. Far below on the lawn, all was quiet. She let her eyes roam over the stretch of velvety grass and peer into the shadows beneath the shrubbery. Nothing. Not even a tomcat on the prowl. What *had* she seen?

A servant boy, or some child from the village. She must have imagined the resemblance. But when she tried to call up the unknown boy's face, even her mind's eye seemed determined to betray her. She could see only Alexander, or a child enough like him to be his—

Nonsense. Alexander's only sibling was Eugenia. And Rosamund did not intend to be party to any arrangement that might give him another.

Stretching out her arm, she caught the shutter, jerked it inward, and latched it tight, throwing the chamber into darkness.

Chapter 2

At the knelling of church bells, Paris Burke swore—blasphemy, no doubt, but what did it matter? He was damned already.

He paused in his descent from Constitution Hill to shake the sound from his head. The call to Evensong at Christchurch? Surely not. The waters of the Liffey must be making the bells echo, doubling their peals. It could not possibly be as late as…

He pulled his watch from his waistcoat pocket, tilted its face toward the fading sunlight, and at its confirmation of the hour, swore again.

During the years of his life when he might have offered ample excuses for running late—the combined and sometimes competing demands of the law and his hopes for Ireland's liberation—only once had he failed to keep an assignation. The disastrous effects of that mistake would haunt him for the rest of his days. Fortunately, the consequences of missing an appointment with Mrs. Fitzhugh were not so dire. Nonetheless, he regretted what it revealed about the kind of man he'd become.

Tucking the watch away, he glanced over his shoulder in the direction of King's Inns—not with longing, precisely. Oh, the dinner in the commons had been good enough, and the wine had flowed freely. Time was, the company alone would have been enough to call him back. The brotherhood of jurisprudence. The discussions, the debates.

Tonight, though, he had felt certain absences too strongly. The faces that could no longer join them. The voices that would never be heard again. No matter how many times he had signaled for his cup to be filled, their ghostly shadows had refused to be dispelled.

For the first time, he was not sorry he'd been forced to give up his lodgings closer to the courts. The walk across the city would help to clear his head. And give him time to concoct some explanation for his lateness, though whatever he produced would do little to blunt the disappointment with which he was bound to be greeted.

He took another half-dozen strides, rounding the corner of Church Street to pass in front of the Four Courts. The last of the daylight cast a jagged chiaroscuro across the ground, the building itself too new for its shadows to have grown familiar to his eyes. From the gloom, something slipped into his path. What sort of claret had they been pouring, that it continued to conjure these spectral apparitions, this one with pale hair and paler skin? He swore a third time.

"You ought to mind your tongue in the presence of a lady," the wraith said primly, stepping into the light and resolving itself into the perfectly ordinary figure of a blonde woman wearing a pelisse the color of Portland stone.

No, not *perfectly ordinary*. Perfectly ordinary women did not materialize on the King's Inns Quay. They did not have hair the color of summer butter, spilling from beneath a ridiculous frippery of a hat that looked a little worse for wear. Nor did they have eyes the color of—well, no sea he had ever had the pleasure to know. With another shake of his head, he stepped closer, finding himself in need of the support of hewn granite.

"I'm looking for someone," she said, warily watching his every move. Her brows knitted themselves into a tight frown. "A lawyer. You see, I—"

"You're English." Part observation, part accusation. She wasn't the first beautiful woman his fancy had invented, but never before had his imagination betrayed his politics so thoroughly.

"I'm Miss Gorse," she replied, as if that decided the matter.

Oddly enough, it did. Because only a real woman could have such a prickly name. And such a prickly voice. Which, heaven help him, was still speaking.

"—and his two children—"

Damn it all. His sisters. He'd promised them, when the last interview had turned up no likely candidate, that Mrs. Fitzhugh would surely know of someone suitable. And now he'd have to confess that he'd—

A tongue of wind licked along the river, rippling the water before gusting up the face of the imposing edifice in whose shelter they stood. He pushed himself up a little straighter, bolstered as much by the cool air as by the cornerstone's sharp edge where it fitted neatly along the groove of his spine.

Two children... Was it possible? He'd understood the meeting with Mrs. Fitzhugh to be preliminary, but perhaps she had not waited to speak with him before deciding on the right person for the job.

"You're looking for a lawyer, you say?"

Her mouth, already forming other words, hung open a moment before shaping an answer to his question. "Yes. I thought—"

"Mrs. Fitzhugh sent you to find Mr. Burke at King's Inns, I gather."

"Er—"

"Well, you've found him. I'm Paris Burke. Barrister. Of course, you'll really be in my father's employ. A man without children isn't likely to need a governess, now is he?" His wry laugh ricocheted off the stone walls, startling a flock of drowsy rooks who cawed their disapproval.

Her lips were parted once again, but this time no words came. She was watching him with wide eyes that did not narrow, even when she at last closed her mouth and jerked her head in some uncertain motion, neither disagreement nor agreement.

"My sisters will be delighted to meet you, Miss Gorse. I am surprised, though, that Mrs. Fitzhugh didn't send you directly to Merrion Square."

"I don't—" She paused, wetted her lips, and appeared to weigh her reply before beginning again. "Is it far?"

"No more than a mile. An English mile, to be precise," he added, curving his mouth into a sort of smile. He would not have guessed that Mrs. Fitzhugh had a sense of humor. To send him, of all people, an Englishwoman… "At least we've a fine night for a stroll."

After a moment's hesitation, she dipped her head in a nod. "Indeed, Mr. Burke. I had no thought this morning that the day would take a turn for the better."

"Ah, well. It mightn't've, you know." Turning, he set off along the quayside. "An Irish spring is not to be predicted."

"This is my first," she said. "My first Irish spring, that is."

Last spring, then, she'd been elsewhere. In England, presumably. Far from the turmoil that had enveloped Dublin and the surrounding countryside. Far from the rebellion that had taken the lives of so many. And for what? For naught, for naught…

The warm glow of the claret guttered like a candle, struggling to withstand the damp, clammy mist rising from the Liffey. He had not realized he had lengthened his stride until he heard the sounds of someone struggling to keep up.

"Mr. Burke?" She had one hand pressed to her side and a hitch in her gait. "I wonder if we might walk a bit more slowly."

When she reached his side, he held out his free arm and she took it, not with the perfunctory brush of her fingertips, but with her whole hand, leaning heavily against him. *Odd.* She was petite, but she didn't look frail.

"Shall I hail a sedan chair, Miss Gorse?" Though truthfully, this was an unlikely spot to hail anything but trouble. And the more he thought of Mrs. Fitzhugh directing a woman to meet him here, in this fashion, the less he liked it. Why, he might have been detained at commons for hours, and she left alone as darkness fell…

Her touch lightened as she bristled. "I can walk." Her step was almost brisk as they crossed the Carlisle Bridge. "So you're in need of a governess?"

"For my sisters. Daphne and Bellis. Aged ten and eight, respectively. You'll find them as ignorant as most girls their age, I daresay."

She drew back her shoulders at that description. "Their previous governess was not firm enough with them?"

"I'm almost embarrassed to admit it, but they haven't any previous governess. They are the youngest of the six of us and shockingly spoiled. My father in particular has always been prone to indulgence where they were concerned."

Some emotion—he hesitated to call it *disapproval*—sketched across her face. "Then whatever made him decide to hire a governess now?"

"He knows nothing of the matter, Miss Gorse."

Those words brought her up short. "Will he not be angry that you hired someone to teach his daughters without reference to his authority?"

He very nearly smiled at such an image of his father. "My parents are in London until the summer. After they left, I determined it would be best if I hired a temporary governess for the girls. I did not expect it would be so difficult."

A group of young men, Trinity students, passed in a noisy gaggle and were gone. Beneath the high walls surrounding the college, the evening shadows were deeper still. But not too deep for him to read a question in her eyes. A question for which he had never yet determined a satisfactory answer.

He'd already done a masterful job of proving himself unequal to the responsibilities of an eldest son and brother. Why in God's name *had* his parents entrusted him with the care of two young girls?

"Not much farther now," he said brusquely. Obligingly, Miss Gorse resumed walking, though her pace had slowed and she was limping noticeably now. But she made no complaint, and he had the distinct impression she would not thank him for enquiring about it.

To cover the sound of her shuffling, irregular footsteps, he passed the last quarter mile regaling her with stories about the girls: Daphne's interest in learning the harp, which he attributed to their eldest sister Cami's unfortunate book—although he omitted that particular detail from his account. And Bell's fondness for a game of cricket, in which both he and their brother Galen had been wont to indulge her.

On the north side of Merrion Square, he stopped. "And here we are."

She climbed the steps of Number 3 as if they were mountains, tottering a bit at the end while he fished for his key and opened the door to let them in. It hardly seemed possible for two girls, both slight of build, to make as much noise as Daphne and Bell as they thundered down the stairs from the drawing room to greet them on the landing.

"Did you see Mrs. Fitzhugh?" demanded Bell.

At the same time, Daphne asked, "Is she our new governe—?"

Miss Gorse looked from one to the other, gave a wan smile, and collapsed on the floor.

Bell's eyes grew round and her lower lip quavered. "I didn't mean to frighten her to death, Paris. Honest I didn't."

"She isn't dead, eejit," Daphne declared, nudging her younger sister with an elbow.

"*Silence.*"

Years of training had given Paris exceptional control over his voice. It could command a crowd. It could compel a confession in the courtroom. But never in all his life had it actually managed to quiet his youngest sisters.

They were both staring at him now, wide-eyed and wobbly-lipped, and he knew in another moment there would be tears. *Oh God, anything but tears.*

"She's just fainted. Bell, run downstairs and ask Molly to make us a pot of tea, will you?" Bellis nodded. With one backward glance at the woman at his feet, she was gone. "And Daphne? If you could…" *Could what?* The clarity that had come with the cool evening air had flown, and the lingering fumes of claret in his brain showed very little interest in forming themselves into a coherent request. He knelt beside Miss Gorse, who was deathly pale and breathing shallowly.

"I'll see if I can find a vinaigrette," Daphne offered.

"Yes. Thank you. And I'll take Miss Gorse upstairs." Because he couldn't very well leave her in a heap in the foyer, though if this was the sort of weak-spirited person Mrs. Fitzhugh recommended for a post as governess to two energetic girls…

He slipped his hands beneath her and rose, expecting to be pulled off balance beneath her weight. But she was no burden at all. Tucking her against his chest, he ascended the stairs, thinking first of the sofa in the drawing room, then bypassing it in favor of a proper bed in a chamber one floor up, the room that Cami and Erica had once shared. As he laid her atop the coverlet, she stirred and murmured but did not wake. His fingers fumbled to unpin her hat. More golden locks sprang free, tumbling over the pillow and across her brow. He brushed them carefully from her eyes. She wasn't feverish, at least. Pray God, it was nothing contagious that had caused her to faint dead away. Perhaps he ought to send Molly for the physician who lived across the square.

He turned his attention next to unbuttoning her gray pelisse with swift, businesslike motions. Then his hands traveled to hers, tugging free her gloves. Her fingers were icy cold, but he paused to note with relief the steady drum of her pulse in one fine-boned wrist. At last, he removed her shoes and found that her hems were damp, stained with grass and fresh mud. The shoes themselves were shockingly worn down. On the sole of one was a hole the size of a three shilling piece. No wonder she had limped! It looked as if she'd walked considerably farther today than the distance from Four Courts to Merrion Square.

Where had she come from? Far enough away that she could have collapsed from the fatigue of her journey? Surely Mrs. Fitzhugh must have known he was more than capable of paying for suitable transportation.

In the bottom of the wardrobe he found a blanket and laid it over her supine form. When Daphne returned holding out a vinaigrette, he shook his head. "I think perhaps we'd best let her rest." Already, some color was coming back into the woman's face.

"But what about her dress?" Daphne's cheeks pinked. "And her—her… *stays*?" The last word escaped in an embarrassed whisper.

His arms retained a memory of the young woman's soft curves. "She isn't wearing any, Daph."

Before his too-precocious sister could ask how he knew, he waved her from the room, pausing on the threshold for one last look.

She put him in mind of the princess in some fairy tale, imprisoned by a wicked spell. In repose, her expression had lost its wariness, its prickliness, and he realized for the first time how young she was. Barely twenty, if he had to guess. Hardly the woman of experience he'd requested.

Silently, he closed the door behind them. The mystery of Miss Gorse would have to wait until morning.

Chapter 3

Noises woke her. The sibilance of children's whispered voices. Likely Eugenia and Alexander plotting just outside her door, though Rosamund could muster very little curiosity about what they were saying. Last night's escapade had caused trouble enou—

She squeezed her eyelids more tightly shut, as if her sight might betray her. But her other senses were quick to muster reassurance. She had indeed escaped Kilready and marriage to Lord Dashfort. Instead of damp stone walls and musty tapestries, she was surrounded now by scents of dried lavender and laundry starch and… Good heavens, was that a whiff of *farmyard*?

Despite the soft surface on which she now lay, her muscles' assorted twinges and aches pushed her to recall yesterday's uncomfortable adventure. The dark, dreary walk from the castle to the village and beyond. Begging a passing farmer to take pity on her. The jouncing, jostling ride in his cart, seated atop a sack of grain, holding a pair of chickens and fending off the advances of a persistent nanny goat that had taken a fancy to her chip bonnet. Another long walk from Dublin's outskirts into the city proper, through unfamiliar streets, amid unfamiliar faces, her destination uncertain. Pain in her feet, her legs, her head…

More wisps of memory floated through her mind, thinner now than high clouds on a summer's day. She'd found herself in the shadows of some hulking building near the river. She'd met…a man. A handsome, dark-haired man. Too handsome to be trusted. But in an extraordinary turn of events, Mr.—Burke, wasn't it?—had claimed to be a lawyer. He'd also clearly been expecting someone. A woman. And she'd…oh, had she really let him imagine *she* was the one he sought? Had she foolishly accompanied him to his home? And had she—had she *fainted*?

Again, her body remembered. Strong arms. The soft wool of his coat and the mingled scents of tobacco and his cologne. The welcome cocoon of heat, when she'd been so cold. He'd carried her up the stairs. He'd put her to bed. He'd—

Involuntarily, her fingers—her ungloved fingers—curled into the textured surface of a quilted linen coverlet.

"Look, Daph! She moved!"

The whisper, somewhat louder than before, came from inside the room.

"I told you she wasn't dead." A second girl's voice, laced with exasperation. "Eejit."

All at once Rosamund opened her eyes, tossed the blanket aside, and sat up, ignoring the protest of muscles whose very existence was something of a revelation, trying not to squint against the morning light. Two pairs of eyes peered over the foot of the bed, staring as if she were indeed a corpse come back to life.

She'd only been able to spare half an ear to Mr. Burke's ramblings about his sisters, focused as she'd been on setting one foot in front of the other and swallowing the gasp of pain that rose to her lips with each step. Something about how he'd found himself unexpectedly responsible for their care and in need of assistance. And he'd assumed, somehow, that Rosamund was a—a *governess.* Absurd, really.

Then again…

A quick glance around the chamber revealed a second, neatly-made bed, a plain, old-fashioned wardrobe, a sturdy desk. A comfortable room in a modest, respectable home. Her brother would never think to look for her here.

In exchange for food and shelter, in exchange for the perfect hiding place, could she pretend to be a governess? Like the Burke girls, she'd never had one. Could she give instruction in French, mathematics, ladylike deportment, and…and whatever else governesses did?

Rosamund shifted her gaze from one sister to the other. They were watching her eagerly now. Expectantly. No, this would be no game of pretend. Not to them.

Well, then. What would a governess do next?

She fixed the elder girl with what she hoped was a stern eye. "You mustn't call your sister an—" Truth be told, she wasn't quite sure *what* the girl had said. But the tone in which the unfamiliar word had been spoken had been sufficient to make its meaning clear. "Ladies do not hurl insults."

The younger gave a triumphant smile. "Yes, miss," her sister murmured, almost penitent.

With Herculean effort she hoped would pass for ladylike grace, Rosamund swung her legs over the edge of the bed and sat, ramrod straight in spite of the hollow feeling in both her head and her belly. She motioned the girls to stand in front of her and studied them for a moment. Their soft brown hair reminded her of Eugenia Carteret's, but there the resemblance ended, for she could by no means imagine their expressions capable of that child's sly knowingness. "I do not believe we were properly introduced last night."

"I'm Daphne," the elder said. "Daphne Burke. And this is Bell," she added, nudging her sister into a curtsy.

"French for beauty," Rosamund observed.

"No," the girl in question corrected boldly. "Bell." She shifted her hips so that her softly rounded skirts swayed in imitation of a ringing bell. "It's short for Bellis."

"We're all named after plants," Daphne explained. "*Bellis* is daisy and *daphne* is—"

"Poisonous!" piped Bell.

Rosamund could not keep her lips from twitching with amusement, but thankfully she managed to avert a very un-governesslike laugh.

"Papa studies botany, you see," Daphne went on, shooting Bell a disapproving look.

"So does Erica."

Another unusual name. "Your…sister?"

"Yes, our middle sister. This is her room. Or was. She's married now, to an Englishman. And so is Cami—Camellia. The eldest of us. She's—she's in…" Daphne screwed up her face as if trying to remember the name of a place, then beamed as she parroted what she'd been told: "She's in expectation of a happy event."

"It means she's having a baby," Bell explained in a confidential whisper, not unlike the one that had woken Rosamund.

Rosamund's lips twitched again. And when she nodded, she kept her head bowed a moment longer than was strictly necessary to hide her expression. *Precocious?* Was that the word to describe the girls' behavior? Would it be her job as governess to check it? What a shame that would be…

"That's why Papa and Mama went to London," Daphne went on.

"We were to have gone with them. But I got the spots." Guilt infused Bell's confession.

Daphne shrugged philosophically. "So they left us with Paris instead."

When she'd heard his name, she'd assumed a reference to Shakespeare or Greek mythology. She'd not imagined its botanical origins. With what sort of plant did he share it? Something striking, she felt certain. And—if Daphne's name was any indication—potentially dangerous.

She remembered that she had given him her name as well. No use in trying to disguise it now. "I'm Miss Gorse."

"Truly?" Bell giggled.

"Papa would say it was a sign you were meant to be a part of this family," Daphne said, more diplomatically. "He's always delighted by anything to do with plants."

At the word *family*, her heart gave a wayward twinge. "And your sister, the botanist? What would she say?"

"Erica? Oh, she'd tell you all sorts of things you didn't want to know. About where gorse grows—"

"Which is precisely *everywhere* in Ireland," Bell interjected.

"And probably some other stuff no one cares about. The shape of its leaves or its root structure or how it survives under adverse conditions."

How it survives under adverse conditions... Perhaps it was in her blood, then, the instinct to fight for survival. She took another quick glance around the room, its pale blue walls brightened by the light of a single, large window. Hardly adverse conditions, even if it wasn't quite the style of living to which the daughter of a viscount was accustomed. "It sounds to me as though you had an eager teacher in your sister."

"Cami was always trying to get us to remember stuff too," Bell agreed wearily, which earned her another nudge. She ignored it. "What's your given name, Miss Gorse?"

Impertinence. She ought to nip it in the bud. Except that the very phrase threatened to bring another smile to her lips. Rather too on the nose when debating how best to discipline the children of a botanist, wasn't it?

"Rosamund. It means—"

"Rose of the world," Bell translated easily.

Hadn't Mr. Burke described his sisters as *ignorant*? Why, this slip of a girl knew as much Latin as her supposed governess. Likely more. When Rosamund could not entirely contain her bemusement, Bell gave a small, embarrassed shrug. "I like words."

"Then," Rosamund declared firmly, setting her hands on the mattress at either side of her hips to push herself to her feet, "we'd best begin our lessons."

She wobbled. Tipped precariously forward. Managed at the last moment to shift her balance so that when she sank down, it was onto the bed and not the floor this time.

"You'd best have breakfast first, I think," Daphne said.

Bell eyed her critically. "And maybe a wash, too."

"I'll send Molly. She's our housemaid."

"Cami and Erica left some things in the clothespress," Bell added with a nod toward the wardrobe. "You can borrow whatever you need until your trunk arrives."

Her trunk. Trunk*s*, actually. But dresses weren't all she'd left behind, hopefully forever, at Kilready Castle. Rosamund hadn't the strength to contain the shudder that passed through her. "Thank you," she managed, though the words came out as little more than a whisper. "I shall join you in the schoolroom in an hour, then."

Bell looked quizzically at Daphne. Daphne shrugged, then turned back to Rosamund and nodded. "Yes, Miss Gorse." With a single, quick curtsy, they were gone, leaving her alone in quiet contemplation of the enormity of what she had done.

How long would it take Mr. Paris Burke—who, for all his good looks, might prove to be as sharp as one of his bevy of sisters—to uncover her deception and send her away?

* * * *

Chasing the fading fragments of a particularly pleasant dream, Paris burrowed deeper into his pillow. But mere goose down could do little to mute the grinding, rumbling, thumping din that had awakened him.

At first, the noise seemed to have its origins inside his head, which throbbed like a fresh wound. Had miniature workmen sawed their way into his skull and taken tiny pickaxes to his brain? *Good Lord.* He must have deceived himself as to the quality—or quantity—of claret he'd consumed last night. Perhaps both.

He ought to know by now that it was little use trying to drown his sorrows; they'd long since learned to swim.

Cautiously he squinted, opening one eye just enough to determine it was midmorning. After a moment, he hoisted himself up on one elbow, tried in vain to force both eyes open at once, and finally collapsed on the pillow in defeat to crawl back into his dream. Something about a woman…

Another grating rumble—from above his head, not inside it, and accompanied this time by Molly's tuneless whistle as she swept into the room—drove away the lingering possibility of losing himself in sleep.

"Och, Mr. Paris, 'tis a fearsome racket they're makin'. I do believe they're after wreckin' the house."

The girls. He might've known. But what could they possibly want in the attic—short of tearing up a few floorboards, if the noise was any indication?

He sat up in bed, scrubbed his hand over the rough growth of a day's beard, and considered his options, the least appealing of which was confronting his sisters over their latest escapade. A year ago, he would've been safely ensconced in his rooms near King's Inns, none the wiser to their mischief. Now, however, the best he could hope was that the ruckus would be muted if he retreated to his father's study, a floor below.

Having deposited a can of steaming water near the washstand, Molly moved to hang freshly pressed linen in the wardrobe dividing his bed from Galen's now empty one. Paris found himself longing for the days when he could have ordered his younger sibling to intervene before the girls brought the ceiling caving in upon them. But Galen had chosen Oxford over Trinity, eager to get away from Dublin—and his only brother.

Crash!

Turning, Molly set her hands to her hips and fixed him with the sort of glare that might have earned her a reprimand in a more rigidly-run household. "A schoolroom, she wanted," the young woman muttered. "An' how's anyone to learn with the likes o' *that*, I'd like to know?"

Paris tried and failed to shape meaning from the housemaid's words. "*Who* wanted a schoolroom?"

"The new governess."

His hand slid absently from his jaw. *Governess?* But he hadn't…

Oh, Lord. The dream. The woman. With golden hair and summer blue eyes and a voice like—

Molly possessed a selection of fine Irish sayings for any occasion, some of which he and his siblings had been known to borrow. But the only words that rose to Paris's lips now were a string of English curses. Fitting, he supposed. Since he'd evidently hired a damn English governess.

Just how much *had* he drunk last night?

"Jesus, Mary, and Joseph," Molly exclaimed when another thump rattled the ceiling and sent down a shower of plaster dust.

"I'll take care of it," Paris declared, rising. Forgetting he had crawled into bed wearing nothing but his drawers.

Ever practical, Molly looked him up and down, lifted one brow, then reached into the wardrobe to hand out his dressing gown. "You'll be wantin' this, then." She winked. "Unless you were hopin' to persuade her to stay."

Chapter 4

A quarter of an hour later—washed, dressed, and grumpy—Paris marched to the upper regions of the house to confront Miss Gorse. Over that brief span of time, however, the din from above had subsided. At the foot of the narrow attic staircase, he paused. If the worst was over, perhaps he could safely ignore it. Except, of course, for the matter of the pretty young stranger he'd met on the quay, brought into his family home, carried to bed, and… *Oh, yes.* Hired to be his sisters' new governess.

He took the steps two at a time.

There was no landing to speak of, and he stepped through the open door into what once had been used as servants' quarters but almost a decade ago had been repurposed for a nursery. The furnishings were sparse: two beds, a washstand, and a lidless box containing dolls' clothes and other playthings, tucked beneath a small square window. Across one corner of the room, a curtain had been hung to form a dressing area, as the ceiling slanted at a sharp angle, altogether too low to accommodate a wardrobe. He had to duck his head unless he stood in the very center of the room.

Perhaps he ought to have insisted that Daphne and Bell move into Cami and Erica's old bedchamber, beside his. But they had responded to his suggestion with open reluctance, and as his gaze traveled around the room, he thought he understood why. He tried to see it as his littlest sisters must. Dust motes twirled and sparkled magically in a shaft of morning light. All was otherwise neatly arranged, but not, so far as he could judge, by Molly's hand. It was not the sort of space that invited intrusion, even of the servant variety.

Good God, was he actually jealous of his little sisters' hideaway?

A low murmur of voices drew his attention to the partition that divided the top floor of the house into bedroom and attic storage. The door in that thin wall stood ajar, and he moved noiselessly to peer through the opening.

He couldn't remember when he'd last looked into the attic. Hadn't it been crowded and rather disorganized? Less crowded now, since five members of the household had put their trunks and traveling paraphernalia to their intended uses. What remained had been dragged to the perimeter of the room and tucked under the eaves; he could see the tracks in the dust on the floor. The broken pieces of a discarded lamp had been swept into a neat pile near the door. Beneath the peak of the roof stood two makeshift desks, side by side. To the right sat Daphne in a Windsor-back chair missing two spokes, her toes tucked into a groove in the floor to keep them from swinging. On his left, Bell perched on an upturned box, her humble seat padded by a shawl he remembered his mother wearing years ago, now darned and wrinkled almost beyond recognition. Books had been stacked at each girl's place, but neither of his sisters was reading. They were looking up expectantly at their teacher.

Miss Gorse stood before them, her back to the room's only window, a mirror of the one in the girls' bedroom: small, square, but west-facing and therefore comparatively dim. No motes twinkled here, though the air was thick with dust stirred up by the trio's morning work. Paris could feel it in his nose and the back of his throat. Still, what light there was caught in her golden hair, setting aglow a few wisps that had worked free from the simple knot at the back of her head. Even across the room, he could make out the brilliant blue of her eyes.

Because, he realized belatedly, she was staring right at him.

Pairing the slight lift of her chin with an arrow-straight spine, she betrayed little trace of the fainting flower he remembered from last night. "Did we disturb you, Mr. Burke? My apologies." Her voice was cool, her accent crisp. *Aristocratic*, he should call it, if he didn't know better.

Bell spun on her seat, bunching the shawl beneath her. Her face was bright, despite a smudge of dirt across one cheek. "Oh, Paris. Isn't it marvelous?"

"Miss Gorse said we needed a proper schoolroom," Daphne explained.

"And this," he said, with a quick and deliberately dismissive glance around the cramped, dirty room, "is your notion of proper, Miss Gorse?"

More proper, perhaps, than the drawing room, where he and his siblings had taken lessons at their father's knee over the course of more than twenty years. Nevertheless, something about the woman's presumption aggravated him. How very like an Englishwoman to burst into an Irish household and begin giving orders about its management, with no concern for how things had always been done or what might suit the people who lived there.

Swiftly, smoothly, she slipped between the desks and strode toward him in a dress that looked vaguely familiar. One of Erica's? Its skirts were streaked where she had wiped her hands. Eddies of dust swirled across the floor in her wake. "Daphne and Bellis—"

"Bell," he corrected automatically.

The governess's lips narrowed as her nostrils flared. "The girls indicated that the, ah—" Her pert nose twitched. "The, ah—" Her eyelids crinkled and she inhaled sharply. "Ahh—"

No one would deny that Miss Gorse was delicate. Her petite, fine-boned features would not look out of place on a porcelain doll. Ladylike in her deportment. The sort of woman one expected to sneeze with petite, delicate, ladylike sneezes, when such an affliction could not be avoided. Perhaps two or three little squeaks in a row: *choo, choo, choo*. Something in the nature of a timid mouse.

Instead, she blasted a single "Ahh—*choo*!" that ricocheted around the small room, bouncing from the rafters to the bare wood floor and into Paris's aching head.

"God bless you," Daphne said after a moment, sounding genuinely worried that the sneeze might have parted the governess's soul from her body. Bell giggled. Wordlessly, he reached into his breast pocket, withdrew a handkerchief, and handed it to Miss Gorse.

"We'll discuss the matter downstairs," he said, fighting to keep his voice stern as she dabbed daintily at the end of her nose. As if they had not all just heard what that instrument was capable of.

"Of course, Mr. Burke." She folded the square of linen but did not offer to return it to him. "I've scheduled a break in the girls' lessons at half past eleven. I'll be glad to speak with you then."

A good barrister was never speechless. Paris was an excellent barrister. His lips parted automatically to form a reply.

When none came, he instead gave a sharp nod—Lord, but if his head meant to split in two, he wished it would just get on with the job—and left the room.

Most of the first floor was taken up by a drawing room that spanned the house from front to back and in which the family did the greater part of both its working and its playing. At the rear of the room stood his father's desk, surrounded by bookcases and faded botanical prints, some sketched by Erica when she was a girl. Occasionally, his father met with clients in that room. In theory, the half containing his desk could be partitioned from the rest of the space by a pair of folding doors that Paris had never in his life seen closed.

If he had not imagined that time and disuse had rendered them immobile, he would have shut them now, though he could not say whether he hoped to close himself in or to close the world out.

In any case, he held no illusions that mere doors would have kept him free of Molly, who once more entered without knocking, this time carrying a laden breakfast tray. Not waiting for instruction, she deposited the tray on his father's desk and set about pouring steaming coffee. He took the cup from her with a nod that quickly transformed into a grimace.

"Still got a head like a bear, Mr. Paris? Well, eat up," she advised. "It'll take the edge off."

Warily, he eyed the contents of the tray: fried eggs, oatmeal, and a dish of what he rather hoped was stewed fruit and not something worse. His stomach quickly joined his head in its protest. With a flick of his free hand, he waved the food away. "They have indeed made a schoolroom in the attic," he said after swallowing some coffee. "Moved everything that wasn't nailed down. That was the racket we heard."

She hoisted the tray to her hip. "Must've churned up a fair bit of dust too."

He could not entirely contain the twitch of amusement that rose to his lips as he recalled Miss Gorse's explosive sneeze. "Indeed."

Molly sighed, presumably at the unwelcome addition to her workload. "May a body ask *why*?"

"The new governess says it isn't proper for children to have lessons in a drawing room." He gestured about himself with the cup as he spoke.

Dark liquid nearly sloshed over the rim but was ultimately kept within its proper bounds by the force of the housemaid's glare. "I should think that'd be for you to say."

He almost nodded in agreement, then thought better of it, for the sake of both his head and his pride. He shrugged instead. "What do I know of educating young girls? I've given her full authority in the matter." Or more accurately, he'd abdicated his own.

Molly turned to leave. "Well, a bit o' peace'll be welcome enough, I suppose," she said. "What will you do with yourself now, Mr. Paris?"

"Work."

She paused to cast a glance over her shoulder, half scold, half worry.

Clever and quick, Paris had been born to the practice of the law. Benefitted in equal measure by his father's reputation and his own savvy, he had never lacked for important cases once he'd been called to the bar. Whenever the atmosphere of the courtroom had grown stale, he had let himself imagine the day he might be elected to the Irish Parliament. Then rumors of its dissolution had begun to swirl. Just a few months earlier, the Irish Bar had passed a resolution against legislation intended to join this once proud kingdom to its enemy.

But by then, Paris no longer cared. Since the rebellion he'd found himself more and more drawn to the sort of work he once would have considered beneath him, defending clients no other barrister would touch. Devastatingly straightforward cases, they'd given him ample time to reflect on his mistakes. So many mistakes. So many cases. And so rarely was justice served.

The law, his great passion, had become his penance. Some days, his punishment.

A punishment he knew he deserved.

The work was never-ending. Sometimes, he suspected that his parents had contrived to leave Daphne and Bell behind to give him some other occupation. A distraction. His mother in particular cherished the hope that he would begin to yearn for family ties. Love and marriage. Children of his own.

Paris, however, knew better than to dream such dreams. Just as he knew that his sisters were far better off under someone else's tutelage and care. Even the sort of governess who seemed more accustomed to giving orders than taking them.

"Did Miss Gorse happen to mention where she last was employed?" he asked.

"Not a word of it to me, sir," Molly replied as she crossed the threshold.

Nor to him. She'd walked a long way yesterday, that could not be denied. He recalled the sharp contrast between the condition of her clothing and its quality. Not exactly well-suited to the schoolroom, and far better than he would have imagined a governess could afford. Where were the rest of Miss Gorse's things? Why had she walked so far? Had something driven her from her previous post, and if so, what?

The steady throb in his temples threatened to drown out those questions, despite their importance. He took another fortifying gulp of coffee and resolved to ask them as soon as she came downstairs. Yes, he trusted Mrs. Fitzhugh's judgment; her employment agency had come highly recommended. But it never hurt to be thorough. Miss Gorse was, after all, quite young.

Not at all what he had been expecting.

Surely he could spare a few moments to look in on the schoolroom now and again. Observe the new governess at work.

For his sisters' sake. Of course.

Chapter 5

When Rosamund had responded to Mr. Burke's peremptory summons by naming the hour she would be willing to meet, she had been thinking only of a way to gain time, acting instinctively to avoid a confrontation, or worse, a dismissal. Until she had seen his expression, the sardonic arch to one brow, she had not fully considered how such a retort might be received from a…well, a servant, she supposed. Or as good as.

She had also neglected to consider the problem posed by the lack of a clock.

Well, there *was* a clock. An ormolu mantel clock shaped like a bird nesting in some otherworldly plant. Broken, like so many other things that had been stuffed into the attic and forgotten for years. Why couldn't Mr. Burke have forgotten about her, too?

For a moment, she had actually let herself hope that the man had drunk enough last night to make remembering impossible. Though of course if he had, he surely would have stumbled when carrying her up the stairs, and then they would have ended up on the floor, dazed and breathless, their limbs tangled together…

"Do you think my brother handsome, miss?"

"I beg your pardon?" She shot a look at Bell, but could not bring herself to meet the girl's gaze. She knew she'd been caught staring, once again, at the spot where he had stood. When he had appeared in the doorway, dark eyes narrowed, dark hair mussed, dark beard unshaven, she certainly would not have taken him for a barrister. A highwayman, perhaps.

"All the ladies seem to," Daphne said. "Some of them even go to the public trials and sit in the gallery, just to ogle him in that silly wig. Can you imagine anything more dull?"

Rosamund reminded herself that her sole interest in Mr. Burke was his legal expertise. Her only concern was freeing herself from her guardian's authority. "I'm sure his cases are fascinating," she insisted, not quite sure whether she was defending him or the folly of her own sex. In any case, neither girl looked persuaded by the argument.

"Maybe." Daphne shrugged. "Anyway, that was mostly before the fighting."

Rosamund knew very little about what had transpired in Dublin last spring, beyond the London papers' staunch reassurances that the Irish rebels had been easily routed and a French invasion thwarted. But yesterday's walk through the compact city had made one thing clear: the upheaval would have been felt here universally.

"Before he joined the Knighted Irishmen," Bell clarified.

"*U-nited*," corrected Daphne, annoyed. She was clearly on the verge of appending the usual *eejit*, then realized what she'd admitted and slapped her hand over her mouth instead.

Rosamund only narrowly stopped herself from mirroring the gesture. Paris Burke was a member of the United Irishmen? But…but they were radicals. Traitors. Why, if that was true, he ought by rights to be in prison. Or…or dead.

"Everything changed because everyone *left*," Daphne explained flatly, glossing over her misstep. "First Cami, then Erica. Now Galen's gone to Oxford. And I know it's only right that Mama and Papa wanted to visit all of them, but…"

Rosamund heard worry in Daphne's voice, more than petulance. "You have one sibling still here." Odd reassurance from one who knew, better than most, the woes that might befall a girl left alone in the care of her brother. She had no means to measure the strength of the Burke siblings' bond except by the weakness of her own. Did Mr. Burke treat his sisters poorly? She would not exactly call his behavior toward them warm or loving. Neither had she observed any signs of fear in Daphne and Bell. Then again, even she had not always been afraid…

Daphne shrugged. "Sort of. He's different now. Too busy."

"Too angry," her younger sister interjected in a hesitant whisper.

"In any case, he's made it clear he didn't want to be stuck with us." A challenge flashed in Daphne's eyes, though it did not entirely mask her hurt. "That's why he hired you."

Rosamund let her gaze wander to the window, streaked with grime like everything else. He *hadn't* hired her. She hadn't the faintest notion what she was about. And the girls—

Wait. Was that a clock? On the face of some building in the distance? She reached up to clean a circle on the glass. Yes. Yes, it was. With narrowed eyes she could just make out the time: a quarter of ten. She wiped once more, then realized she was using Mr. Burke's handkerchief to polish the window. The once-pristine linen was streaked with black.

Balling the handkerchief in her hand, she turned back to her charges and mustered something she hoped would pass for a cheering smile. "Then we'd best get back to work."

When an hour and a half had gone by according to the distant clock, whose hands seemed to move not at all for stretches, then lurched forward alarmingly, she dismissed the girls to their luncheon. One floor below, she found the room where she had slept and slipped inside to wash her face and hands and to comb her hair. She longed to change into a fresh dress, but she hesitated to make free with the contents of the wardrobe without permission from someone other than Daphne and Bell. She could not help having to borrow one dress. Her own was filthy, perhaps beyond repair. But a change of clothes at midday would surely be considered lavish for a governess.

With light, uncertain steps she descended to the first floor. The girls had shown her the drawing room that morning and explained how they often studied their lessons there while their father read, their mother sewed, or their eldest sister wrote. Sometimes all together. Rosamund had looked around the room—the largest in the house, surely, but not overlarge nonetheless—and had foreseen how quickly all would come to grief if she were expected to teach while their brother sat in judgment just a few feet away. So she had wondered aloud whether some other space mightn't serve better as a schoolroom.

In hindsight, perhaps, she had been rather foolish to leap on the girls' suggestion of using the attic. She had an instinct for good hiding places, as it turned out. But she had a great deal to learn about being a governess.

The door to the drawing room was ajar now, but not enough that she might peer inside. No footman waited to announce her. In fact, she'd seen no servants other than Molly and the cook. Rosamund raised one hand to knock, hesitated, and then heard the sound of a longcase clock in the room chiming the half hour. She could not, would not be late. Raising one arm, she rapped her knuckles twice on the door and waited.

No one opened the door. No one called out, "Come in." When she had counted to twenty, she knocked again, this time hard enough that the door swung inward a few inches more, giving her a view of the front half of the room: a pair of tall windows facing the street, groupings of comfortable furniture, a spinet. Cautiously, she pushed the door further and stepped across the threshold.

"I'll be with you in a minute."

Paris Burke's voice, soft yet forceful, came from her left. She turned to face him, but he remained bent over some papers spread across a large desk, his pen moving swiftly while the fingers of his other hand traced down and across the spread pages of a book. This work occupied him fully for several moments more, and she had no choice but to wait. Punishment, she supposed, for her pert reply in the attic.

Her gaze roamed over the rest of the room's furnishings, the overstuffed bookcases, the amateur artwork adorning the walls. The Burkes seemed to be reasonably well-off; the room was neat and tastefully fitted up. Still, it looked quite as one might expect a room regularly occupied by a half-dozen members of the family might look. Here and there she spied a scuff mark in the wallpaper, a worn spot in the upholstery. Blemishes that would never have been permitted in the house where she had grown up.

Well, no, that wasn't entirely true. She had the vaguest sense that things might have been different when Papa was alive. Less strict. Happier.

Doubt scuttled the memory. If it *was* a memory. Charles would have told her it was a figment of her imagination. Would have explained that things were now as they had always been, that he had ordered everything just as their father would have wanted it done.

The walls and chairs and carpet of the drawing room were insufficient to hold her attention for long. Her gaze persisted in wandering back to Mr. Burke, though she would not allow herself to stare. She had called him a highwayman in her thoughts, and given what his sisters had revealed, perhaps she hadn't been far off the mark. *A United Irishman.* A dangerous rebel against the Crown.

Well, she'd hoped to find someone ruthless, hadn't she?

When he had visited the schoolroom, he had been fully dressed, but now he sat, most shockingly, in his shirtsleeves; his cravat had worked loose and he had cast his coat over the back of another chair. Though he had not looked up from his work, she could see enough of his face in profile to realize he still had not shaved. The strange intimacy of that scruff of beard, ink black like his hair, startled her almost more than his state of undress. As if she were peeping at a man just roused from his bed.

The gentlemen of her acquaintance did not appear so in front of ladies. Charles would have insisted that Mr. Burke was no gentleman. But recent events had not exactly increased her faith in her brother's opinion.

With a rough noise in his throat, a sort of exasperated-sounding laugh, Mr. Burke shoved the book away and tossed his pen onto a tray, then ran one hand through his already disordered hair. Unruly waves fell over his brow and brushed his collar, and her first prim thought was that he ought to visit a barber and have it tamed.

So why did her fingertips tingle with the unexpected desire to smooth one silky blue-black wave from his dark eyes?

Pushing back from the desk, he came to his feet and fixed her with an assessing look. "Do sit down, Miss Gorse." With one hand he snatched his coat from the nearby chair, while motioning her toward it with the other.

She wanted to decline. It would mean giving up some of the aloof dignity that a standing posture conveyed. It would mean moving nearer to him. But something about his voice made him difficult to refuse. She suspected he lost very few cases.

As he shrugged into his coat, she seated herself facing him, her spine rigid, not touching the back of the chair. Though he was of average height and slender build, Mr. Burke had the presence of a much larger man. He reminded her of an actor who had once brought his traveling troupe to perform at Tavisham Manor when she was fourteen. Charles, who had happened to be visiting at the time, had sent him away and tried to persuade her she wanted nothing to do with such amateur spectacles. But even a glimpse of the man through the drawing room windows had been riveting.

She could not exactly blame the women of Dublin for haunting courtrooms to catch a glimpse of the handsome barrister.

Tugging a sleeve into place, he seated himself at the desk again. "Have you a great deal of experience with children, Miss Gorse?"

No pleasantries. No pretense at conversation. And how was she to answer such a direct attack? For a moment, she could only watch as he idly straightened the papers on the desk with the fingers of one hand. She could not meet his eye. But the longer she hesitated, the more damning the truth would be. "No, sir."

"*Any* experience?" He spoke with the assurance of a man who was accustomed to asking questions and having them answered.

She swallowed. "In my—in my last, ah, situation, there were two children. A boy and a girl. Of an age with your sisters." *Shading the truth*, people called it. God forgive her.

"And why did you leave that post?"

"I, ah—"

"Were you dismissed?"

"I was not." She jerked her chin up and met his gaze at last. His eyes were indeed black—or such dark brown as to make no difference. But not cold, as she had imagined them from a distance. Sharp. Lively. And every bit as compelling as the rest of him. "I left. The children's father seemed to imagine that I—" Heat rose in her cheeks and she let her eyes drift from his face again. "That he was entitled to certain liberties."

For a moment, Mr. Burke sat perfectly still, perfectly silent. Then—

"His name, Miss Gorse?"

She did not think he meant to inquire after a reference. "The gentleman in question is a person with a great deal of power, sir. I cannot—"

She broke off when Mr. Burke's fingers drummed on the stack of papers beneath them. "The 'gentleman' in question is no gentleman." A pause. "What of his wife? Would she not intervene?"

"She is dead."

He rose and stood before the window at the rear of the room, his hands crossed behind his back. When he spoke again, his voice was gentler. "So you walked away. Quite literally. And after traveling some distance, I gather you found your way to Mrs. Fitzhugh, who sent you to us."

It was not a question, so she felt safe in making no answer. He had mentioned Mrs. Fitzhugh the night before. The woman must run some sort of employment agency. One word from her and Rosamund's story would unravel.

He turned back to the desk, opened a drawer, and withdrew a cash box, of the sort from which household expenses were generally paid. Rummaging beneath the blotter, he found a small key and fitted it to the lock on the box. "Under the circumstances, I suppose we ought not to expect your previous employer to forward your trunk," he said, a wry twist to his lips that might have been either grimace or smile. "And you cannot go on rummaging for castoffs in my sisters' wardrobe. An advance on your salary is in order, I believe." Twisting the key with one hand, he opened the lid of the box with the other, then reached inside without looking. "Will that do?" he asked as he set a stack of coins in front of her. Five pounds, at least.

"You are very generous." She did not reach to take the money until he had moved his hand away, not wanting to reveal how desperate she was. "Thank you, Mr. Burke."

When he sat down again, both his expression and his posture had softened. No less a performance to produce the answers he wanted, however. He leaned toward her. "Are you certain you're fully recovered from yesterday's ordeal, Miss Gorse?"

"Quite." She blinked away the tears that had sprung to her eyes and folded her hands in her lap, the money carefully contained within one palm. "Did you—did you wish to discuss your sisters' program of study, Mr. Burke?" Dangerous, no doubt, to invite further questions. But his quiet concern for her, the scrutiny of his dark eyes, was more dangerous still.

She nearly heaved a sigh of relief when he settled back into his chair. "Was it Daphne's suggestion to make use of the attic, I wonder? Or Bell's?" His gaze left her face to travel to the far end of the room. "I suppose I haven't made this place too welcoming of late," he said, not waiting for her answer.

"Children learn better in an environment free of distractions." She had no notion if it were true, but it seemed a sensible, governess-like position to take.

One corner of his mouth lifted. Still not a smile. In profile, his features were hard, angular. His eyes remained focused on some distant point. "Perhaps that explains why I was such a poor student."

A contradiction sprang to her lips, and she pressed them tightly together to contain it. He had never been a poor student. Of that she was certain.

Her mouth was still in that same thin, disapproving line when he suddenly turned his head and looked back at her. He laughed. Rather wryly, to be sure, but nonetheless, a few of the harshest lines disappeared from his face, and his eyes twinkled. "Oh, very good, Miss Gorse. I confess I had my doubts about you. But another such frown and you'll have *me* conjugating Latin verbs."

She dared an answering smile, and his expression shifted again. A fire lit in the depth of his eyes and its warmth spread across his face. She found herself suddenly aware again of his shadowed jaw and the scandalously loose knot of his cravat. "*Venisti, vidisti, vicisti,*" he murmured, the smile still playing around his mouth.

She came, she saw, she conquered.

Rosamund straightened in her chair—when had she leaned toward him?—and said, "I'm afraid my own accomplishments run in a somewhat narrower vein, Mr. Burke. If you require instruction in Latin, I cannot satisfy you. Instruction for your sisters, I mean," she added hastily.

He too sat more upright, although the warmth still lingered in his eyes. "French?"

"I—er, yes, of course. As well as the rudiments of both Italian and German."

Surprise lifted his brow and slid as quickly away. "History? Geography? Mathematics?"

When Rosamund's mother had died, Charles had hired the granite-faced and silent Mrs. Sloane to be her companion. That woman's sole redeeming virtue had been her lack of curiosity; no reader herself, she had not thought to forbid Tavisham Manor's modest library. Rosamund's chin lifted with a surge of fledgling defiance. "You may examine me if you like."

He dipped his head, but not before she caught a flare of something in his eyes. "That won't be necessary." With restless motions, he began sifting through the papers on his desk. "You may return to your pupils, Miss Gorse. Make of them what you will." He sounded relieved to be free of the responsibility.

She rose. He did not.

The lack of acknowledgment stung her pride—her foolish, foolish pride. Charles had not eradicated it as thoroughly as he had intended, it would seem. Instead of accepting her dismissal, as a servant would, she laid the fingers of her free hand on the very edge of the desk. "It's an important case, then?" She nodded toward his papers. "Whatever you're working on."

Too important for him to be persuaded to put it aside in favor of her own?

He reached for the book he had closed earlier and began to thumb through it, giving her no opportunity to read his expression. "It was." The words were edged with bitterness.

When he dipped his pen and said nothing more, she turned and walked to the door. But on the threshold, his voice gave her pause. "You will dine with me. And my sisters," he added, but not before her pulse had begun to rattle in her veins. Although he was doubtless too absorbed in his work to see her reply, she nodded her agreement. What choice did she have?

Mr. Burke's changeable nature did not bode well. It was one of the flaws in the Irish national character her brother had warned her about. She recalled the girls' description of their brother as angry. Over the course of their brief acquaintance, she'd watched him shift from morose to mordant and back again in a flash. He seemed to take no particular pleasure in her company. Why then was he insisting on it?

The answer came before she had taken another step.

"I should be just as happy if you ate with your charges in the schoolroom. But Molly would resent having to carry the trays." She heard paper rustle, the click of the pen against the ink bottle. "No doubt such matters are ordered differently in other families," he said. "But you shall have to accustom yourself to our strange Irish ways."

Chapter 6

Overhearing her huff of—surprise? outrage? perhaps a bit of both—as she left the room, Paris allowed himself the slightest of smiles. Miss Gorse, with her rudimentary Italian and her soft, well-manicured hands, had not been born to be a governess, he felt certain. A countess, perhaps…

Well, and suppose she had? he argued with himself. *What of it?* Even if her father *were* an aristocrat, he might have planned poorly and left his daughter at the mercy of the unforgiving marketplace. Many Irish households were eager for the supposed prestige an English governess conveyed, according to Mrs. Fitzhugh. And the world abounded with unscrupulous men waiting to prey on the vulnerable.

If he required proof of what Miss Gorse had told him about her previous post, he had only to think of the hole in her shoe. Did it matter that the shoe itself was an elegant little slipper designed for the sort of lady who never had to walk farther than the distance from the dining room to the drawing room? In some ways, that was the most damning evidence of all, a clear sign that she had fled without forethought, desperate to get away.

Nevertheless, it went against his nature to believe people. Years of courtroom experience had only exacerbated his skepticism. No one was ever entirely honest, and he knew, with the certainty of both a born cynic and a well-trained lawyer, that she had not been entirely honest with him.

He might have dismissed her for it. But weeks of fruitless searching had taught him how difficult it was to find a governess willing to accept a temporary position.

And God knew, even if his parents didn't, that his sisters deserved better care than he could provide. Daphne and Bell missed their mother and their elder sisters. Without the qualities imbued by those three very different women—Mama's gentleness, Cami's stability, Erica's energy—the whole household suffered.

Besides, everyone had something about themselves they would rather not show to the world, including him. Why should Miss Gorse be an exception? Her blue eyes, clear as a cloudless summer sky, yet somehow opaque, gave the impression *she* was hiding, however. Hiding deep within herself. So deep that for a moment he had felt certain she was lost and needed help finding the way out…

What a load of fanciful rot! Cami could put it in one of her books. As if one's eyes revealed such things. As if he were in any way qualified to guide a lost soul.

With a vigorous shake of his head, he forced his attention back to the papers before him, an important case that might have been his, if circumstances had been different. Instead another barrister had taken it to trial and lost in spectacular fashion. Sometimes Paris amused himself—if *amusement* it could properly be called—with laying out the arguments he would have made. If circumstances had been different.

He could not say how much time had passed when shouted voices pulled his fitful attention from Blackstone. The noise was coming from the small garden behind the house. Pushing away from the desk, he rose and went to the window. A damp, gray morning had slid imperceptibly into a damp, gray afternoon, though it was not raining at the moment. He could only conclude that Miss Gorse's schedule included exercise at… He tugged his watch from his waistcoat pocket. Three o'clock already?

In any case, the girls and their governess were playing cricket.

Well, *playing* might be an exaggeration. Miss Gorse was bowling, and the longer he watched, the more convinced he became that she had never even watched the sport before. Bell waved the bat about; there was hardly space in the back garden to swing it properly. Why hadn't the three of them gone into the large and lovely garden at the center of the square? Though since Daphne appeared to be more interested in coaxing the neighbor's cat through the wrought-iron fence than she was in fielding, perhaps a narrower compass for their game was best.

In an extraordinary act of sportsmanship, Miss Gorse called out words of encouragement to Bell, then screwed up her face in concentration as she prepared to bowl. Was she actually closing her eyes? Not that it mattered much. Bell almost certainly had *her* eyes closed waiting for the ball to come her way; Galen had never managed to break her of the habit. The first genuine smile in…oh, *months*…slipped across his lips as he watched

Miss Gorse release the ball. Bell swung the bat wildly, elbows jutted out at fierce angles.

"Brilliant!" he exclaimed under his breath at the unexpected *crack* of contact. And then—

Strange how everything seemed to freeze: Bell's and Miss Gorse's arms upraised in celebration. The ball at the zenith of its arc. Then a rush of noise and motion: the ball's sharp descent, Daphne's scream of warning to Miss Gorse, who was oblivious to the danger. He was away from the window before the ball struck her, down the stairs and into the garden before either Bell or Daphne had reached her side.

He had expected to find her collapsed on the ground, in much the same posture as the night before. But she was sitting up, one hand and arm covering half her head, the other hand outstretched to his littlest sister.

"I'm all right, Bell. Truly," she insisted, though she sounded pained. "I'm so proud of you."

"Eejit, eejit, eejit," Daphne was muttering as she came within earshot.

He was on the point of reprimanding her when Miss Gorse said gently but with surprising firmness, "What did I say about calling your sister rude names, Daphne?"

Daphne stopped a few feet away, her face set in a fierce frown. "I wasn't talking about Bell."

"*Daphne Burke*." The voice that could compel a noisy courtroom to silence only made his sister fold her arms defiantly over her chest. "Go to your room. I'll deal with you later."

With a jut of her chin, she flounced away. Bell burst into tears, dropped the bat, and followed her. Ignoring them both, Paris sank to one knee beside Miss Gorse. "How bad is it?"

She shook her head, the slightest of movements, and her free hand turned from welcoming Bell to warding him off. "How could you, Mr. Burke?"

He rocked onto his heels. "How—how could—?" he echoed, bewildered. "*What?*"

"Could you not see that Daphne was upset? She needed…she needed… comfort. From her brother." That little speech seemed to require a great deal of effort.

"Comfort?" Clearly, the blow had rattled the woman's brain. "You're the one who's been injured, Miss Gorse."

"I'm fine," she repeated, though the words were no more convincing this time. "Besides, Daphne was right." What he could see of her face was curved into a feeble, self-deprecating smile. "I ought to have been more attentive."

In his experience with such matters, which was not insignificant, innocent people were far more likely to shoulder blame than guilty ones. Why was she so ready to accept responsibility for an unfortunate accident?

The explanation grew clear when she added—no, begged, "Please, do not punish your sister."

Did she fear the girls needed protection from him? Evidently, she had not yet discovered that salutary neglect was more his family's style. Though in his case, it might better be described simply as *neglect.*

"Surely you are not suggesting that Daphne be allowed to speak to her governess in such a manner?" he said, testing.

Her head dipped lower, hiding her expression entirely. "She spoke without thinking. She was frightened, that's all."

"And so—" He bit off the next words. *And so was I.*

The realization shocked him. Frightened? For Miss Gorse?

Her heavy blond hair had slipped from its pins to caress her swan-like neck. He recognized the base impulse that urged him to gather her body against his, to press his lips to the curve of her throat and capture the wild thrum of her pulse. *That* impulse had nothing to do with fear.

But still, his heart rattled in his chest. Oh, yes. He was afraid.

"And so was I, Miss Gorse," he said, when he could be certain the words would come out in his customary mocking tone. "It would be a great inconvenience to have to seek out another governess."

She twisted her head to fix him with one disbelieving eye. Splat! A cold raindrop pelted her cheek and rolled away like a tear.

"It's about to come down in earnest," he predicted. "Allow me to help you to your feet."

Too late. As he rose, the scattered drops became a heavy shower. Wrapping his hand around her forearm, he lifted as she scrambled to get her feet beneath her. When she proved a trifle unsteady, he gathered his resolve and settled his other arm around her. His hand fitted neatly to the curve of her waist, as it had the night before. Dangerously comfortable. Carefully, he led her toward the house across ground that was already growing muddy and slick. By the time they reached the door, they were soaked. "Molly," he bellowed as soon as they were inside. "Fetch some towels to Miss Gorse's room."

"I can make it from here," the governess said, reaching out to lay her palm against the stairwell wall to balance herself, since the hand on the bannister side was still clutching her head.

He knew he should let her go.

He did not.

"Forgive me, Miss Gorse," he said. "But I'd rather you didn't go tumbling down into the kitchen."

"You mean, you'd rather not have to carry me up again." Her voice was a curious mixture of teasing and embarrassment.

Fighting the instinct of his right hand to pull her closer, he gripped the bannister more firmly with his left instead. "I can think of worse fates," he said, intending to sound reassuring. But even his voice no longer seemed to be quite within his control. The words left his lips as a seductive murmur.

She made no answer, but once they were inside the room, she slipped from his supportive arm and made her way unaided across the floor. Heavily, she sat down on the bed that had been Cami's. On the threshold, he hesitated. No desire to leave. No pretext to stay, either.

Well, then, he would invent one. "Will you permit me to look at your injury?" he asked. "I wish to reassure myself you are not seriously harmed."

She hesitated. Finally, for answer, she removed her hand from her face and let her arm sink slowly into her lap. He came to stand beside her. The room was dim. With fingers he half-expected to tremble with foolish anticipation, he reached up and touched her, the lightest brush along her jaw, urging her to turn toward the comparative brightness of the rain-streaked window. She complied readily. Too readily. He had no chance to relish the petal softness of her skin. No excuse to linger.

Expecting to see the bloom of a black eye, he looked down in surprise at her unmarked face. Seeing his confusion, she reached up with one hand to lift the damp hair away from her brow, revealing a gash at her temple, surrounded by an angry-looking welt.

Stepping to the washstand, he wetted the corner of a towel in the washbasin and returned to dab away a trickle of blood. She winced. Gently, he laid the cool cloth over the wound, then reached for her hand where it lay in her lap. He settled her palm over the cloth, then rested his own hand lightly over hers for a moment.

When the compress was secure, he sank onto his haunches beside the bed in order to meet her eyes. Pain mingled with uncertainty in their blue depths. But her gaze was focused, clear. "Headache?" he asked.

She started to nod, winced again, and whispered, "Yes."

"Let me call the physician who lives across the square. Sir Owen—"

A flare of alarm. "Oh, no. That's not necessary. I'm fine. I will be fine," she corrected.

"When Molly comes in with the towels, you must ask her for anything else you need. Anything that would make you more comfortable."

Miss Gorse looked doubtful. "I wouldn't want to cause her any trouble. I'll just rest until dinner, if I may. The girls—"

"Leave them to me."

Another flare of worry lit her eyes, but she did not speak.

He rose, mustering a sort of smile. "Don't worry. I had nothing in mind more severe than a tongue lashing, I do assure you."

The answer did not satisfy her. In her lap, her free hand curled into a determined fist. "That sort of lashing can inflict as much harm as the other, Mr. Burke. More lasting harm, at any rate."

The chill that settled over him had little to do with his rain-soaked clothes. She spoke with the certainty of someone who knew from experience the sort of damage words could do. Perhaps that explained why she had been so quick to accept blame for a simple accident. Someone—but who?—had badgered and bullied her into submission.

Or rather, had tried. He glimpsed in the depths of her eyes a flicker of something. Something that hinted her spirit had not been entirely subdued.

"Besides," she said with clearly unpracticed boldness, "you hired me to manage your sisters, did you not?"

Something like a laugh rumbled in his chest. "I may be a barrister, Miss Gorse. But even I cannot argue with that."

* * * *

He was out the door before Rosamund could reply, and in another moment, Molly entered. In that interval of solitude, albeit brief, Rosamund came to two conclusions.

First, she felt certain that when Daphne had described her brother as angry, she had misstated the case. Rosamund had some experience with *angry*, and it was not how she would describe Mr. Burke. Which was not to say he was *happy*, either. Quite the opposite, in fact. If she were forced to choose just one word with which to label him, it would be *sad*.

Oh, he was quick tempered at times, witty at others. Changeable, as she had noted from the first. But the more opportunities she was given to study him, the more she felt certain that sorrow, or something very like it, had etched its mark on his features and his voice. He conveyed a sort of weariness, a sort of wariness, that the occasional sharp retort only reinforced. His determination to have the last word, to manage every exchange as he saw fit, was but one of his ways of holding people at a distance, of keeping them from probing too deeply.

Her second conclusion was that she had been right to think of Mr. Burke as dangerous. Certainly, he was dangerous to her. His touch, instead of being shocking or unwelcome, made her feel safe, when in reality she was the furthest thing from it. What might he say or do when he discovered that she was not at all the woman he believed her to be?

Molly's arrival prevented her from dwelling on the probable consequences of her deception. A spasm of disapproval flashed across the servant's face as she took in Rosamund's disheveled appearance—an expression not unlike the one Mr. Burke had been wearing when he'd burst from the back of the house. All at once Rosamund had been a child again, facing her brother's wrath over an innocent mistake, quickly realizing that what had happened was all her own fault. Then and now, she instinctively curled her arm tighter to hide the injury, to shield herself.

Molly softened when she spied the compress at Rosamund's temple. "Let's have a look, then." She deposited an armload of towels at the foot of the bed, then turned to inspect Rosamund's wound. As she gently lifted the damp cloth and studied what was beneath, she clucked her tongue and shook her head. "Cricket." On her lips the word was an epithet. "I thought you fine ladies had more sense. Well, you've a lump the size of a quail's egg, and you'll soon have a fine poppy bruise to go with it. Perhaps that will help you to remember not to go messin' about with balls and bats."

Carefully, Rosamund nodded. Play had formed little part of her solitary childhood, and when Daphne and Bell had described the game, it had sounded harmless fun. Now, of course, she knew why such rough and tumble stuff had been forbidden in her youth. Charles often said she had to learn things the hard way.

Still, there was something comic about Molly's exaggerated frown. And something joyful in the memory of the light in Bell's eyes when she'd hit the ball. A wayward smile twitched at the corners of Rosamund's lips and laughter burbled in her chest.

Perhaps her mind really was addled if she could see any humor in her current predicament. Perhaps Charles was right.

Certainly Molly was looking at her as if she feared the knock on the head had done more than superficial damage. With another shake of her head, she replaced the compress. "After we get you dried off, I'll fetch a plaster to stop the bleedin'." As Rosamund reached up to hold the damp cloth in place once more, Molly grabbed one of the towels, snapped it open, and wrapped it around Rosamund's dripping hair. "Not a soul will notice it beneath all this English gold."

Her Englishness had been the first thing Mr. Burke had remarked upon. And his tone had not been complimentary, either—not surprising, given what his sisters had revealed about his radical politics. Yet she was not the only English person who had become a part of this household… "Daphne and Bell told me that their sisters married Englishmen." As she could no longer see Molly's face, Rosamund felt safe in probing.

"They did indeed. High-born ones, too. Mr. Paris got himself into a right state when Miss Cami brought her man home. But then, those two always did enjoy a row. Comes of being so close in age. Now, Miss Erica… well, she does as she likes, mostly." Molly paused and let the towel sag. Rosamund glanced back in time to catch a sly smile curving the servant's lips. "An' she was smart enough not to tell her brother what she'd done until it was too late."

Rosamund murmured in reluctant admiration of such daring, the sound thankfully muffled by the towel. "The elder Misses Burke sound like spirited women. I believe I can see their influence on Daphne and Bell."

Molly nodded, and the smile shifted into fondness. "The dear loves do miss their sisters so."

"I'm surprised they did not accompany their parents on the visit to England. I understand there was some childhood malady, but surely—"

"Between you and me, Miss Rosamund," Molly said, lowering her voice, "they might've gone and been none the worse. But I think Mr. Paris was grasping for an excuse to stay here. Work, he says, and God knows he takes on enough of it. But since those three left Dublin—Miss Cami, Miss Erica, and their brother, Mr. Galen," she explained, seeing Rosamund's puzzled expression, "he's had nothing but harsh words for them. I've heard him swear up and down that he'd sooner drown than cross the Irish Sea."

Somehow, Rosamund did not think it was fear of the water that kept him firmly planted on his own island.

She thought again of his involvement with the United Irishmen. "I suppose most of your countrymen share his prejudice."

"Well…" Molly stretched the word into several syllables. "I don't know about *most*, but a fair few do, and that's a fact. Then again, his mother's English, and he thinks the world o' her."

Half English, yet somehow entirely Irish. Did he never feel himself caught between the two worlds?

When her hair was sufficiently dry, Molly helped her shed her damp dress and offered a faded nightgown from the bottom of the clothes press. "Why don't you have a lie down? I'll bring up your dinner in a while."

Rosamund could not help but think of Mr. Burke's instructions regarding meals. "I don't want to be a burden."

The servant waved such concerns away. "Och, go on. You need your rest after a great thump like that one."

When Molly had tucked her securely into bed—an odd yet comforting feeling in the middle of the afternoon—she promised to return in a few moments. "I'll fetch that plaster for your head."

"Thank you, Molly. And please, I wish—I wish you would call me Rosamund. At least in private." It was a liberty she had never before allowed. Charles would have fired any servant who had dared to take her up on the offer. But Molly was friendly and young—about her own age, Rosamund guessed—and might be an ally. She hadn't had one of those since her mother had died.

Molly regarded her skeptically for a moment, then shrugged. "If you say so, miss."

When she had gone, Rosamund leaned back against the pillow and closed her eyes, hoping to quiet the throbbing behind her eye. Solitude did nothing to quiet her mind, however.

Far from providing answers, the conversation with Molly had only further piqued Rosamund's curiosity. She could almost admire Mr. Burke's willingness to stay in Dublin with his youngest sisters—her own brother often spoke of the many sacrifices he had been required to make on her behalf. But to hear Molly tell it, Mr. Burke's actions had actually required little sacrifice at all. He'd wanted an excuse to maintain the distance between him and the rest of his family and had leaped on one when it had presented itself.

Had his decision been driven purely by his dislike of England and the English? Was his siblings' choice to leave Ireland the source of his deep sorrow?

Or was something else to blame?

Chapter 7

Paris laid his palms flat against the cool leather of the chair's arms but made no other effort to rise. It was late and the house was silent. Past time to retire. But he knew with the certainty born of a hundred nights' previous experience that he would not sleep if he went to bed.

Restlessness was nothing new. It had been driving him all his life. For as long as he could remember, he had wanted what lay just beyond his reach. He had believed anything was attainable with effort.

As he'd grown from a boy to a man, he had focused all his energies on securing an independent future for Ireland. He'd joined the radical Society of United Irishmen as a matter of course, though membership in the organization was considered treason. A proud patriot, he'd been more than willing to take a personal risk if it might in the end benefit the cause of Irish independence.

It's good to chase your dreams, his father would occasionally remind him, whenever he found him still poring over a stack of law books as dawn streaked the sky, or caught him slipping out to a clandestine meeting under cover of darkness. *Just don't let them chase you.*

Then, last spring, the spark of rebellion had caught and flared to life. Everything had been destroyed in the subsequent conflagration. He'd lost his oldest and dearest friend. He had very nearly lost his brother. His life's work had been reduced to a pile of ashes.

His father had been right, as he was about most things. Paris's dreams had indeed turned the tables on him. How quickly they had become nightmares.

Was that why he refused his bed? Good God, he was worse than his baby sisters, cringing at every shadow and afraid of being alone. Enough childishness. He heaved himself from the chair and picked up the snuffers to extinguish the candles. A noise behind him gave him pause. The creak of hinges. Slowly he turned, the thin metal implement still gripped in his hand, the feeblest of weapons. A figure slipped into the room, and the candlelight caught a gleam of gold.

Rosamund!

Curse Molly for her discovery and letting it slip. Of course the woman had a given name as unusual, as beautiful as she. Well, he simply wouldn't let the association take root in his mind. No silken petals dewed by a passing summer shower. No delicate perfume that lingered on the warm air.

He let the snuffers clatter onto the tabletop, watched in satisfaction when she started at the noise, then gave a mocking bow. "You're up late, Miss Gorse."

"Or early," she replied in her quiet, contrary, oh-so-English way.

Yes, that was it. *Gorse*. Prickly. Perfectly ordinary. Vaguely pleasing in appearance at certain seasons, but only from a distance.

She came closer. Over her nightclothes she wore a brown flannel dressing gown he guessed had belonged to Cami, as its hems dragged along the carpet with every step. It should not have been an appealing costume. Nevertheless, he found it difficult to tear his gaze away.

He blamed her hair. The way it cascaded down her back in loose waves. The way the candlelight rippled through it with every step she took. Did it still smell of spring rain?

Then he glimpsed a bit of court-plaster near her temple, too little to disguise either the bruise or the lump. The sight of it chastened him. "You are recovered from this afternoon's incident?" he asked, softening his voice.

She smiled. "*Incident* seems rather grandiose." A few feet from him, she stopped, dipped into a shallow curtsy. The movement sent more sparks shimmering through her golden hair. "You must imagine I make a daily habit of falling into a swoon."

"No, I..." An uncertain laugh broke free. "*Do* you?"

Instead of widening, the smile slipped from her lips. "I am sorry, Mr. Burke. You hired me to relieve one burden and instead I have become another." Worry skated across her features. He might almost have called it fear. Then she rallied, drawing back her shoulders in that way she had and lifting her chin in a posture of determination. "But it won't continue. You have my word that from here on out, I shan't cause you another moment's trouble."

He didn't believe her, of course. Wasn't even sure he wanted to believe her.

"Miss Gorse," he said, at once reassuring and teasing, "I have five siblings. What is a day without trouble?" Her smile slid back into place, though it retained a hint of wariness. "Speaking of, you're having trouble sleeping, I take it."

"Yes. Er, not exactly. At Molly's insistence, I rested all afternoon. And all evening. I—I couldn't lie in bed another moment. I thought perhaps a book…"

Her gaze shifted to the compact library that surrounded his father's desk, and his own followed. "There's plenty on those shelves that would cure insomnia, to be sure," he said. "Legal tomes, scientific works…"

"I confess I was hoping for something a bit lighter." Her hand crept to her injured temple, throwing her expression into shadow. "I do still have a touch of the headache."

He could offer no fashion plates or magazines. Not even, at the moment, many novels. Their family's subscription to the circulating library had largely been made use of by Mama and Cami. But he knew of one other possibility. He stepped past the desk and ran one finger along the spines on the uppermost shelf until he came to a thin folio. "Perhaps this?" he said as he withdrew the book and extended it to her.

Forced to step closer still, she took it with one hand and examined it in the light. "Botanical prints?"

"Yes. My father's hobby. I've never shared his interest, certainly not to the degree my sister Erica does, but I find the pictures soothing." As a boy, he'd been allowed to thumb through the expensive volume of hand-tinted illustrations on the rare occasions when he was declared too sick to go out and play. He hadn't looked at them in ages. But he still remembered his fascination with the strange arcs and lines of petals and stems.

When he'd been very young, Bell's age, perhaps, he'd imagined them to be maps of planets no one could ever visit. A few years later, he'd noted a resemblance to more familiar, feminine territories in those alluring curves and hollows, and he'd dreamed of charting them himself. His father had moved the book to a shelf beyond his adolescent reach.

"Thank you." She tucked the oversize book against her hip rather awkwardly. "I should let you return to your…" Her quick glance traveled from the empty desktop to the empty table beside the chair in which he'd been sitting. "Your solitude," she finished uncertainly.

At various points in his life, Paris had constructed elaborate plans of all he would accomplish if ever he had a room, or an hour, to himself. Four sisters and a brother in a modest-sized townhouse had a tendency to interfere with one's concentration. When he'd reluctantly returned to Merrion Square to care for Daphne and Bell after many years on his own, however, he'd discovered that the boisterous Burke household had grown considerably quieter in his absence, its occupants now scattered, some never to return. As a result, he knew now what he could not have known six years, or even six months, ago: Silence could be a greater distraction than noise. Sometimes, he quite disliked being alone.

But what did he expect? What more did he deserve?

Knowing her eyes were on him now, he nodded toward the partner of his chair, opposite the table and further in shadow. "I couldn't sleep either," he confessed. "Will you stay and talk?"

He fully expected her to say no. When she moved with hesitating steps to the chair and perched herself on the very edge of its seat, the book strapped to her chest by her flannel-covered arms like a breastplate of armor, he wished she *had* said no.

He ought to have considered the lateness of the hour, her dishabille, the story she'd told of her last employer's improprieties. What a callous suggestion he'd made, one she was poorly situated to refuse.

Nevertheless, he did not rescind his offer.

Instead he wandered with apparent aimlessness to the far end of the room, hoping to reassure her that his intentions were not malicious. As he passed the spinet, he trailed his fingers lightly over the keys.

"Do you play?" The distance between them was insufficient to muffle the surprise in her voice.

For answer, he plucked out a few bars of a popular Irish air, not bothering to seat himself at the instrument. "Mama was determined that we all would," he said, looking back at her. "Galen is the only real talent among us. Cami is proficient, as she is in most things, though I do not believe it gives her any particular pleasure. Bell shares Erica's impatience and never practices. And Daphne—"

"Would rather learn the harp."

He'd told her as much. On the walk from King's Inns Quay. Or at least, he presumed he had. "Yes. I wasn't sure you'd remember."

"Oh, I remember."

The lightest stress on the pronoun made clear to him that she had expected *he* would not. She seemed to place great store in his forgetfulness, and he knew very well why. "I owe you an apology, Miss Gorse, for not realizing how fatigued you were last evening. I was—"

"Drunk?" The prim note in her voice grew stronger.

He'd never known a lady to use anything other than a polite euphemism for the condition. *Foxed*, perhaps. Or *a trifle disguised*. He cleared his throat. "*Selfish*, I was going to say."

"Ah." He watched her gaze travel to the decanter of Irish whiskey that sat on the corner of his father's desk. "Well, I hope you do not often find occasion to be…*selfish*, Mr. Burke."

By God, was she a Methodist? Who else would be so inclined to scowl at a man's sins? Annoyance prickled near the base of his spine, then traveled upward, stirring the air in his lungs, prompting him to retort with sharp words.

He bit them back, turning toward the window to look down on the empty street.

Given the vulnerable position in which she had found herself, he could hardly blame her for wanting to stake out some little piece of territory on higher ground. Well, he was willing to concede that much to her. Tonight, the stopper had remained in that bottle. But if he was honest, there had been other nights, lonely hours in the semi-darkness, when he had not been so wise.

"You also play, I assume." It was the most innocuous question he could think of. Really, not even a question. A signal, after a few moments of uncomfortable silence, that the previous line of discussion was closed. And really, not much reassurance that he was any more gentlemanly than she believed. His voice was surprisingly gruff to his ears, and he only glanced over his shoulder as he spoke, rather than facing her. Serve him right if she got up and left.

She did not, however. She slid deeper into the chair—not so far that her spine touched its back, of course; he wondered if she ever allowed herself to relax enough for that—and laid the book across her lap. "I do. Will you wish me to continue your sisters' lessons? Or have they a music master?"

A puff of laughter escaped his lips. "You must already have guessed the answer to that last, Miss Gorse, seeing as they did not even have a governess. And as to the first, you are at liberty to set the curriculum, so long as my sisters are no worse off when you leave us."

When you leave us. An unexpected pang accompanied those words. In just twenty-four hours, she had made an indelible impression. Her departure, when it inevitably occurred, could not fail to be felt.

Her pursed mouth softened just enough to curve into a mocking smile. "What extraordinary license you give your employees, Mr. Burke."

He had not noticed before how plump her lips were. How mobile. He wanted, suddenly, to make a project of discovering all their moods.

With a thump, he seated himself at the spinet and picked up the thread of his earlier tune. What was it he had told Molly about focusing on his work? Oh, he needed employment, all right. Some task. A goal. One in which his sisters' governess's lips played no part.

"I?" He took care to keep his tone as wry as her expression. "I have no employees." He gestured around the room with one hand and continued to play with the other. "My father's household. My father's servants. My father's children." His second hand joined the first on the keys. "My authority, such as it is, merely borrowed and no doubt ill-fitting."

When he came to the end of the piece—a fumbling stop, as he'd forgotten half of it—she spoke again. Had she been waiting impatiently to speak, or had the interval of his performance given her time to gather her thoughts?

"When my father died, my brother assumed his mantle." One fingertip traced the edge of the book in her lap, and her eyes were watching its movement. "I wish—" With a little gasp of breath, she caught herself, and the wish remained unspoken. Though perhaps not entirely unspoken. "He did not choose to wear it as lightly as you have," she said.

Those words could have meant many things…anything, really. Perhaps she disapproved of Paris's negligence. Or perhaps little Rosamund had been a hellion once. Perhaps she'd fancied a stable hand and her brother had wisely dismissed the man. No cause to imagine her brother had acted inappropriately or unjustly. No reason to assume he had been the one who had tried to cow her with harsh words—or worse.

No matter how Paris longed for an excuse to go to her and comfort her through this interminable night.

"Is his mismanagement responsible for the necessity of your seeking employment?" Though his fingers still lay on the keys, Paris's attention was focused squarely on her, waiting for her answer to a question he'd had no business asking.

"Mismanagement?" She bristled. "My brother has been an excellent steward and fulfilled his responsibilities admirably. He cannot be blamed for the difficulties he inherited."

She defended him with conviction. So much so that Paris nearly persuaded himself he had imagined the rote quality of her speech. As if she were repeating something she'd often been told. By her brother, if he had to guess.

"Forgive me." He dipped his head, less penitent than he ought to be. "I have had my doubts about whether you were raised with the expectation of becoming a governess. Perhaps I was mistaken."

For a moment she said nothing, then gave a nod of reluctant acknowledgment. "You're not entirely wrong. One might say I wouldn't be here now if it weren't for my brother." At that confession, her lips twisted into something more like a grimace.

The expression did not make him want to kiss her any less.

From some dusty corner of his memory, he dredged up another song—a livelier tune, this time; why did those Irish airs always sound so melancholy?—and began to play. Out of the corner of his eye, he caught her tapping one finger against the cover of the book, keeping time with the melody.

"He is still comfortably at home, I suppose?"

At his question, the tapping stopped. "I do not know where he might be at the moment. I was never privy to his plans."

Even that was no real cause to fault her brother. After all, he did not always trouble to acquaint Daphne and Bell with his comings and goings. And if Rosamund's voice had been laced with annoyance at her brother's inconsiderateness, or had prickled with displeasure at the forwardness of Paris's question, he might have let her answer pass by. But what he heard when she spoke this time was an undercurrent of fear. This time, he was sure of it. She was afraid of her brother.

When he finished the song, he asked, "Where is home?" Partly because he was sorely tempted to hunt down her brother and see to it that no one had cause to fear him again. And partly because her answer would serve as a useful reminder that she was English and therefore the very last sort of woman any self-respecting Irish patriot should want.

Certain parts of him seemed to require such a reminder.

She hesitated. Only for a moment, but experience had made him suspicious of such pauses and the truthfulness of the answers that followed them. "I grew up in Berkshire. That house belongs to my brother now, of course. And as for *home*..." Another pause, though this one might better be characterized as a gasp. A gasp of realization. Of pain. "Why, I suppose I haven't any, anymore."

Before he could offer any reply at all, she twitched her shoulders and lifted her chin again. With that movement, her ordinary gorse-like demeanor returned. "Berkshire is in the southern portion of the country," she explained in her governess voice, primed to deliver a geography lesson. "West of the capital."

"Yes, I know."

"I beg your pardon." The stiffness of her voice undercut the words of apology. "I did not wish to presume any particular familiarity. Molly made clear your disdain for the sister island."

His laugh, though humorless, propelled him to his feet and sent him a half-dozen steps closer to her. "Oh? Did she also make clear that my mother is English? As are the two unfortunate gentlemen who have saddled themselves with my sisters and whom I must therefore claim as brothers."

Really, it should not have been possible for her spine to straighten further. "She, er...she might have mentioned it, yes."

Ah, so the lady-governess did not like to be caught gossiping with servants? "If she was so forthcoming about our family history, then I daresay she cannot have failed to mention that I myself lived in London for some years?" He could tell by Rosamund's wide eyes that Molly had said nothing of the sort. "Through a quirk of custom, even an Irish lawyer must serve his time at the Inns of Court before he can be called to the bar, you see. Time and travel gave me some knowledge of the southern portion of the 'sister island,' as you call it. Including the general proximity of the capital to such quaint country villages as may be found in Berkshire."

He stood close enough now to watch her throat work. Perhaps swallowing one's pride was not always a figurative act. "Well, then, you doubtless know your way better than I, for I have been to London only once," she said. "When I was a very little girl, my father took me. We saw the menagerie at the Tower." The soft fondness of her voice was paired with a shadow of memory in her eyes.

"I suppose you pitied the poor wild things trapped in cages." Right now, he felt positively savage, though he refused to let himself think about why.

The slightest hesitation, and the shadow in her eyes deepened. "Not then, I didn't." She rose. "Forgive me, Mr. Burke. I find I'm more tired than I realized. I should return to my room."

"An excellent idea, Miss Gorse," he said with a bow of his head. "My sisters no doubt look forward to the resumption of their regular lessons in the morning."

Her lips parted, a question clearly poised on their soft curves. But she merely said, "Yes, sir. Good night." And with a shallow curtsy, she was gone.

As soon as the door shut behind her, he flung himself into the chair she had abandoned and was rewarded with a sharp jab to the ribs. Muttering an oath under his breath, he groped beneath his arm for the object that had attacked him: the corner of a book. When she'd risen, the slim folio of botanical prints had slid into the groove between the arm of the chair and the seat and lodged there, awaiting its victim.

He tugged it free and flicked his hand to toss the book onto the table. Halfway through the motion, however, he paused, then slapped the volume onto his knee where it wobbled for a moment before coming to rest.

Damn, but he was tempted to reach for that decanter now, though he was torn between drinking from it and smashing it to pieces. Instead, he leaned his head against the back of the chair and closed his eyes.

Despite his exhaustion, sleep was no closer than it had been an hour ago.

With a sigh, part weary resignation, part bitter laugh, he opened the book and began to flip idly through the collection of pictures. Where a boy had once seen fantastic landscapes, and a randy young man had once discovered the rounded swell of a woman's breast, or the pouting curve of her lips, he now saw nothing but flowers, leaves, and vines. And yet there was still more than enough in its pages to call Rosamund to mind. Her soft blue eyes in the petals of one bloom, her barbed words in the thorns of another.

What did he care whether she mourned her father or feared her brother or missed her childhood home? Whether her head still ached from Bell's first-ever strike, or whether Molly had stuffed that same head with nonsense about him?

His absolute and only concern was whether Miss Gorse was a suitable governess for his sisters. And if his past record was anything to judge by, his concern was likely to be both warranted and short-lived. He would wonder how things were getting on, mean to inquire, let himself be distracted from his responsibilities, and that would be the end of it. In a matter of months, she would be gone. If she didn't trust him enough to lay her life's story at his feet, then she was…wise.

And surely wisdom was a desirable quality for a governess to possess.

Chapter 8

Rosamund was an eejit, just as Daphne had said.

How else to explain what she'd revealed to Paris Burke? She'd mentioned her brother. She'd named the county in which she'd lived. How easily he could use that information against her. And if he discovered the truth, would he send her away? Back to Charles? Back to Lord Dashfort?

How else to explain lying awake until nearly dawn, listening for his footsteps on the stairs, the creak of the door to the bedchamber adjacent to hers, the squeak of his bedstead as he lay down upon it? Waiting and wondering and worrying, until every inch of her ached with awareness of how near he was. Not because she feared having him so close, but because she…*oh.* Oh, dear. Because she *didn't.*

And how else to explain sleeping through the start of lessons?

She hadn't known the exact hour, of course, until she'd gone up to the attic, walked across the makeshift schoolroom, and peered through the dirty window at the distant clock. But she could tell from the expressions on Daphne's and Bell's faces that she was late.

When she turned away from the window, Bell glanced furtively at the plaster at her temple and then to the floor. Daphne slid a book from the stack on her desk and pretended to be absorbed in it.

No use in asking herself how a proper governess would handle such a situation. A proper governess wouldn't have overslept. "Thank you for waiting patiently," she said. "Now, if you'll—"

"Paris told us to." Daphne explained, a petulant note in her voice.

"You—you've seen your brother this morning?" Was he not still asleep?

Bell nodded. "At breakfast."

"He said he had an appointment." Was it her imagination, or did Daphne sound unhappy?

"And that we were to let you sleep as long as you needed. On account of—of—" Bell's gaze flicked once more to Rosamund's brow.

Automatically she shot up a hand to hide the injury from prying eyes, flinching when she brushed against the tender spot. Paris's touch had been infinitely gentler. She hardly knew what to make of such kindness. It would be unwise to let herself need it. "I appreciate your solicitude, and his, but I'm perfectly fine."

The words were very nearly true. The bleeding had stopped, though she hadn't taken the time to remove the court-plaster. The bruise looked a good deal worse than it felt. Even her headache was mostly gone, and what lingered could not entirely be attributed to a wayward cricket ball.

Clearing her throat, she worked up the courage to ask the question she'd been unable to give voice to last night. "He was not unduly harsh when he reprimanded you?"

"Reprimanded us?" Daphne screwed up her face in obvious puzzlement.

"You mean about yesterday?" Bell shook her head. "Paris didn't scold us, miss." Tension she hadn't known she was holding eased from Rosamund's shoulders. "He just reminded us that all cricket players, whether batting, fielding—"

"Or bowling," Daphne added with a significant look.

"—must keep their eye on the ball." Bell glanced at Daphne. "Always."

Focus. Singleness of purpose. Excellent advice. She would do well to take it, rather than allow herself to be distracted by an untoward interest in…people and matters that were none of her concern. If Mr. Burke chose to discipline his sisters in a manner altogether different from her own brother, that was certainly his prerogative. And if he chose to treat all the members of his household with a surprising degree of kindness and generosity, it was still no excuse for her to slacken in her duty. "We will begin this morning with mathematics," she said in her best governess voice. "If you would kindly tell me where you left off in your lessons…"

The girls looked to one another, then back at her. Neither reached for a book or a pencil. Rosamund's heart sank. She knew what that meant. Yesterday, following a similar inquiry about their previous study of history, she'd discovered that the girls' father had not limited himself to the traditional methods of reading and recitation. Instead, he had had his children act out the speeches of Demosthenes ("while wearing tunics made of our bedsheets!" Bell had exclaimed), and build a model of the Battle of Agincourt, using chess pieces, candle stubs, and the contents of their mother's sewing basket.

"The last mathematics lesson I remember was going to market with Molly," Bell said, "and having to figure all the pounds and pence in our heads."

"No, that wasn't it," Daphne countered. "Have you forgotten the mouse?"

Though she was almost afraid to ask, Rosamund echoed, "*Mouse?*"

"Papa told us there was a mouse who wanted to visit every house on this side of Merrion Square. We had to tell how many feet and inches the mouse would go if he started in our drawing room, chewed a hole through the wall behind the green sofa and into the Daltons' drawing room, and so on." In the air, she sketched the mouse's journey. Rosamund narrowly contained a shudder, though she couldn't deny the girls had learned *something* when Daphne concluded, "Nine hundred eighteen feet and a half, assuming every drawing room is a uniform width, though I don't believe they are. I wanted to measure them, but Papa said we mustn't disturb the neighbors."

"And what did your mother say to all this?" Rosamund asked weakly.

"Oh, *now* I remember that lesson," said Bell. "Mama said a real mouse would've gone considerably farther, because she'd never yet met one who wouldn't find his way into the kitchens too."

Rosamund wasn't sure whether to laugh or cry. *You are at liberty to set the curriculum*, their brother had told her, *so long as my sisters are no worse off when you leave us*. But how, exactly, did one measure such things in the Burke household?

Dropping her chin, she fixed her gaze on the toes of her shoes, peeping from beneath her skirts. Her own dress, which Molly had brushed and pressed, though it would never be the same again. And her own shoes, with a heavy piece of paper fitted into the sole of the left one to cover the hole. One damp excursion and the patch would disintegrate; the bottom of her foot was still sore.

But she had five pounds now, didn't she? Five pounds and the beginnings of an idea. "All right, girls," she said, lifting her head and mustering a smile, "get your wraps. This lesson is going to combine mathematics, domestic economy, and art. We're going shopping."

"We've done that already," Daphne pointed out as both girls got to their feet.

"Dress shopping," Rosamund clarified. "You'll have to figure yardage and price per yard, both fabric and trimmings. On a very strict budget."

"Where's the art lesson in that?"

"In choosing the proper colors," Bell said firmly. "And style."

"Yes, that's right." Rosamund laid an arm around the younger girl's shoulders. "Dress making is an art."

Daphne continued to look skeptical, but Rosamund managed to herd both of them toward the door to their room with little resistance. "Meet me in the front hall in ten minutes."

Once more in her own chamber, she stood over the washbasin to remove the bandage, then rearranged her hair to cover the bruise as Molly had recommended. Afterward she donned her pelisse, slightly worse for wear than her dress but still serviceable. Her chip bonnet, however, was nowhere to be found. Doubtless Molly had determined it beyond repair. Groping about on one of the high shelves of the wardrobe, hopeful one of the Burke sisters had left behind a hat, her fingers brushed some sturdy fabric and tugged it from its hiding place. *A cap.* What luck! Except…

Turning it over in her hands, Rosamund wondered if she'd at first been mistaken. She'd never seen anything quite like it, except perhaps in an old-fashioned painting of rosy-cheeked Dutch girls. Still, she couldn't very well go out without something on her head, and this, er, bonnet, however unfashionable, offered the added advantage of disguising her hair, shielding her face, and covering her bruise. Carefully, she put it on, trying her best to arrange the shapeless fabric.

When she reached the front hall, Bell took one look and slapped a hand over her mouth to stifle a giggle. Daphne's brows lifted. "I wondered what had become of that cap. Mama bought it for Erica, because she was forever going outside with her head bare. Mama said she'd never find a man who'd tolerate her freckles."

Bell let a snicker escape. "I guess the duke didn't mind."

Rosamund, who had been self-consciously trying to rearrange the monstrosity on her head, let her hands drop. "I beg your pardon. Did you—did you say…*duke?*"

"Mm-hm." Daphne turned to open the door. "She married the Duke of Raynham in October."

Molly had told her the Burke sisters had married "high-born Englishmen," but Rosamund hadn't imagined anything quite like this. "And your other sister?"

"Oh, Cami's very proper," Bell assured her. "She always wears a bonnet."

Daphne rolled her eyes in exasperation. "She's Lady Ashborough now, though she always swore she didn't even want to get married."

"*Lady Ashborough.* The—the author?" The London newspapers had been full of the story of the marchioness and her scandalous book, and even Mrs. Sloane couldn't very well forbid the *Times*.

"Mm-hm," Daphne said again.

Vaguely, Rosamund thought of correcting her. A child speaking to her governess ought to say, "Yes, Miss Gorse," and "No, Miss Gorse." But her brain was too busy trying to piece together what the rest of the girl's words had meant. How, in all of Dublin, had she managed to insert herself into a household with so many ties to England? And not just any ties, but family ties to the highest ranks of the English aristocracy. Gentlemen who might know her brother from one of the clubs or even the House of Lords. What if Paris wrote to his father or sisters and mentioned her by name? She recalled the papers spread across his desk. *What if he already had?*

While the girls were busy tying their own bonnet strings and buttoning their pelisses, Rosamund forced one calming breath after another into her lungs. Her brother had always been too concerned with appearances to have broadcast her escape. And even if he had, why should a member of the Burke family, learning the name of the new governess, make the connection?

Nevertheless, when Daphne opened the door, more panic fluttered through her. It might prove unwise to stay in this house, but was it not equally unsafe to leave? Part of her expected to see her brother standing across the street in the familiar posture, arms folded over his chest, one booted foot tapping impatiently, waiting for her to appear so he could fetch her back to Kilready. After tugging the absurd bonnet even lower to shield her face, she ushered the girls onto the steps.

Yesterday's rain had given way to a remarkably fine morning, though the chill in the air still spoke of March. Charles was nowhere in sight. The quiet was disturbed only by birdsong coming from the green and the clip-clop-rattle of a passing gig.

"Which shop?" Daphne asked as they descended to the street.

"You must choose," Rosamund replied. "Wherever you think you will get the most for your—er, *my* money."

"This way to Grafton Street," said Bell and tugged her by the hand, leading her along the same streets she recalled following with her brother, although this time, they traveled only a fraction of the distance.

Daphne pointed out various landmarks as they passed, Leinster House and St. Ann's to their left, and for almost the entirety of their short journey, the greens and gardens of Trinity College to their right. "Galen was meant to be a student there," she explained, "as Paris was. But he chose Oxford instead, where Papa went."

Bell whispered confidentially, "When Galen told the family his decision, it made Paris say naughty words."

"Nothing can *make* you say naughty words," Daphne opined. "Except maybe stubbing your toe in the dark."

"Or perhaps an unexpected hit during a game of cricket?" Rosamund suggested, arching one brow, then wincing at the movement. Daphne tucked in her chin and said nothing more.

Soon Grafton Street was spread before them in all its mercantile glory. Rosamund's eyes darted from tea shop to tobacconist to toymaker. Men, women, and children of all classes and sorts strolled or bustled to their destinations. Automatically, she clasped one hand to her side. Beneath her bodice, she had pinned Paris's handkerchief, and in it were wrapped half the coins he'd given her. The rest she'd secreted in her room in case of an emergency. Bell took her other hand in hers as her sister urged, "Come on."

After a quick survey of the goods in one dressmaker's shop, they abandoned it for a second, where the proprietress, Mrs. Teague, quickly got into the spirit of the game. "It's to be a bargain hunt, is it? Well, let us see..." Bolts of fabric appeared, and pattern books; the girls carefully tallied every ell and counted every shilling.

Eventually, Rosamund was presented with their choice, a simple style, though with the newly-fashionable high waist. Bell clutched an armful of smoke blue woolen, far coarser fabric than that of any of the gowns Rosamund had left behind, but well-suited to both her new station and her budget.

Once more, she fingered the pouch of coins at her waist. Together with petticoats and stays, the purchase would seriously deplete her little stash of wealth, which might be needed for another hasty escape. But in that moment, the gleam of satisfaction in the girls' eyes was wealth enough. "It's perfect."

With brisk efficiency, Mrs. Teague produced a tape and began to measure Rosamund. Bell came to stand nearby. "Daphne said a governess should wear gray or brown." Rosamund had never heard the girl's voice so quiet, though a small smile curved her lips. "But the blue goes with your eyes."

"Blue is my favorite color," Rosamund reassured her.

Bell's smile widened. "Paris's too."

His predilections in such matters were of course none of Rosamund's concern. Besides, the style the girls had chosen was perfectly governess-like. Almost severe. Nothing to attract a gentleman's notice.

Not even if she wanted it.

"Tut-tut," Mrs. Teague admonished Rosamund. "Hold still now, dear. We're almost finished."

Afterward, as Rosamund paid for her purchases, the proprietress assured her that the dress would be promptly done. "And no charge for delivery," she added as Daphne wrote out the direction in her neatest hand.

Back in the midday sunshine, Rosamund found herself reluctant to return to Merrion Square, although the lesson, such as it was, had been completed.

"Anything else, Miss Gorse?" Daphne asked, purposefully staring at Rosamund's head.

Thinking of her dwindling coins, Rosamund at first hesitated. But she could hardly deny her need for a new bonnet, and new shoes too. "The milliner's, I think. But first, let me stop in here," she said as they passed an apothecary's shop.

Quickly she bought two sticks of barley sugar to treat the girls, who stood waiting outside. Having never been allowed so much as pin money by her brother, she felt a tingle of trepidation pass through her fingers, for all that she passed the clerk nothing more substantial than a farthing.

But perhaps that strange, electric sensation wasn't trepidation. Perhaps it was power. Was this what the heroines in books meant when they spoke of liking their independence?

As she turned to leave, another customer entered, a sensibly-dressed woman of middle age. At the same time, Daphne called for Rosamund, a note of urgency in her voice. The stranger stopped in the doorway, glanced back at the girls with something like recognition in her eyes, and then gave Rosamund an assessing look that quickly settled into disapproval. Lifting her chin a notch higher, the better to look along her nose, the woman strode sharply past without speaking. Though Rosamund had never set foot in a London ballroom, she suspected she had just experienced the dreaded cut.

But why? "Do you know that lady?" she asked Daphne as the girl scurried to her side.

Distracted, Daphne did not even glance over Rosamund's shoulder. "I don't know, Miss. Oh, do come."

Across the way, a group of rowdy boys scuffled and snickered over something, and to her horror, Rosamund saw that Bell had inserted herself into the fray and was standing, arms folded over her chest, facing the leader with a furious scowl on her face.

Rosamund thrust the paper packet of sweets into Daphne's hands and rushed across the street. "What's all this?"

At first, the boys paid little heed. All but one of them were taller than she, although they looked to be only a few years older than Daphne. Well-dressed enough that she took them for schoolboys, not urchins.

The leader leaned toward Bell. "Give 'im up," he demanded.

Bell stomped one foot. "No."

Only then did Rosamund see that Bell held something wrapped in her arms. Something living, although she couldn't determine what sort of creature the girl had rescued. With a silent prayer that she wasn't about to endanger the girl further, either by angering the boys or frightening a wild animal, Rosamund whipped the ridiculous bonnet off her head and began slapping them with it. Shoulders, faces, whatever she could reach.

The boys stood their ground for a moment, too surprised to do otherwise. Then two or three of them peeled away from the group, arms upraised and disbelieving expressions on their faces. One swore—or at least, she assumed the string of unfamiliar syllables that burst from his lips were curses, based on the wide eyes of his friends and the tinge of scarlet on his cheeks as he spouted the forbidden words. The leader stood his ground the longest beneath the onslaught, until one of the others tugged at his sleeve and jerked his chin up the street, giving either direction or warning. Rosamund lifted her bonnet for another swat to urge him on his way.

A moment later, the boys had melted into the bustle of the noonday crowd. Passersby seemed not even to have noticed the altercation. Rosamund wrapped her arms around Bell. As Daphne hurried toward them, Rosamund steeled herself against the girl's favored imprecation.

But her first words were not at all what she expected. "That was brilliant, Miss Gorse!"

An unexpected blush prickled in her cheeks as she eased her hold on Bell. "I figured this hat ought to be good for something," she said with a laugh as she looked down at the mangled and now grimy piece of linen.

Into the bonnet, Bell deposited the creature she'd rescued, turning the wad of fabric into a makeshift nest. A tiny gray kitten looked at them through blue eyes, and its head wobbled as it opened its mouth in a silent cry. "I couldn't let them kill it." Bell's voice trembled.

"No, of course not," Rosamund murmured as she cupped her hands more securely around the frightened animal.

"I really think it was your shrieking that drove the boys away," Daphne said, reaching out one finger to stroke the kitten's fur. "Though that hat would be enough to scare anyone."

"Shrieking? I…*shrieked*?"

Bell nodded solemnly. "Like a banshee."

Rosamund didn't know what that meant, but she doubted it was a good thing. Certainly not ladylike—or governesslike. Dimly, she registered the disapproving woman still standing in the doorway of the apothecary's shop, watching them.

"Come, girls. Let's go home." Kitten clutched in her hand, she set off in what she hoped was the proper direction.

"You mean, we can keep it?"

The creature was hardly old enough to be separated from its mother. Scrawny, probably sickly. Doubtless crawling with fleas. Molly would have a fit. Mr. Burke would have yet another reason to dismiss his sisters' governess.

"Of course."

Bell squealed, startling the kitten. Daphne grinned. "I'm sorry I called you an eejit yesterday, Miss Gorse."

Rosamund gave what she hoped was a stern look. "Apology accepted, Daphne." But she kept any note of triumph from her voice. Because, in the end, Daphne was right—she was an idiot.

The sort of idiot who played at being stern, then told her charges they could keep a pet without consulting their brother.

The sort of idiot who had laid awake for hours poring over every word the man had spoken. And many he had not.

The sort of idiot who had just bought a dress she could hardly afford because it would set off the gold of her hair and deepen the blue of her eyes. And who could not wait to see his reaction to it.

Chapter 9

When Molly had delivered Eamon Graves's early note, asking Paris to meet to discuss a case, he'd never once considered declining the invitation. To be sure, he had no particular desire to talk with the man. But anything that got him even half an English mile away from Rosamund Gorse was better than the alternative: lying in bed for another moment, knowing she was lying in a similarly situated bed just a wall's width away. Plaster and lathe were proving inadequate antidotes to his interest.

As expected, he found Graves in Dublin's most popular coffeehouse at a table framed by a window, a spot that inevitably drew the eyes of passersby, both inside the shop and on the street. Graves coveted attention.

"Burke." The man's voice boomed as he rose and gestured toward the seat opposite, almost as if he were genuinely enthusiastic at the meeting. The man was a consummate actor, Paris would give him that. Because of those skills, some reckoned him a better barrister than Paris. Because of those skills, Paris knew better than to trust him.

"Graves." The chair scraped noisily across the floor as Paris pulled it from beneath the small table. With leisurely movements, he removed his hat and pulled off his gloves before sitting down. Dark paneled walls absorbed much of the light from the window, casting the alcove into dimness. Cozy, he supposed one might call it. If one fancied cozying up with a snake.

"I'm pleased you could meet me on such short notice." Graves signaled to a waiter to bring another cup. "I expected you to cry off, claim you were too busy playing nursemaid."

"I've hired a governess for my sisters," Paris explained shortly, resentful of being made to think about Miss Gorse.

"Good. The courtrooms of Dublin have missed you."

Graves faked sincerity well. All in all, Paris thought it might be the man's most dangerous skill. Yet, he was tempted now to believe that expression of regret. Oh, not because he imagined Graves worried about injustice or his fellow man's well-being. But because, as Paris knew, the drama of the courtroom soon fell flat without a worthy adversary.

So Graves was bored. Well, well, well…

The waiter returned, bearing a cup and saucer in one hand and a small silver pot in the other. As soon as the coffee was poured, Paris lifted the cup to his lips to disguise the involuntary smile that played about them.

"Careful, Burke," Graves cautioned, idly stirring the contents of his own cup. "You'll get burned."

Paris returned the cup to its saucer with a clatter. "What is it you want, Graves?"

Not to be hurried, the other man laid his spoon aside and lifted his cup to his mouth. A cooling breath rippled across the dark surface of the coffee. "Your opinion on a matter of some delicacy." Rather than say anything more, he sipped, swallowed, then settled the cup in its saucer, taking care to square the handle.

"A case?"

He tipped his head, not quite assent.

Enough. Paris laid his palms on the edge of the table as if preparing to push away.

Graves's hand shot out and gripped his forearm to prevent him from rising. In that instant, everything about the man's expression and demeanor had changed. Gone was the superciliousness, the thinly-veiled mockery. In its place, determination. If Graves were capable of true sincerity, it would look like this.

Though tempted to shake off the staying hand, Paris waited instead, watching as remorse slipped over the other man's features and self-control returned. At last Graves's grasp eased and slid away, and the window into his thoughts slammed shut. "Forgive me. But I believe you'll find the case has some intrinsic interest to men like us."

Men like us. The pair of them had always inspired comparison. Both Trinity men. Both barristers. Both, ostensibly, patriots.

In the last few months, however, Paris had grown more attuned to their differences.

The foremost figures of the rebellion had been drawn from the ranks of the Irish bar, and Paris had counted many of them friends. But when the uprising had failed, the voices of those who had claimed to remain loyal to the British Crown had grown louder. Some of the men suspected of involvement with the United Irishmen—those who had survived—had been shunned for traitors. Paris would surely have been among them if he had not chosen to step aside from the most high-profile cases. His politics had not changed. Only his priorities. But because he had largely removed himself from the society of his peers, they seemed to have come to believe he could safely be ignored.

Graves, however, whose patriotism Paris had always suspected as more for show than substance, had taken a different approach. Having once given vocal support to the cause of Irish independence, he now actively courted the good opinion of the loyalists. With certain men, he spoke critically of the uprising and warmly of the proposed union with Great Britain; with others, however, he still voiced feelings quite opposite. No one could say for certain which side Graves was on. His own side, Paris suspected. The man clearly wanted something more than a life as a Dublin barrister and would say what he must to get it.

Now, Paris made a show of straightening his sleeve as he weighed the man's words. *A matter of some delicacy.* Against his better judgment, he nodded once. "Go on."

Graves leaned back in his chair. "It concerns a half-starved boy arrested for theft." He was savvy enough not to drop his voice and thereby draw attention to their conversation. "Caught red-handed by the baker as he snatched a loaf from his cart."

"What makes you assume I would be interested?" Paris demanded, though of course he was. The poor child, punished for trying to assuage his hunger…

"I can think of several reasons." Graves paused for a sip of coffee and to nod to an acquaintance as he passed by their table. "But I'll offer just one: It seems the boy is from Kilready."

Kilready Castle, on the northern border of County Dublin, belonged to the nominally Irish Lord Dashfort. For many years, however, the earl had been an absentee, supporting himself in style in London by charging rack-rent to his tenants, who had been driven to the point of desperation—and beyond. The man's neglect had surely driven some of them into the grave.

Whenever possible, the United Irishmen had made use of the unrest at places like Kilready to drum up support for their cause. But Dashfort's unlooked-for return to his Irish estate after more than a decade away, followed by the stationing of British soldiers near the castle to protect both his life and his property, had necessitated a change of plans. A change that, like many other aspects of the uprising, had been poorly communicated and executed, resulting in yet more bloodshed—in this case, the life's blood of

Paris's oldest and dearest friend. Unavoidably delayed by a grave injury to his brother, Paris had arrived too late to support Henry Edgeworth's mission. Too late to save Henry.

At the name *Kilready*, a sudden rush of blood through his veins paralyzed Paris for a moment. At last he managed to cross one booted leg over the other and fingered the handle of his spoon. "And what has that to do with 'men like us'?"

Graves's expression shifted to something that was not quite surprise. "The boy claims he left home because he's grown a conscience about his role in a ring of smugglers. No one believes his tale, of course, but one wonders..."

"You mean you suspect D—"

Under pretense of reaching for his cup, Graves made a slicing movement with one long finger, cutting him off. "Ah, Lord Castlereagh. Good morning, sir," he said, rising. Reluctantly, Paris followed suit to greet the Chief Secretary, the man who had made it his personal mission to quash the rebellion. Graves bowed and received a nod of acknowledgment in return; Paris's spine refused to bend. Castlereagh moved on without speaking.

As Paris and Graves leaned in to resume their seats, Graves spoke low. "You need to spend more time in the pubs and with the gossip columns. If you did, you'd know all about Dashfort's trial in the court of public opinion. When his wife died a year ago, under suspicious circumstances, he was forced to leave London with a cloud of scandal hanging over him. Or so it is said."

Paris nodded his understanding. He was well aware of the rumors. He also knew that Dashfort had brought his son and daughter with him to Ireland. Despite his utter disdain for the man, Paris nevertheless pitied his two young children, mourning their mother, caught up in a cruel circus, and now uprooted, ferried "home" to a place they had never seen. "But you suspect there was more to Dashfort's decision to return when he did?"

Graves lifted one shoulder. "It could prove beneficial to the man who discovers what's going on at Kilready Castle."

Smuggling... Even Dashfort would find it difficult to avoid trouble if it could be proved he was involved. Paris settled into his chair. "Beneficial to your case, you mean."

"*My* case? My dear fellow, I am at present fully occupied with my preparations for the dispute over Mr. Halloran's lease. Why," he reached out and lifted his drink to his lips once more, "I hardly have time for a cup of coffee."

"I see." Paris drummed his fingers on the tabletop. "I suppose no one is eager to take on the boy's defense."

"It isn't the sort of case on which reputations are built," Graves agreed, a sneering twist to his expression. "But I didn't think you'd mind."

No, Paris cared little for his reputation now. And evidently, Graves was counting on that fact.

If Paris succeeded, then the boy—doubtless another Irish pawn exploited by his master, whether or not any laws had been broken—might be saved. And if Dashfort's crimes were exposed, Paris would have gone a little further toward atoning for his mistakes, particularly where Henry Edgeworth was concerned. Of course, revenge wouldn't restore Henry's life, nor the lives of so many others who had been lost in the fight for freedom or executed afterward. But it would be better than nothing.

Wouldn't it?

"One question, Graves." He curved his hand around his cup. "Are you trying to save me, or destroy me?"

Graves chuckled. A shade too heartily, perhaps. "If you have to ask…"

Paris gave a humorless laugh in reply. Nevertheless, after a moment's reflection, he raised his cup in a sort of toast to seal his fate. He drank deeply, though the coffee had gone cold.

"Very good," Graves said. "I knew you would see things in the proper light." He reached into his breast pocket, withdrew a folded paper, and slid it across the table to him. "The information you'll need…"

Paris palmed the note without reading it. This was neither the time nor the place to indulge his curiosity. With a nod, he rose to leave, but not before he snapped a coin onto the table. Best not to be indebted to Graves, not even for the price of a cup of coffee.

Chapter 10

"So glad you could join us, Miss Gorse."

At first Rosamund assumed Paris's words were sarcasm, a gibe at her lateness, though she hadn't heard any clock in the house strike the hour. But his face was…well, she knew no better word to describe his expression than *keen*. Sharp as a whetted blade.

Standing at the head of the table, he radiated a strange, yet compelling energy. His garnet colored coat, a striking shade under any circumstances, was especially so given his dark coloring. The boyish, tousled waves of his black hair hinted that he had spent the better part of the day brushing it out of his eyes, evidently his habit when he was preoccupied. One persistent lock slipped forward even now. And from beneath it peered eyes that made her feel…well, *wanted*.

The sensation was more than a little unsettling.

Thankfully, Molly chose that moment to step into the room with a tray full of steaming dishes. Quickly, Rosamund seated herself. Not opposite Paris, as he had suggested with a nod of his head, but beside Bell on one of the long sides of the table, at an angle that put him out of her direct line of vision, and she out of his.

For the next few moments, they were absorbed in filling their plates. The only words exchanged were those to the purpose, to "pass the creamed turnips" or "mind the salt" when the cellar was nearly overturned by a careless hand.

Accustomed to quiet dinners, she thought little of the silence that fell over the room as they began to eat. Mrs. Sloane had been at best a taciturn companion, and in recent years Charles had rarely visited Tavisham Manor.

Over time, she had learned that if silence did not exactly aid digestion, it was better than complaint and derision.

But of course silence was not the norm in the Burke household. Paris cleared his throat. "I can't recall a meal in which my sisters had so little to say."

Rosamund suspected that the girls had decided not to speak at all, rather than risk the truth slipping out. That afternoon, the four of them—Molly included—had come to a grudging agreement: to say nothing to Paris about the kitten until the moment was right. *Wait until he's happy about something*, Bell had insisted, to which Daphne had replied that the kitten would be a fully grown cat if they waited so long as that.

"Perhaps," Rosamund ventured, "they are simply putting into practice the old maxim that children ought to be seen and not heard."

Daphne's face contorted as if she were trying to make sense of words spoken in an unfamiliar language. "What sort of rubbish is that, Miss Gorse?"

Sardonic humor twitched at the corners of Paris's mouth. "An English maxim, I daresay."

Bell looked thoughtful. "I've never heard Mama say that. But if she ever did believe in such a rule, I suppose Erica broke it so often, she grew weary of repeating it and gave it up."

"Paris would have broken it first," said Daphne matter-of-factly.

"Girls!" Rosamund exclaimed, both horrified and, God help her, envious. What would it be like to speak to one's brother as Daphne and Bell spoke to theirs? Not to fear some wounding reply…or worse?

"Do you doubt I was a rule breaker, Miss Gorse?"

She stabbed blindly at her plate and put a forkful of something—roast beef—in her mouth to give herself a moment to think of a suitable reply. It was too tender to provide an excuse for much delay, but nevertheless she chewed thoroughly and swallowed and dabbed her lips before answering. And even then, she did not meet his eye. "I'm not persuaded that you have any great respect for the rules even now, Mr. Burke."

Silence fell again as she awaited the inevitable reprimand. Teasing banter was not a skill she had had occasion to perfect—not a skill a woman in her position would ever have occasion to perfect.

Then a sound that wasn't precisely laughter rumbled from the far end of the table. "Quite so, Miss Gorse." His low murmur lodged somewhere near the base of her spine, sending an unexpected shiver of pleasure through her. "And that being the case, I certainly do not require silence from my young dinner companions." Rosamund at last glanced up in time to see him look from one of his sisters to the other, one dark brow bent in a playfully suspicious arch. Her heart lifted with it. "Well? Cat got your tongue?"

Bell choked and sputtered. Molly, who was nearest, gave her an unceremonious whack on the back.

Daphne, however, seized the moment, perhaps inspired by the teasing note in her brother's voice. "Now that you mention it, Paris, we did have a lesson in zoology today."

"Oh?"

"No, art," squeaked Bell, her face contorted with worry.

"Mathematics and economics." Rosamund forced herself to speak again. "I took the girls shopping."

Bell gave an eager nod. "Miss Gorse bought a dress."

Paris's dark eyes sought her out. Was he displeased that she had taken his sisters without asking permission? Displeased by her purchase? But there was a flicker in the depths of his gaze that hinted at something quite other than displeasure. Along with a twist of his lips that wasn't quite a smile. "Shoes, too, I hope."

Her reply caught in her throat. How did he know? The faintest memory—or perhaps fantasy—sketched through her mind, of strong fingers caressing along her stocking-covered calf and over her ankle, slipping her ruined shoe from her foot.

"No," Daphne answered for her, a hint of exasperation in her voice. "Just a dress."

"And underthings," added Bell.

He had not taken his eyes from her. Was it her imagination, or did they grow darker? She did not know how to read that expression, but it turned her insides to jelly, and she did not like—oh, *twaddle*. She might be lying to everyone else, but there was nothing to be gained by lying to herself. She *did* like the way it made her feel, though she knew she should not. Of all the foolish things she had done in the last three days, allowing herself to be attracted to Paris Burke was undoubtedly the most foolish of all.

"I did not wish to keep the girls from home too long, Mr. Burke." Her cheeks stung with heat. "Any additional items I may require can wait for another occasion."

"If I were you, Miss Gorse, I should get a bonnet next," Daphne said, chewing as she spoke. Turning toward her brother, she added, "She wore that awful sunhat of Erica's today, but thank God, now it's ru—"

"I must remind you that a young lady does not talk with her mouth full." Rosamund spoke across her, firmly but gently.

"Another English childrearing maxim, Miss Gorse?" Paris took a bite of bread. "I confess I'm curious about one thing, though," he said after making a point of chewing and swallowing. "Where did the zoology lesson come into it?"

China and silver rattled against the tray on which Molly was stacking the serving dishes. "Och, you know Grafton Street, Mr. Paris. Beastly when there's a crowd."

Both of Paris's brows lifted in patent disbelief. He once more looked from Daphne to Bell and last to Rosamund. Beneath the table, she could feel Bell's legs bouncing with nervous energy. She scrambled for another line of conversation, anything to keep the secret of the rescued kitten. "Your sisters told me you had a meeting this morning, Mr. Burke. It went well, I hope?"

"Unexpectedly so." His feverishly bright gaze pierced her, unblunted by the awkward angle between them. Was the meeting, or its subject, the cause of his strange energy? "Rather exciting stuff, if I do say so myself. A case of possible smuggling at—"

Daphne rolled her eyes. "That's done it, Miss Gorse. Both he and Papa will talk about their cases for hours if you'll let them. It's always *exciting* and *interesting* and—"

"Forgive me," he said, looking anything but chastened. "I am prone to forget that everyone does not share my fascination with the law. Dare I hope you do, Miss Gorse?"

A trap, surely. And she was teetering on the brink. If she blinked, drew breath, she would topple headlong into it. Did he suspect that she had deliberately sought out a man of his profession? Worse, did he know that she was fascinated by him?

Leaning back from the table as if from a precipice, she lifted her napkin from her lap and folded it beside her plate. "I have had no occasion to be involved with legal matters, Mr. Burke. *Thankfully*, I suppose most would say."

"*Regrettably*," he countered with an expression just shy of wicked.

She made herself look away. "If you're quite finished, girls, we ought to excuse ourselves."

It would not have surprised her in the least to learn that in the Burke household, the ladies lingered at table with the gentlemen. It would hardly have surprised her even to be told that they all, from youngest to oldest, took port together. But whatever their previous custom, the girls scrambled to their feet now, tired of dancing around the subject of how their day had been spent and eager to check on the kitten. "Yes, Miss."

Paris stood too. "You'll join me for tea, I hope, Miss Gorse? After the girls are in bed?"

Swallowing against temptation, she curtsied. "A generous offer, sir. Thank you. But I believe it would be best if I retired."

As they neared the top of the house, they could hear the kitten mewing piteously. Daphne and Bell hiked their skirts to their knees and raced up the remaining stairs. Rosamund stumbled to follow them. In the girls' bedroom, they found the little ball of fluff hanging from the curtain that covered their dressing area, unable to free itself to either climb higher or descend.

Daphne rushed to unhook its tiny, translucent claws, then gathered the complaining creature to her chest. "Oh, poor thing. You're all right now."

"I've been thinking. I want to call her Eileen." Bell touched the soft fur, no longer gray, but silvery white after a thorough but careful wash with a rough scrap of cloth Molly had sacrificed for the purpose, dipped in a pan of warm water. "It means *bright*."

"But we don't even know it's a girl," Rosamund observed.

Bell frowned, unconvinced, and scooped the kitten from her sister's hands. "What else would she be?"

Soon Molly entered with a can of hot water, shooting a frown at the kitten as she filled the washbasin and muttering under her breath as she stacked clean linens and laid out the girls' nightclothes. Nevertheless, Rosamund could have sworn she saw her give the tiny creature a tickle under the chin and a wink before she left.

While the girls washed and dressed, Rosamund wandered into the schoolroom. Curious, she examined the stack of books on Daphne's desk. Surprisingly standard fare, primers from a generation ago, perhaps acquired when Paris and the elder siblings were young, before their parents had embarked on what Rosamund had begun to think of as their "educational experiment."

The exception was a small, illustrated book called *The Botanic Garden: A Poem in Two Parts, Containing "The Economy of Vegetation" and "The Loves of the Plants."*

Of course.

With a small sigh, she picked it up and returned to the bedroom. Daphne had already slid between the sheets, the kitten held close. Bell stood beside Daphne's bed, a jealous frown notched into her brow. "Shall I read to you?" Rosamund asked, holding up the little book. In a corner of her heart she kept the fragment of a memory, one of the few memories Charles had never managed to make her doubt: the sound of Papa's voice as he read to her.

"What is it?" Daphne sounded suspicious. Rosamund read the title aloud. "Oh. Erica left that behind. It's bound to be deadly dull stuff."

With a parting glance of longing at Eileen, Bell at last clambered into her own bed, leaving room for Rosamund to sit at the foot. "The second part sounds promising."

"Let's give it a go, shall we?"

Rosamund opened to a page that had been marked by a sloppily embroidered slip of silk ribbon, and found the lives of plants fancifully rendered as fair damsels and gallant nights and—*oh*. Oh, dear. Some of the flowers seemed not always to behave with ladylike deportment. How else to read lines such as this?

Each wanton beauty, trick'd in all her grace,
Shakes the bright dew-drops from her blushing face;
In gay undress displays her rival charms,
And calls her wondering lovers to her arms.

With a smile Rosamund closed the book and rose. "That's enough for tonight, I think." The girls protested, thankfully oblivious to most of the poem's suggestive symbolism. "No, no. We've a busy day tomorrow. Geography. And French." She thrust the book under one arm before bending down to tuck the covers under Bell's chin. She then turned to Daphne. "For the time being, Eileen will stay downstairs with me."

"Oh, but Miss Gorse, that's not fair."

"Fair or not, it's what's best for all of you. Otherwise I predict that none of you would get a wink of sleep. Kittens especially need their rest."

Though it would be an exaggeration to claim that her words had persuaded them, the girls at last relented. "Good night," she said, picking up the kitten in one hand and the candle in the other.

Once in her room, she placed the candlestick on the desk and laid both the kitten and the book on her bed. Eileen soon began to creep over the mountains and valleys of the rumpled coverlet, an eager explorer. Rosamund watched for a moment before turning to the washstand and studying her face in the small square of glass that hung above it. In the uncertain light of the candle, the bruise on her temple nearly disappeared into the shadow of her hairline. With practiced fingers, she unpinned the heavy coil, then wove the locks into a neat braid, looser than usual so as not to make her head ache again. Finally, she went to the wardrobe, slipped out of her dress and into her nightgown.

When she turned around again, Eileen was nowhere to be seen. Quickly, her eyes darted to the doorway. But the door was closed. She shrugged. The kitten couldn't go far.

Ready for bed, but unready for sleep, she sat on the edge of the mattress and with one fingertip, traced the corners of the book of poetry. Scandalous poetry. Surely, she had imagined it… But ladies didn't imagine such things, did they? Ladies did not spend any time at all thinking about…

She lifted the cover.

How the young Rose in beauty's damask pride

Drinks the warm blushes of his bashful bride;

Without conscious thought, she drew the slender volume closer, into the circle of candlelight. Onto her lap.

With honey'd lips enamour'd Woodbines meet,

Clasp with fond arms, and mix their kisses sweet—

"Oh!"

The book leaped out of her hands and onto the floor. From nowhere, Eileen had launched herself onto Rosamund's back and was now hanging, one set of fragile claws hooked in her braid, another in her nightdress. First with one hand, then with the other, Rosamund flailed behind her back, reaching for the kitten. Her long sleeves hampered her efforts. Neither from above nor below could she touch anything more than a wisp of fluff—either the tops of Eileen's ears or the tip of her tail. How on earth was she going to—?

"Miss Gorse? Are you all right?"

Oh, God above. She was well and truly punished now for looking into that book. "Quite all right, thank you, Mr. Burke."

Through the door, she heard him take a step closer. "Are you certain? You sounded as if you were in some pain."

The latch shifted slightly. He'd laid his hand upon it. Oh, dear. Screwing up her courage, she rose and went to the door to reassure him. With every step, Eileen gripped harder, holding on for dear life, and the tiny daggers at the ends of her paws sank through the nightdress and into her skin.

Forcing a smile onto her face, she opened the door. "Perfectly certain, thank you," she managed as her chin jerked a notch higher, tugged by the weight of the kitten. "I'll wish you good night."

He'd been on his way to bed but not in it, by the looks of things. He still wore the dark red wool coat. Beneath his loosened cravat, she could just glimpse the notch at the base on his throat, disguised as a shadow in the folds of his linen.

He quickly looked her up and down, took in her state of dishabille, and fixed his iron and ebony gaze somewhere on the far wall. "Are you—are you hiding something behind your back, Miss Gorse?"

If she shook her head in denial, as she so desperately longed to do, the kitten would grip even harder. Resigned, she turned slowly and rather stiffly away from the door but made no move to close it.

She knew the moment he saw Eileen and understood her predicament.

Gruffly, he cleared his throat. Almost the sound he had made at dinner. Not quite a laugh. "Ah. The subject of the zoology lesson, I take it?"

"Yes."

He stepped closer, and the warmth of his hands seeped through the cambric of her nightgown as he proceeded to disentangle the kitten, claw by claw. "Perhaps 'animal husbandry' would be a more fitting description of today's lesson. Did *you* rescue this creature?"

"Bell," she whispered. "She is fearless, you know."

"My sister, or the kitten?" When he had worked the last claw free, Rosamund turned slowly to face him. The kitten was curled in his cupped hand. "I suppose she and Daphne are determined to keep it. Does Molly know?" His expression was stern. "Because I certainly will *not* be the one to tell her."

"She knows. Which is not to say she approves…"

He held out the ball of fluff, clearly expecting her to take it. But to do so, she would have to step closer. Touch him. Slide the back of her hand into the curve of his palm. The muscles of her arm ached with longing as she curled her fingers into her nightgown.

At last he gave up waiting and twisted just enough to tip Eileen onto the bed behind him. When he faced Rosamund again, his eyes still respectfully averted, he bowed his head as if to say goodnight. The movement must have brought the fallen book into his line of sight, for instead of rising to go out, he bent further to pick it up. "What's this?" Turning the spine toward the candlelight, he read the title aloud. "Something of my sister's, I suppose." He glanced up at her, and his hair fell forward, shadowing his eyes. "Were you reading it?"

"I—yes," she confessed after a moment, and her hesitation seemed to pique his curiosity. Heat flushed up her neck and into her face. "It's quite, um…*fascinating*, really."

She hadn't meant to repeat his word. The word he'd used to describe his interest in the law. The word that more accurately described her interest in him.

When he leaned forward to hand the book to her, she reached for it at the same moment and nearly knocked it from his grasp. "Oh, dear. Forgive me. I didn't—"

Only the width of the book separated them now. With a trembling hand she once more reached out…and up…and…*oh*. That stubborn, misbehaving lock of black hair was silky soft, tickling through her fingertips as she swept it off his brow.

Never in her life had she been so bold. So reckless.

Not even when she had escaped Kilready Castle.

Surprise flared in his dark eyes, and as her hand fell away, his rose. Lightly, he caught her wayward wrist. The frantic tattoo of her pulse would tell him everything she couldn't. Oh, how she longed for the courage to speak. Though what to say? An apology would be a paltry thing at this juncture—and a lie, to boot.

"I—" She swallowed but did not break her gaze. "I'm not sorry."

"No?" His thumb swept a lazy arc across her palm, the same practiced touch that had made the spinet give up its music. "Is there something else you wanted, Miss Gorse?"

She had so little experience with men. But some experience, at least, with her own desires. Desires on which she'd begun to think she would never have an opportunity to act. Why, if Erica's book was to be believed, even flowers indulged now and then in a… "A—a kiss?"

Before he could respond to that daring request, before either of them could come to their senses, she stretched up on her toes and brushed her lips against his.

As she drew back she watched a mischievous smile play around his mouth. Slowly, he shook his head. "No." With a flick of his wrist, he tossed the forgotten book onto the desk. Out of the corner of her eye, she saw it slide across the polished surface, coming to a stop near the far edge. Then his newly-free hand settled at her waist, and all her attention was taken up by the delicious heat of his touch as it seeped through her nightgown and into her skin. "A *kiss*."

She let her eyelids fall as he lowered his mouth to hers, more than willing to lose herself in the senses that remained. Her fingertips curled against the soft wool of his coat when he brought her hand to his chest. The woodsy scent of his cologne was an invitation to wander into shadowy, forbidden places. But best of all was the sound of his breath, that delightful catch of anticipation just before their lips met.

He'd been right, of course. Her swift peck had not been a kiss—not if one judged by the sweet, soft movement of his mouth over hers. And she felt quite certain that she would measure any future kisses against this one.

A muffled whimper of pleasure rose in her throat as his mouth grew firmer, more demanding. Awareness shot through her, every place where they touched and even where they didn't. Her pulse fluttered in her chest and in the second, secret heart between her thighs. When the gentle pressure of his lips coaxed hers to part, she gave in to the inexplicable need to taste him, to take him into herself and to be taken.

As if startled by her eagerness, he stiffened and jerked her closer, her breasts tight against his chest. Below, she could feel the growing sign of his arousal. Lifting his head, he broke the kiss and his eyes bored into hers. "Miss Gorse," he began, his voice a gravelly whisper.

"Rosamund," she corrected brazenly.

His brows lifted. "*Rosamund*, then. Will you do me the great favor…?"

It was her turn to catch her breath. "Yes?"

"…Of informing me as to whether or not my sisters have given this infernal creature a name? I wish to be precise when I rain curses upon it."

Baffled surprise warred with mortification, then stifled laughter, as the soft tips of pink ears appeared over his shoulder, followed closely by the rest of the kitten. Eileen wobbled a bit before finding her balance and sitting down near Paris's collar, her white fur set off nicely by his black hair and the color of his coat.

"I *am* sorry," he said. Was he was apologizing for kissing her, or for stopping?

Either way, the spell was broken. Rosamund slipped free of his embrace and reached up to retrieve Eileen, who was clearly pleased at last to have made a successful climb, purring as she curled into the hollow of her palm, still warm from Paris's touch. Rosamund stepped back and tucked the kitten close to her breast, cradling her with both hands, while Paris tugged his coat collar into place.

When he was done, he shot a narrow-eyed glare at Eileen—at least, Rosamund hoped he was looking at the kitten. The thin, old nightgown she was wearing didn't leave much to the imagination. "I suppose an interruption from some member of this household was inevitable," he said. *And fortunate?*

She nodded, darting her eyes toward the door, then back to him, not allowing her gaze to fasten on any one feature, in the vain hope she would not be tempted to catalog them when he had gone. "Good night, Mr. Burke."

"Good night, Miss Gorse."

He closed the door behind him, but she waited until she heard his booted tread descending the staircase before she allowed herself to sink to the bed and cuddle the kitten to her burning cheek.

For just a moment, she had forgotten to be the prim governess. A moment more and she might have let herself forget to be a proper young lady.

Never had she exhibited such a shocking lapse of judgment. Yet she regretted only Eileen's disruption. She'd wanted that kiss, the heat of his palm rising from her waist to brush the underside of her breast. But she wanted something else, too.

Behind that wry smile that occasionally turned up his lips—the one he deployed so ruthlessly, both shield and weapon—she'd glimpsed something else. And for some reason she couldn't quite put into words, she wanted to know what it was. She wanted to see inside him.

Eileen squirmed, asking to be set free, and Rosamund obliged. In another show of daring, the kitten leaped from the pillow to the desk and explored for a bit before sitting down atop *The Botanic Garden* and beginning to groom herself, making it impossible for Rosamund to resume reading.

Probably for the best.

When Rosamund collapsed backward on the bed, Eileen paused in her ministrations to send a firm glare of blue-eyed disapproval. A huff of silent laughter lifted Rosamund's chest at the sight of the kitten's pink tongue paused in mid-lick. If only the library below contained books that had to do with something other than plants. Or the law. She needed an entirely different sort of book. A guide to animal nature. Preferably one with a chapter on cats.

And two chapters at least on men.

Chapter 11

Paris woke with the sour tang of whiskey in his mouth. Too familiar, but surely preferable, at least in some small way, to waking with the sweet taste of Rosamund's kiss on his lips. Waking to proof he'd fallen so far, he was capable of debauching the governess. The prim, prickly, oh-so-English governess…

Unfortunately, that string of adjectives was proving far more appealing than he liked.

But by God a gentleman was accountable for his actions, even if he could not always control his wayward thoughts. He deserved every pang of guilt that had wracked him through yet another interminable night. Even now he could not be certain what he'd meant to do when he'd grabbed her wrist. Stop her from issuing a second invitation, he'd told himself.

If only he'd been strong enough to decline the first.

Molly appeared in the doorway to the drawing room bearing coffee on a tray, for once a welcome distraction. "Och, here you are, Mr. Paris," she called as she sailed into the room and deposited the tray on the table beside his chair. "Up early I see." For a housemaid who found his bed undisturbed more mornings than it had been slept in, she oughtn't to sound so surprised.

He'd fully intended to retire last night, though. He'd even allowed himself to imagine a night of undisturbed rest. Then he'd heard Miss Gorse's muffled cry of distress from the neighboring room and the evening had taken rather a different turn. Afterward, he'd been unable to bear the thought of lying for hours in the darkness of his own chamber, knowing Rosamund slept just a few feet away. So he'd retreated to the darkness of the drawing room instead, taking a perverse sort of comfort in the least comfortable chair he could find. He'd allowed himself a single dram of liquor, just enough to dull the too-sharp memory of her lips and what might have happened if not for…

"That damned kitten," he muttered aloud—a phrase he'd never expected to say. Certainly not in a voice tinged with jealousy. But he could not deny that he'd wanted to be the beast cradled against Rosamund's perfect breast last night.

Molly sighed and shook her head as she poured. "Likely it won't be any worse than Miss Erica's hedgehog."

How could he have forgotten that poor creature? Rescued by his sister a year ago—no, two, of course. How time did fly. She'd found it during one of her botanical expeditions to the very outskirts of Dublin, farther afield than she was supposed to wander alone and therefore forbidden. For that reason, she'd been determined to keep the hedgehog a secret. She'd almost succeeded, until the night it had escaped its box and somehow made its way down to the kitchen, where Cook had heard it grubbing about and gone, skillet upraised, to investigate. Molly had reacted just in time to prevent the slaughter of innocents—both the hedgehog and Erica.

Erica had made a sort of pet out of the thing. Only she had ever managed to learn the trick of persuading it to unroll from its defensive ball so its soft belly could be stroked. He remembered once joking in a low voice with Henry Edgeworth, who had often dined with the family: *"How do hedgehogs mate?"*

Henry had regarded him with an unreadable expression for a long moment before cracking something meant to be a smile. *"Very carefully."*

Shortly thereafter, Henry had proposed to Erica and been accepted. Paris had thought it an odd match, persuaded Henry's interest lay in another direction and believing Erica unsuited to marriage at all. No doubt a true friend and a responsible elder brother would have tried to keep the two of them from making a terrible mistake.

Paris had merely shrugged off his concerns and offered them his felicitations.

"Do you remember what became of that hedgehog?" he asked Molly.

"Not I." The maid looked thoughtful. "You don't suppose Cook managed to sneak it into a stew?"

As he sputtered into the coffee he'd been sipping, Molly began straightening the piles he'd left on the desk. Wordlessly, she placed last night's dirty glass on her tray, but the assessing look she sent over her shoulder drove him from the room.

Outside the door to his bedchamber, he paused. He'd listened to the girls troop down to the kitchen for breakfast and Rosamund's lighter ascent to the schoolroom sometime later. Molly would be occupied downstairs for some time. He would be safe, finally, in collapsing into oblivion. But a comfortable bed was the last thing he deserved.

Instead, he went in, removed his wrinkled coat, and hung it over the back of a chair. Molly had left hot water. Somehow, she managed the near-impossible task of keeping the household running smoothly, even anticipating its occupants' needs. For that, he was more than willing to put up with a little sauciness. After shedding his waistcoat, cravat, and shirt, he shaved—though where he was going, no one would notice if he looked like death warmed over—then donned fresh linen and a brown coat that he knew from experience wouldn't show the grime.

When he left the house, a steady drizzle was falling. He flipped up the collar on his greatcoat, tugged his hat lower over his ears, and considered a hackney. But cabs were few and far between on the Dublin streets, and none would want to take him where he was headed. He'd reach his destination sooner on foot.

In an hour—during which time the drizzle had turned to rain and he'd been splashed with mud and worse by a passing dray—he stood before the hulking gray stone walls of the New Gaol in Kilmainham, larger than its predecessor but already almost as fetid.

Even outside, the odor of unwashed bodies hung thick in the air. The guard recognized him and let him through the gate with a sneer. Of late, Paris had expended all of his considerable legal acumen trying to save at least a few of those whom the system was designed to damn. He almost always failed, as Graves had surely known when he'd presented him with the Kilready case.

Part of him wondered whether he was supposed to fail this time, too.

Inside the jail, men, women, and children were penned together indiscriminately, murderers beside pickpockets, like hogs allowed to fatten by feeding on one another as they awaited slaughter. On every visit, Paris fought the temptation to clutch a handkerchief over his nose and mouth to filter the air, too thick with the stench of human misery to breathe. Each time, he made himself go on without it. If the prisoners could survive it, he could too.

Of course, a good many of them would not survive. A steady noise of moaning, coughing, and keening nearly drowned out his footsteps as he walked through the dark corridor lined with cells.

But silence would be more frightening still.

A few eyes had already begun to follow him. "Fagan?" he called out, dreading what would follow. "I'm looking for Thomas Fagan."

The replies, as always, ran the gamut. Some men claimed an identity that wasn't theirs, clutching at the mere flicker of hope it offered. Others, whose hope had long since died, loudly denied the existence of such a fellow. From the shadows, someone offered to suck his cock. Whether the lewd words were intended to draw him closer or drive him away, Paris had never tried to determine.

The women and children were quieter, though they watched him with hollow eyes from the corners of the crowded cells, where they'd been driven by the men. While he stood waiting, one elbowed her way to the front of her cage, snarling at those who would refuse her passage. "'Tis here you'll find him, sirrah."

It might have been a trap. Nevertheless, Paris stepped closer. "Yes?"

"T' lad took sick in the night," she explained, and she bravely nudged a few more bodies aside so that he could see a figure lying on the dirty straw, his face turned toward the wall.

"You, there," Paris called to the guard at the far end of the corridor. "I need to speak with this prisoner."

With a great show of reluctance, the man rose from the battered table at which he'd been seated, dealing himself a solitary hand of cards, and slowly approached. Paris had never seen him before. He must have been newly appointed to his post. "How's that?" the man grunted.

"I need to enter this cell." A wiser man wouldn't have made a habit of it. No one inside that cage had a thing to lose.

But Paris had also lost a great deal. Too much to fear disease or a makeshift knife between the ribs.

The guard looked from the gathered prisoners to Paris and gave a mirthless laugh, revealing a mouthful of rotted teeth. "It's your funeral." He shrugged. "All right, then. Back, you. Back!" he shouted, rattling the bars with a club to drive the men away. The ring of keys at his side jingled, but there was no merriment in the sound.

The woman who'd called Paris over had returned to the boy's side. "What ails him?" Paris asked her. Typhoid, cholera...the possibilities were legion.

That foolish question earned him another guffaw from the guard. "Naught but what this club would cure."

Paris caught the end of the man's cudgel in one hand and shoved him backward with it. "Enough. Unlock the cell."

The guard's eyes narrowed, clearly weighing whether or not to use the weapon on Paris. Paris held his ground. At last, the man grabbed his keys and thrust one into the lock. On rusty, squawking hinges, the door swung open just wide enough to admit Paris, then slammed shut again. Once more the key grated in the lock. By sheer force of will, Paris contained the familiar shudder of dread that accompanied the sound.

Privacy was a thing unheard of in prison. He'd planned defenses and heard confessions within these cells, while other prisoners chimed in with unsolicited advice and opinions. But this time, perhaps because of the boy's illness, the crowd held back a bit, leaving as wide a berth as possible around the body curled on the mangy straw. Only the woman stayed close enough to hear their quiet conversation.

"Do you know him?" Paris asked her.

She hesitated, then shook her head. When she laid her hand on the boy's shoulder, he moaned. "Fever," she explained. "Though not so's t' make 'im mad. Come now, Tommy, show yourself. Here's Mr. Burke come t' halp ee."

He couldn't remember having seen the woman before. But perhaps he had. Or perhaps his reputation had preceded him—whatever it might be. He squatted in the muck and joined the woman in her efforts to rouse Tommy Fagan.

At last the boy eased from the coil into which he'd wound himself and rolled onto his back, eyes still tightly closed. Paris could not prevent a gasp from escaping his lips. Fagan was crusted with dirt. Tracks had formed on his cheeks where tears had fallen and not been wiped away. Neither the dirt nor the tears surprised him. Beneath the layer of grime and the slight flush of fever, however, the boy's skin was almost translucent, like a creature born and raised in utter darkness. His hair, which poked through the holes in a tattered wool cap, was whiter than Rosamund's kitten. The effect was unearthly: a child formed of smoke or light, liable to be snuffed out by a strong breath of wind.

Nevertheless, his grip was firm as he fumbled for and found Paris's hand. "Help me," he whispered through dry, cracked lips.

With the woman's assistance, Paris lifted the boy to a sitting position, then slipped a flask from the deep pocket of his greatcoat. "Water," he explained.

The woman lifted one shoulder. "Pity."

Tommy drank greedily, the flask fastened to his lips so that not a drop escaped. When he'd drained its contents, his eyelids at last fluttered, then lifted, revealing surprisingly ordinary brown eyes, dull with fever. "Thank you, sir."

"You're Thomas Fagan?"

"Aye."

"And you came to Dublin from Kilready Castle?"

The eyelids drifted closed again. "Aye."

"What made you leave?"

"I couldn't go on—" He drew a rattling breath, eyes still closed. "Couldn't go on doin' his biddin'. 'Tis wrong, what he's doin'. Same as stealin'."

"I've heard there's smuggling going on near Kilready, Tommy. Is that it? Is that what you've been involved in?" The boy nodded. "Will you tell me who's behind it?"

He did not answer. The woman, still supporting one of the boy's shoulders, gave him a gentle shake. "Go on, then, Tommy. Why should you hang for another's crime?"

"Th' agent. Mr. Quin."

Paris was careful to keep his voice calm, matter-of-fact, though a great deal rode on the answer to his next question. "And from whom does Mr. Quin take his orders?"

Tommy's chest rose and fell with a labored breath. "'is lordship. Who else?"

"The Earl of Dashfort."

"Aye."

The exchange had cost the boy a great deal of effort, and Paris thanked him. "It's my hope that if Dashfort's involvement can be proved, the law will deal more lightly with you, Tommy."

"An' more harshly with 'im?"

"A peer has certain protections under the law. But I'll do my best to see justice served."

"Tain't right, is it?" he cried.

"The inequalities in our system? No, indeed. But—"

Tommy went on speaking, apparently without hearing Paris's reply. "Tain't right for a boy to wish 'is da ill. But 'e don't…" His narrow shoulders shook with a sob.

A quiver started low in Paris's gut, part excitement, part trepidation, and part reaction to the horrors that pressed in on him from all sides. Tommy Fagan was Dashfort's byblow? Had Graves suspected anything of the sort? Did Dashfort himself know?

"Och, me poor mam," Tommy cried. "She's naught but a washerwoman. Quin'll see to it she starves if he finds out I turned traitor."

The woman ran a grimy hand down the boy's cheek. "Hush, now," she soothed. "Don't you worry about your mam. She's a strong woman. She'd not want to see you take on so."

"I'll do everything I can, Tommy. You have my word." He squeezed the boy's hand, though Fagan's grasp had grown weaker. When he rose, the woman did too. "Tell me his mother's name."

She shook her head. "An' how should I know it, sirrah?"

"But you said she was a strong woman. I assumed—"

"Ain't met a washerwoman yet who weren't, Mr. Burke."

He swallowed the epithet on his tongue. "Of course." In prison, people either knew everything or nothing. One glance around the cell told him that Fagan's fellow inmates, who had no doubt overheard enough of the conversation, were content to pretend the latter. They cleared a wider path this time as he made his way back to the cell door and called for the guard, who took far longer than necessary to find his keys and release him.

"I'm going to send a physician to look after the boy," Paris told the man, who showed even less interest than the prisoners. "If he's not treated, the sickness may well spread."

"Save us the cost o' the rope, that will," he replied with a chortle.

Paris let his hand curl into a fist at his side, but he did not raise it. A brawl might mean he'd be forbidden to return. "Fever is no respecter of persons, my good fellow. Why, it might even spread to the guards."

That caught the man's attention. His shuffle increased to a trot as he escorted Paris to the mouth of the cavernous building. "You won't delay, Mr. Burke?"

"I wouldn't dream of it."

Outside the rain still came down. Despite its chill, he stood for a moment in the courtyard and let it sluice over him, washing away what it could of New Gaol. Some stains, of course, could not be touched with mere water.

Eventually he made his way east through the city, past houses that gleamed with the glow of lamplight, though it was only just past midday. The people who lived in them would never know the horrors inside the prison that hunched in their shadows. Soon enough he found himself near Trinity. The coffeehouse beckoned, warm and dry. He might yet have refused its lure, if Graves had not been sitting in his favorite window.

Paris went directly to the man's table. "You've been to Kilmainham," Graves observed. "I can tell by the smell." His quill continued to scratch along his paper. "And?"

With a flourish, Paris tossed his wet hat onto the table, spraying water onto the work spread across its top. Graves gave an exclamation of annoyance. But he also looked up at last.

"Send a doctor to the boy," Paris said flatly. "Without delay. Otherwise there'll be no case at all."

Graves set his mouth in a grim line and nodded. Quickly he wrote out a few words on a clean and mostly dry sheet of paper, folded it, and then signaled for a waiter. With the exchange of a few low words and a coin, the note was soon dispatched. Paris prayed the physician himself would soon follow.

"What did you learn?" Graves asked when they were alone again.

"More than I hoped. More than I liked, to be perfectly honest. The boy claims Dashfort is a…relation, we'll say. A close relation."

Graves lifted his brows, though not exactly in shock. "I wonder the man doesn't take a more personal interest in the case."

"I mean to see that he does. I'm going up to Kilready to investigate."

Graves's mild expression transformed into a grimace. "I wouldn't if I were you, Burke."

"Ah, but you are not I—a fact for which you no doubt give daily thanks." Certainly such a trip would not be the most pleasant thing Paris had ever done. But staying home had its own difficulties and dangers. "Good day, Graves." Retrieving his hat, Paris turned on one heel and left before the man could utter more feeble words of caution.

The rain had lightened, and Grafton Street was now crowded with shoppers who had been delayed in setting out. He was almost past the milliner's shop when a display of spring bonnets in the window caught his eye. He had hoped this morning's excursion would put last night's exchange with Rosamund out of his mind, at least for a little while. Yet even in the darkness of prison, she had lingered at the edge of his thoughts, the way the fragrance of her namesake perfumed a room even after the window onto the garden had been closed.

Good God. What had he done? The woman had fled the improper advances of her last employer. He had no right to be thinking of her as anything other than his sisters' governess. And had he not hired a governess to relieve himself of the burden of having to think of certain things at all?

He laid a hand on the shop door. Perhaps one more act of penance was in order…

When the door swung inward abruptly without any assistance from him, he nearly lost his balance. A bell jangled harshly, masking his exclamation of surprise as a woman charged from the shop and almost collided with him.

He collected himself enough to step backward into the street and bow. "Why, Mrs. Fitzhugh, fancy meeting you here."

With a glare of stern disapproval she looked him up and down, her frown deepening as she took in his dripping clothes and the grime he'd accumulated over the course of the morning. "I beg your pardon. Have we been introduced?"

"Paris Burke, ma'am," he said, touching two fingers to the brim of his hat. "At your service."

Her demeanor changed instantly, although not for the better. She jerked her head in a single nod that made the bedraggled feathers atop her hat sag lower.

"My sisters and I are most pleased—"

She spoke over him in a clipped voice. "I am most severely displeased, Mr. Burke."

Though he knew she had cause, the strength of her reaction took him aback. "I apologize for missing our meeting, ma'am, but I—"

"Without even the courtesy of a note informing me you'd filled the post. And with whom, sir! Why, when I first saw her, I took her for a scullery maid, and even then, I could scarce believe my eyes. To entrust your dear sisters to someone so slatternly and neglectful of her duties?"

"You cannot mean Miss—"

"Then, to hear your sisters address her as Miss—"

"Gorse." They spoke the name together, her voice sharp with disgust, his uplifted on a questioning note.

Her lips, her entire face, pursed. "Wherever did you find such a person, Mr. Burke?"

It behooved a barrister to be skilled at disguising his surprise. He managed to keep his reply between his teeth until he could speak it with the necessary detachment. "I regret most sincerely that I was not in touch sooner about the matter. Thank you for your concern, Mrs. Fitzhugh."

His unwillingness to explain only increased her affront. She stiffened, setting the feathers in motion once more. "Well!"

But Paris remained unmoved, though his thoughts were spinning. "Good day, ma'am." This time, he lifted his hat, and the rain that had collected on the brim spilled between them, spattering her skirts. She fixed him with a glare that conveyed without question her opinion of him. Then again, who could approve of the sort of man capable of hiring a perfect stranger off the streets of Dublin to serve as governess to his sisters?

As she turned and marched away, he bit his lip to quell the laughter determined to rise in his chest. If that laugh escaped, it would sound mad enough.

Christ above. He'd wondered at Mrs. Fitzhugh, sending him a governess with so little experience. Sending the woman alone to meet him in a part of town where the women who walked unaccompanied were generally members of quite another profession. But he'd tucked his concerns away behind the knowledge of Mrs. Fitzhugh's sterling reputation. Behind his own selfish needs.

When he finally succeeded in swallowing the laugh once and for all, it turned into something more akin to a growl. He'd suspected Rosamund of not telling the entire truth. But this? This chance meeting with Mrs. Fitzhugh was proof of the extent to which he had been duped. As soon as he reached Merrion Square, he ought to summon the demon that had been prowling about the corners of his mind all day and dispel it. Dismiss her.

But hardly had he turned in the direction of home when he caught a glimpse of several pairs of ladies' shoes in the window of the cobbler's shop across the way. His mind was quick to conjure the memory of Rosamund's delicate slipper, ruined beyond repair by a desperate journey.

Where had she come from if not Mrs. Fitzhugh's agency? Why had she been at King's Inns Quay? She'd said she was looking for him, hadn't she? Certainly she'd said she was a governess…

Three days had made his memory of that evening no clearer. Was it possible he had assumed…? And she, fleeing something—no, some*one*—had let him?

People often misunderstood the law as a search for truth. But any barrister worth his salt knew that the truth was sometimes an inconvenience. Less likely to ensure justice than a story, carefully constructed and conveyed. A *lie*, as laypeople were wont to call it.

In a courtroom, one side put together the pieces of a broken vase in a way that made it look whole and appealing, all the while hoping it wouldn't leak. The other side held it up to the light to reveal its cracks.

As the bustle of Grafton Street flowed around him, he stood, savoring the remembered taste of Rosamund's lips, despite his best intentions, and trying to decide which side he was on.

Chapter 12

The morning after the kiss, Rosamund woke with a weight on her chest. Embarrassment at her wanton behavior like a hot stone pressing against her heart, like a—

Eileen stretched, lifting herself from Rosamund's breastbone and lightly touching her paw to Rosamund's chin.

No. No, she *wasn't* embarrassed. She tested the thought as the kitten stretched, one soft paw chasing the smile that settled over her lips. Well, maybe a *little* embarrassed. But not sorry. Why should she be? Why shouldn't she like Paris Burke? He was witty and passionate about his work and easy-going with his sisters and—

That unaccustomed spasm of defiance gave way almost immediately to a more familiar emotion: doubt. He used his wit and his work and his careless manner to hold himself apart from everyone. Had she really let herself imagine that he would let down his guard if she touched her lips to his? And why in heaven's name did she care if he did? *Anything* might be hiding behind his handsome, sardonic mask.

Worse yet, perhaps *nothing* hid behind it. Maybe that was simply who he was.

A shaky breath left her. Eileen, who liked neither the movement of Rosamund's chest beneath her nor the ruffling of her fur, jumped to the floor.

The fact of the matter was, Rosamund *did* care. For Daphne and Bell, who were bright and eager students—though surely she had learned more from them than the other way around. And for their brother, who intrigued her and challenged her and made her want to kiss him again.

He ought to dismiss her for her spectacular errors in judgment. But she didn't think he would. Partly because he didn't seem the sort who relished going to the trouble of dismissing servants. And partly because she suspected he liked having her there—and not just because it relieved him of caring for his sisters. Despite her inexperience, she felt certain his had not been the kiss of an indifferent man.

Freeing one hand from the tangle of sheets and blankets, she laid her palm softly against the cool plaster that divided her bedchamber from his. Perhaps at this very moment, he was on the other side of that wall thinking not of telling her to leave, but of asking her to stay. Perhaps he—

She snatched her hand away, shut her eyes, shook her head—but none of it stopped the next thought from forming. That cricket ball must have done more damage than she realized. Paris wasn't planning a proposal after one foolish kiss. And she wasn't free to accept him if he were. However eager Charles had been to marry her off, he would certainly object to any future for her that involved Merrion Square and an Irish barrister. So long as he was her guardian, she wasn't free to choose.

"Good mornin', Miss Rosamund," Molly sang out as she backed into the room carrying hot water and fresh linens. Eileen shot between her legs and through the open door. "Never tell me you had that creature in here with you last night?"

"She was an excellent companion and protector, Molly."

Molly spun, training her sharp eyes on Rosamund. "An' just what is it you need protectin' from?"

At the memory of the kitten climbing over Paris's shoulder, Rosamund only smiled, ignoring the question. "Is Mr. Burke up?"

After another searching look, the maid moved to fill the washbasin. "I've not seen him yet this morning. But his room's empty."

"Oh." The note of disappointment in her voice earned her a puzzled, backward glance from Molly as she left.

Quickly, Rosamund washed, dressed, and went down to the kitchen, where she met the girls and they all ate breakfast together. Eileen was already there, too, greedily lapping milk from a chipped saucer Cook had placed on the floor. Half an hour later, with the kitten curled contentedly on a pile of rags near the hearth, Rosamund ushered Daphne and Bell up to the schoolroom. Still no sign of their brother, though she noted in passing that the drawing room door was shut.

The girls slid into their seats as she walked to the window and looked out. "We'll begin with geography, girls," she said briskly, spinning to face them. Surely the wide world contained sufficient distraction from the question of what would happen when she saw Paris again.

Several hours later, Molly opened the door to the schoolroom. "Beggin' your pardon, but I—"

She broke off, eyes wide, forcing Rosamund to make an honest assessment of the mess the girls had made with their papier-mâché topographical map of North and South America, which covered the surface area of both desks. Bell was wrist deep in pulp, working on raising the Andes to disproportionate heights. Daphne looked comparatively neat, although the smears and speckles on her face suggested she might have employed her chin in carving out Hudson Bay. Rosamund carefully wiped the starchy paste from the ends of the hairpin she'd been using to trace the path of the Amazon and tucked it back into her loose chignon.

"I, er..." Molly continued. "I'm sorry to disturb your, uh, lesson, Miss Gorse, but Mr. Paris sent word that I was to pack his things for him, and all the bags are up here."

"Is he—is Mr. Burke leaving, Molly?" Rosamund could not give a name to the catch in her chest. Whatever resolution she had imagined, it had not been this one.

Daphne slapped her palm onto the board, wiping out a goodly portion of the eastern seaboard of the newly-minted United States of America and splattering her pinafore in the process. "I knew it. I knew he'd go back to his rented rooms once he found us a governess."

Rosamund's first instinct was to contradict her, but she bit the words back. How ironic that she should find herself leaping to the defense of a man whose own sister was so quick to assume the worst.

Molly, however, came down on Rosamund's side. "Now, Miss Daphne," the housemaid said in a surprisingly reassuring voice. "T'isn't that at all, at all. He went out early this morning for a meetin', then along come a note saying he's got to speak with someone about a case and guessed he might be gone overnight. Two days, at most."

Daphne looked unpersuaded. "Everyone leaves us."

Bell crossed her arms protectively over her chest, smearing her dress with would-be mountaintops. Tears welled in her eyes. "At least the others told us they were going."

"I won't leave you," Rosamund promised rashly. Not even if she should—for her own good. She was letting her wild imagination get the best of her again, making excuses for a man who didn't exist. Daphne and Bellis knew the real Paris. *Angry. Selfish. Neglectful.*

"That is," she corrected gently when Bell rushed to her side and wrapped her arms, coated in laundry starch paste, around Rosamund's waist, "when it comes time for me to leave, I will be sure to say goodbye."

As many as two days would pass before those words would have to be spoken. Perhaps between now and Paris's return, he would have forgotten about the kiss. After all, from his perspective, it might have been utterly forgettable.

And perhaps she—*no.* She had no hoping of forgetting. But she could use the time to figure out what do to about the fact that she wanted much more from him than mere legal advice.

* * * *

By the morning of the third day, the weight on Rosamund's chest was far heavier than a kitten. Colder and harder too. A solid lump of dread. Why had he stayed away so long?

Last night, Daphne and Bell had begged to stay up late and await their brother's arrival. Rosamund had read to them from *The Botanic Garden* for more than an hour, in part because she knew her listeners would hardly hear a word. When at last she had insisted upon bed, she'd left Eileen with them, an even better distraction than a book. She herself had sat up in the drawing room until the longcase clock struck one. Still, Paris had not returned.

Nor had he sent any message informing them of a delay. Molly did her best to behave as if all was as it should be, but the girls were clearly worried. Rosamund was too, though she dared not admit it—not even to herself.

At least the day had had the decency to dawn fair. "Excellent weather for safe traveling," Rosamund said aloud as she rose, repeating the words to Molly when she brought the water, and again to the girls over breakfast.

Rosamund feared that skepticism was soon to become the permanent expression of Daphne's face. "He's not coming back," the girl declared. "Not to stay. You'll see. He's back in those miserable rooms near Henrietta Street without a care for us."

She'd said as much on each of the previous days. Then, Molly had corrected her. Today, the maid said nothing.

Bell, wide-eyed, offered an even less consoling option. "Perhaps he's hurt and can't come home."

Rosamund realized that, despite her own anxiety as to the cause of his prolonged absence, it was down to her to distract them all. "Come, come, girls. No moping. I propose we spend today in the drawing room."

Daphne shifted from skeptical to petulant. "Doing what?"

She thought for a moment. "Sketching. The light is good, and we can use the botanical prints in your father's study for our models. When we've had our fill of that, we'll practice on the spinet. And if you're very diligent scholars," she said, taking Bell by the hand, "we'll have dancing when we're through."

"I like that idea, Miss Gorse," Bell said. "Except for practicing the spinet."

Rosamund only smiled and directed her toward the stairs, and the girls trooped out with minimal grumbling. Molly motioned for Rosamund to hang back. "You don't suppose—?"

"No, Molly. I don't," she said, hoping to convince herself. "Either his work has delayed him, or the condition of the roads. Don't you recall how it rained the day before yesterday?"

"Speakin' of his work, I think he's come to like the drawing room undisturbed."

"All part of my secret plan. He'll sense that his domain has been invaded and come charging home to restore peace and order."

Molly laughed but shook her head. "Mr. Paris never showed any sign o' bein' fey, Miss Rosamund. Why, for all that black hair, he's only got half a drop of Irish blood in 'im."

"Well, we'll just have to hope it's enough."

At midday, a sharp rap on the door to the street rattled Rosamund, who had managed to keep the girls absorbed by their sketches. "My brother isn't likely to knock at his own front door, Miss Gorse," Bell pointed out.

"No. No, of course not."

"Unless," Daphne suggested while sharpening her pencil, "he's lost his key."

So they all sat in hopeful alertness, waiting for his tread on the stairs. And they all sagged with disappointment when Molly appeared in the doorway with a paper-wrapped parcel. "For you, miss. The boy said he come from Mrs. Teague's."

"Oh, the dress," cried Daphne, brighter than she had been all day.

Bell jumped up and down. "Try it on!"

To distract them, and to give herself something to do, Rosamund obliged. In her chamber she changed out of the dress she'd borrowed from the wardrobe—her own muslin had borne the brunt of the papier-mâché paste—into the new smoke blue wool. It fit well; Mrs. Teague knew her craft. When she peered into the looking glass, she could see how the blue of the dress deepened the blue of her eyes, just as she'd imagined. Paris's favorite color.

But would he ever see it?

Plastering a smile on her face, she went back down to the drawing room, where she was greeted with Molly's vigorous nod of approval, Bell's squeal, and Daphne's brusque, "It'll do."

"Such a fine gown calls for dancing, don't you think, Miss Gorse?" Bell asked.

It wasn't fine, of course. It was perfectly plain. Nothing to grace a ballroom. Nothing compared to the dress she'd ruined with a long walk through wet grass, a ride in a farmer's cart, the mud and muck of the streets of Dublin, and two handfuls of pulp suitable for map-making.

Rosamund twirled. "Of course."

At first she played the spinet while the two girls took turns dancing in rollicking steps with Molly, and then with one another when the housemaid declared she had work to do. After several songs, she invited Daphne to sit down at the instrument and was pleasantly surprised by her musical skill. If Paris returned she would suggest that harp lessons might be in order after all. *When* Paris returned. To the strains of the same Irish tune he had played just a few nights ago, Rosamund taught Bell the chassé and the allemande.

The dancing lesson was also interrupted by the sound of the doorknocker. Once more they listened as Molly made her way to the door. An exchange of words, muffled by distance. Then Molly again appeared in the doorway. "Two packages for you this time, Miss Gorse."

Baffled, she allowed each of the girls to untie the strings of a box, unfold the paper, and open it. "Ah," exclaimed Bell, peering into her sister's box. "A bonnet, of course." Then she tipped up the box she had opened to display its contents. "And shoes."

"But when did you find time to shop for them?" Daphne wanted to know.

"I, uh… I sent Molly." Pray God the maid would play along, for she too must know that Rosamund could not have bought them. "With very specific instructions."

The items could only have been chosen for her by Paris. And only after that night… He had asked about her purchases over dinner. They'd kissed. Then, the next morning, he'd disappeared. But before leaving town, he must have gone to Grafton Street and ordered these items to be delivered to her. Why?

"Och, aye," Molly said, sounding slightly startled. "And didn't I do well, Miss Rosamund?" Her sharp eyes took in every detail of the dainty bonnet as Rosamund traced a fingertip along the unblemished sole of one shoe.

"You did, Molly. You did indeed."

The arrival of these items required another fashion show. The shoes fit almost perfectly—how on earth had he managed that? The hat was trimmed with pink roses and blue ribbon a shade lighter than her dress. Almost the color of her eyes. It was difficult not to conclude that he'd chosen it specifically with her in mind.

The hat's shape made it necessary to rearrange her hair. As she took it down and prepared to pin it up again, Bell gasped. "Your bruise, miss. It's almost gone."

Automatically, the fingertips of her right hand went to her temple. Had she really been here as long as that? "Why, I'd almost forgotten about it," she murmured, though of course, she hadn't. She was still dwelling too often on the feel of Paris's arm about her waist as he'd helped her up the stairs afterward, the look of concern in his dark eyes as he'd examined the injury.

Once the bonnet was in place, Bell tied an uneven bow beneath Rosamund's left ear, and the others both admired it. When she reached up to remove the hat again, Daphne shook her head. "Oh, please, Miss Gorse. It's so pretty. Won't you leave it on for just a little longer?"

The clock behind her cleared its throat and prepared to strike four. At the sound, she jumped and worry flitted into the girls' eyes. The better part of another day gone and still no sign of Paris.

"You must fancy a cup of tea, miss," said Molly. "Come, girls. You can help me put together a tray. Perhaps Cook will have baked something special…if that kitten hasn't been after causin' too much trouble downstairs."

Over the tops of their heads, Rosamund mouthed her thanks to Molly. Molly only shook her head.

When the rumble of footsteps on the staircase had dissipated, the house returned to awful silence. Rosamund plucked out a few notes on the spinet, but it was too dear a reminder of Paris's half-hearted attempt to play the instrument. So instead she returned to the table to put the pencils in their cases. Absently, she shuffled through the girls' sketches. Not bad. Not terribly good, either, though Bell showed some promise. Perhaps she took after her sister Erica, whose drawings, she'd been told, lined the walls. Rosamund scanned the framed pictures and realized that what she had at first imagined to be the difference between amateur and professional work was simply a gradual increase in the young woman's skill. Some, carefully inked and tinted with watercolors, might have come from the pages of the book Paris had given her to help her sleep.

Oh, he was everywhere and nowhere in this room, in this house, and she could not quite decide whether the greater mistake had been kissing him that night, or letting him go.

The rattle of the knocker on the front door made her jump. She waited a moment, but when the visitor knocked again and Molly gave no sign of coming up, she went down to answer it herself.

The gentleman who appeared on the other side of the open door was not Paris, though he shared the same dark hair and eyes. Taller, by a bit. And not half so handsome. "Ah," he said, looking her up and down. She did not like the feel of his gaze on her. "You must be the new governess."

Who was this man? And how had he recognized her? Panic fluttered through her chest, then sank through her stomach to lodge in suddenly wobbly knees. She gripped the door handle for support. "May I help you?"

He was still studying her. "You were on your way out, I see. Well, I'll not keep you. Just tell Burke I've come, or I'll show myself up—" He moved as if to go past her.

"Mr. Burke is not here," she said, narrowing the opening between the door and its frame to the width of her face. "If you'll give me your name, I'll make sure he knows you called."

"Not here? Never say he's still at Kilready."

The cold metal of the door handle bit into her hand as she clutched more firmly to keep herself from fainting. Her fingertips went numb. But she hardly noticed the discomfort, too distracted by the buzz of a single word in her ears. *Kilready.* Paris had gone to Kilready?

"I should've thought half a day there would tell him what he wanted to know," the man was saying when she could focus her attention on him again. "Well, let us hope he gets the information we need. Oh." He tipped his hat and smiled at her again. "Tell him Eamon Graves was here."

Somehow she managed to nod. "Yes, Mr. Graves. I'll see that he gets the message."

Another appreciative look. "Enjoy your walk, ma'am."

She shut the door without answering him. Without even hearing him. Paris had gone to Kilready Castle. He must have discovered, somehow, where she'd come from. And by now Charles and Lord Dashfort must know exactly where she was.

Oh, God.

Her hands rose to her temples, encountered the brim of the new bonnet, and in that instant, her decision was made. As Mr. Graves had so astutely observed, she was already dressed to go out. And go out she must—far away from here.

Stepping lightly, she hurried up the stairs and snatched her pelisse from the heavy old wardrobe. She still had a few of the coins Paris had given her. Was it wrong to take them? Wrong to keep his gifts, keep the new clothes the rest of his money had purchased?

Wrong to leave?

She'd promised the girls she wouldn't go, and she hated breaking that promise. She also hated to add to poor, overworked Molly's burden. But she couldn't possibly stay here and wait for Charles's arrival. And without any money, she would be right back where she had started. Quickly she gathered the remaining coins and tied them in a handkerchief. The handkerchief Paris had given her that first morning, still grimy from her attempt to clean the window with it. Between her thumb and forefinger she rubbed the rough embroidery of his initials stitched into one corner. By the loving hands of one of his sisters? Probably Bell, as the stitches were a trifle uneven.

After tucking the tiny bundle into the pocket beneath her skirt, she sent one last look around the room. If only there were some way to tell Daphne and Bell how sorry she was. Some way to say goodbye. In the drawing room, of course, were pencils and paper. If she went back there, she might write a note. But she hadn't a moment to spare if she wanted to get away without being seen.

Well, when Paris returned—*if* Paris returned—he could explain it to them. The discovery of her duplicity would erase any sorrow the girls or Molly might feel over her abrupt departure.

She reached up one hand to adjust her new bonnet and tried not to think of why Paris had picked it. But it was impossible not to wonder whether he'd chosen a bonnet and a pair of shoes because those were the items that would allow him to send her on her way with a clear conscience. Oh, if he'd been disappointed in her work, shocked by her forward behavior, dismayed by her deception, why couldn't he have simply dismissed her? He'd had no call to go to Kilready, reveal her whereabouts to Charles, and ruin everything.

Chapter 13

Paris had deliberately rented the shoddiest gig he could find, so as not to arouse suspicions. But the broken-down jade in its traces had been unintentional insurance. By the time they arrived in the village of Kilready, the gelding was favoring his left hind leg.

"Needs rest," the blacksmith announced after taking one glance. "Three days, at least."

Three days? Paris did not think it wise to argue with the burly man, who was evidently also the farrier and, for all he knew, the closest thing Kilready had to a cattle doctor. "Then can you recommend—?"

The blacksmith jerked his chin in the general direction of "up the road."

"Much obliged." Heaving his valise from the gig, Paris marched up the narrow track that led into the heart of the village. A dozen or so ramshackle buildings skulked in the shadow of Kilready Castle, perched high on the cliff's edge in the distance. In the ancient days, the chieftain's men would have seen invaders coming from miles away. Was that excellent vantage point being put to more nefarious uses now?

He directed his footsteps to the pub. Hanging crookedly above its lintel, a sign proclaimed "Good, Dry Lodgings." He had his doubts about the accuracy of either adjective, but especially, given the moldering thatch, the latter. His spirits lifted, though, when he noted another hand-lettered sign, higher up and considerably more faded, which identified the establishment as belonging to one "P. Fagan." Might the proprietor be some relation to the imprisoned boy? Could Paris put the unexpected delay in Kilready to good use?

Once he had entered and spotted the man behind the bar, he understood why the sign was faded. It must have been erected when P. Fagan was young, some sixty or more years ago. The pub was otherwise empty, though evening was coming on.

Despite his wizened stature and bent back, Mr. Fagan's voice was strong when he called out, "*Céad míle fáilte*."

A hundred thousand welcomes, the traditional Irish greeting to a stranger. The words echoed off rough, dingy walls. But Paris needed to be thought of as something other than a stranger if he hoped to get useful—incriminating—information about Dashfort's involvement in whatever was going on at Kilready.

"Thank you kindly, Mr.—Fagan, is it?" He tried to keep himself from sounding too eager. The man might not be related to Tommy at all. "I was passing through when my horse took lame, and the blacksmith tells me I must trespass on your hospitality for a bit."

Fagan looked him over, with curiosity rather than hostility. Nevertheless, Paris was glad he had not changed out of the clothes he'd worn to Kilmainham. Anything needlessly fine would attract the sort of attention he'd rather avoid. Something like recognition flickered into the older man's eyes. "Sure, an' you must be one of the Englishmen passin' through to measure up the roads. 'Tis welcome you are to the best room I've got."

What luck! A party of surveyors, of which Paris could pretend to be a member. It would give him a reason to be in the vicinity, and he could explain away his lack of equipment and maps by saying they'd been sent on ahead.

Nevertheless, his first impulse was denial. *English* surveyors… How could this man mistake a Dublin patriot for an—?

Doubt crept in before the thought could be completed. He was, after all, more than half English by blood. And he'd spent all his life with an English accent in his ear. Had it somehow become *his* voice too?

Not quite, surely. Oh, he might have picked it up a trace of it from his mother, or any number of Londoners he'd encountered during his time at the Inns of Court. But his mind went first to the voice that had struck him so forcibly a few nights back on the King's Inns Quay. The one he caught himself listening for at odd hours. And though he knew that Mr. Fagan expected some reply, he could not bring himself to speak.

The barman seemed to sense that his remark had rattled his guest. "No matter, sir, no matter. Englishman or no, we bid ye kindly welcome to Kilready."

Paris swallowed and forced a single word past his lips. "*We?*" Despite the empty pub, was the man was extending the greeting on behalf of the people of the village?

"My daughter lives here with me. Will I show you the room, then?"

Conscious suddenly of the shape of every sound that passed his lips, Paris nodded and removed his hat. He was exhausted, though the time spent in that rattletrap gig had contributed only a small share to his fatigue. How long since he'd had a decent night's sleep? Or at least, one unaided by the stupor of a bottle. Almost a year…

Lately, however, it hadn't been the old nightmares that kept him wakeful. New dreams had begun to creep into his heart.

Apparently, he had not yet learned how dangerous it was to dream.

The stairs were steep and narrow and led into a low-ceilinged attic. Nothing about the cottage ought to have been familiar. Still less should it have reminded him of the modern comforts of Merrion Square. And yet every creaking step called to mind a certain makeshift schoolroom. And its occupant. *Rosamund*. The governess who wasn't a governess at all. Rather than bringing order and system to his home, she'd turned everything even more topsy-turvy.

He ought to be angry at her deception. His first concern upon discovering that he'd be delayed in Kilready ought to have been for his sisters, left longer in her care. Instead, he had wondered whether he would get back to Dublin in time to see her open the packages he'd sent. Would the bonnet he'd chosen please her? Would the blue ribbon match her eyes?

Would she kiss him again to express her thanks?

Just as he shook his head to clear it of such wayward thoughts, Fagan flung open a door and turned to say, "Here we be." Seeing Paris's fleeting expression of annoyance, a shadow crossed the old man's eyes. "Tain't much, I know. Not for an Englishman…"

"I'm not—" Paris began, then forced himself to break off his confession. It didn't matter. Not really. He might call himself an Irishman, but he was not Irish in the way the people of Kilready thought of themselves. As far as they were concerned, he might as well be English—he was close enough as to make no difference to them.

Well, with any luck, they would show more interest in an exotic curiosity from that island across the sea than they would in a mere countryman. In the time he was going to be forced to spend here, perhaps they would even offer to educate him, as the Irish characters tried to teach the English ones in his sister Cami's book. "I'm quite satisfied, Mr. Fagan," he said, no longer as worried about his voice betraying him. "It's a fine room."

No doubt it was the finest room in the cottage, though it was not fine by any of the usual standards for measuring such things. Fagan crossed its entire length in a half-dozen steps and flung open the shutter covering the small, unglazed window in the gable end. The gray light of a dreary afternoon picked out the room's scant furnishings: a sagging rope bed, a washstand with a chipped basin, a battered chair. Though musty with disuse—there was little in Kilready to attract regular visitors—the room looked clean. Clean enough.

"Shall I fetch you some hot water?" Fagan offered, returning.

At first, Paris did not hear him. After setting his bag on the chair and placing his hat on top of it, he had stepped to window, and his attention had been captured by the sight below. A woman, barefoot and bareheaded, paused in her labors to swipe the back of her hand across her brow, pushing damp, straggling hair away from her face. With the other hand, she pinned a loaded basket to her hip. She was spreading laundry over bushes and hanging it from branches to dry, though the air was cool and heavy with the promise of more rain. The sleeves of her ragged dress were rolled above the elbow, and even at this distance, he could see the pink scars of burns up and down her corded forearms. A strong woman.

Ain't met a washerwoman yet who weren't, Mr. Burke.

Tommy Fagan's mother, hard at work? She would likely be able to reveal a great deal to the person who asked the right questions. It was part and parcel of a good barrister's skills to know just the questions to ask. And when he did not allow himself to be distracted by foolish dreams, Paris was a very good barrister.

"Thank you, Mr. Fagan." He replied to the man's almost forgotten question without turning his head. Steam or smoke or both wafted across the grass. He could picture the boiling kettles hung over peat fires at the rear of the cottage. "But there's no need for you to trouble yourself. I'll fetch it myself."

He waited until the old man had gone down before descending, jug in hand. Rather than entering the pub, he ducked through a doorway that promised to lead to the rear of the house. Instead, he found himself in a large room that served the family as kitchen, parlor, and bedchamber all at once. He'd been right. The room he'd been given was undoubtedly the finest room in the house.

If the rebellion had succeeded, would people like the Fagans have been any better off? He and others had been caught up in ideals of liberty and self-governance; had they forgotten the harsh reality, the thousands of their countrymen with liberty only to starve?

He could have crossed the room and left the house through the back door, but even the thought of trespassing in such a way felt disrespectful.

Quickly, he reversed course and went into the pub, where two men had joined Fagan and were chuckling into their pints.

"Sure, an' it's the Englishman," one of them called out and lifted his mug. "Welcome to Kilready."

Automatically, Paris bowed a greeting, then wished he could recall the gesture when he saw how it made the three men shift awkwardly in their seats. "Good afternoon, sirs. I was just on my way to get some water."

That announcement produced more merriment from the two newcomers. "My girl's out back," Fagan said, quieting them. "She'll help 'ee." Paris nodded and stepped to the door.

"I'd take care, Paddy." One of them spoke low, though perhaps not as low as he imagined. "She's gone soft for an Englishman afore."

Dashfort. But of course everyone in the village would know if a local girl had borne the earl's illegitimate child.

"Maybe he's hopin' she'll do it again," said the other man, and though the words were once more punctuated with a laugh, Paris heard no humor in the sound. "With one that'll take 'er off 'is hands this time."

"Shut it," Paddy Fagan retorted good-naturedly.

Paris chose to imagine the words had been directed at him and shut the front door firmly behind him as he went out. He deliberately walked toward the end of the house where he'd seen the woman at work, hoping to approach without startling her.

Instead, she surprised him. "Who are you?" she demanded, whirling around, her basket still on her hip. "What do you want?" She was his own age or perhaps a bit older, with reddish brown hair and a round face, despite her wiry build. He could see nothing of Tommy Fagan in her.

"My name's Trenton," he answered after a moment, choosing the middle of his three names, his English mother's maiden name. *Burke*, he suspected, would serve him poorly here. "My horse took lame, so I'm staying in Kilready for a few days. Staying here." He darted his gaze toward the cottage and back, and then held up the jug. "I came out for some water."

She looked him up and down, jerked her chin toward the rear of the house, and went on with her task. Working one-handed, she struggled to pull a single item from the basket it and hang it straight.

Carefully, he set the jug in the damp grass and took a step closer to her. "May I help you with that?"

He would have assumed she had not heard him if she hadn't eventually asked, "Why?"

"Because it seemed as if you might need some assistance. It was merely a friendly gesture."

With one hand, she snapped a man's shirt—made of fabric too fine to belong to her father—like a whip. "You're no friend o' mine."

He bent to retrieve the jug. "I'm sorry to have bothered you, ma'am." Behind the cottage, he found several large tubs and kettles each employed in various stages of the laundry process. A washboard stuck up from one, while another hung over a fire, bubbling away with the distinctive stench of lye soap. The mangle sat atop a tree stump, a bedsheet half in, half out. Not family laundry; he doubted Paddy Fagan had more than two shirts to his name. Not villagers' laundry either, for they were doubtless as poor or poorer than the Fagans. Kilready Castle laundry, if he had to guess. Who else in the vicinity would have so much?

He did not fault the woman's sharp tongue. *Imagine being forced to make a life by cleaning the dirty linen of the man who'd fathered your child.* The story had the makings of a tragedy, and he suspected he didn't know the half of it.

" I s'pose you're a friend o' his?"

He jumped at the sound of her voice behind him and splashed water down the front of his waistcoat. "A friend of whose?" As he turned to face her, he could guess the answer to his question.

"His lordship's."

Everything this woman was or had ever been was buried behind a brick wall of bitterness. He, usually so adept at reading people, could see nothing beyond it. In some strange way, her expression called to mind the one he'd seen in Rosamund's eyes, the sensation that she was hiding not just something, but someone. Hiding herself.

"If I were," he pointed out mildly, "wouldn't I have a room at the castle?"

She weighed his response as she sucked her thumb, drawing blood from a cracked chilblain so it wouldn't get on the clean clothes. With a practiced pucker, she spit onto the ground. "Fair enough."

After another assessing stare, she dropped the basket of wet laundry and came toward him with one hand held out. "Here. I'll fetch your water."

"There's no need," he insisted, but she was not to be put off, so he surrendered the jug and while she was ladling water into it, some from a bucket of cold water, some from a boiling kettle, he reached into the basket, pulled out a cravat, and draped it over a nearby branch.

When the jug was full, she set it on the ground, then stepped to the mangle and began to turn the handle, making no remark as he continued to hang items to dry. "I'm Mary Fagan," she said at last when she paused to shake the stiffness from her arm.

An overture? "Pleased to meet you," he said. But to his nod of greeting she said nothing in reply. After he'd hung the last of the items in the basket, he picked up the jug. Best to return to the cottage, before the water turned cold. He could make another attempt at conversation later. "Thank you, ma'am."

She made no acknowledgment of his departure. Inside the pub, two more tables had filled with men whose dirty boots proclaimed them farmers. Tenants of Dashfort's, no doubt. This time, whether anyone spoke to or about him, he could not be certain, for they conversed entirely in Irish. Quickly, he crossed the floor and went up the stairs to his room.

He was a stranger here, all right. Cami's fable about the possibility of sympathetic Anglo-Irish relations had been just that: a fable. Three days in Kilready—hell, three years—would not be enough for a supposed Englishman to earn these people's trust.

And without it, he had very little chance of saving Tommy Fagan and even less chance of bringing the Earl of Dashfort to his knees.

Chapter 14

Paris had misjudged the people of Kilready in one respect. Three days was more than enough time to learn the story of Mary Fagan's downfall. In sordid detail. From the mouth of almost every resident of the village… except, of course, for Mary herself.

He knew, for instance, how Mary had got above herself and dreamed of becoming a parlor maid at Kilready Castle. How, instead of being grateful to the housekeeper for taking on a clumsy girl, Mary had shocked the village by "throwing herself on His Lordship's, er, *charity*." Later, when the earl had gone to London and brought back a bride, the countess—"God rest 'er"—had straightaway sent Mary home in disgrace, rounded belly and all.

It took no great feat of imagination to construct another narrative of events, one in which Mary was not villain but victim. But the people of Kilready stuck stubbornly to their version, perhaps because Mary herself was too stubborn to contradict them—*cold, hard, proud* were the words he heard used to describe her again and again.

"What became of her child?" he had asked on occasion, always with the image of Tommy Fagan, lying ill in prison, burned onto his mind's eye.

That question had invariably been met with shrugs. "Och, his mam's not likely to be after showin' off a bastard, now, is she?" he'd been told. Not a soul seemed bothered by the boy being hidden away. Not a soul seemed to realize the boy was likely gone from Kilready for good. And if these people did not care, for what sort of future was Paris attempting to save him?

On the morning of the third day, Paris awoke filled with a sense of desperation. How much longer was he going to be trapped here? He'd largely failed to persuade the people of the village that he was a sympathetic ear for their troubles. He was wasting his time in Kilready, time better spent helping Rosamund out of whatever predicament had forced her to flee. Time better spent persuading her to trust him, no matter how he'd behaved in the past.

After washing and shaving in what little water was left in the washbasin, though it was cold, he dressed in his last clean shirt. He was knotting his cravat when Mary Fagan rapped on the door.

"The blacksmith was just here, sir," she called from the corridor. "Left your horse and gig waitin' outside."

He stepped to the door and opened it before she could leave. "Excellent news."

She glanced around the room, pausing over the coat lying at the foot of his bed, the finest one he'd brought. "Looks like you're after goin' somewhere."

"I need to talk with Mr. Quin, Lord Dashfort's agent." He doubted the man would be foolish enough to reveal anything of value. But at least then Paris could tell himself that he'd be as thorough as possible in his investigation.

"You'll likely find him at the castle." Like her eyes, her voice was wary.

"I'll call there on my way out of town. Thank you."

She nodded, turned to go, then paused. "Before you go to the castle," she murmured over her shoulder, "you'd best know it's haunted."

"Oh, come now, Mistress Fagan," he scoffed. "Surely you don't believe—"

She chuckled. Or perhaps *cackled* would have been a more accurate description. "Gor. *Mistress Fagan*," she repeated disbelievingly. She turned around to face him again and quietly shut the door behind her. "Go on. Have a seat." She nodded toward the rickety wooden chair, over which he'd flung his greatcoat.

When it appeared he had little choice but to obey, he eased himself onto the chair. "All right."

She perched on the edge of the bed. Facing her across the narrow room, he saw for the first time the remnants of prettiness in her face. Had circumstances all but stripped her of her youthful beauty? Or did she hide its signs deliberately now, knowing she'd caught Dashfort's eye and hoping to catch no one else's?

"I hear tell you like a story, sir," she said after a moment. "Leastways, I know you've heard mine."

Her words left no room for denial, though he would have liked to have made one. With one finger, he traced a crack in the chair's joinery. "I have. But as to this nonsense about a ghost—"

She wagged a gnarled finger at him. "Hush. I know there's a ghost. Seen him wit' my own eyes, haven't I? An' so's Mr. Quin. That's why I'm tellin' you."

He parted his lips to express something—his disbelief, his incomprehension—but a sharp look from her kept him silent.

"If you go up there, he'll be worried you came back because something got missed. A road he wants on no surveyor's map, that's certain."

She smoothed a hand over the wrinkled bed linens, carefully avoiding his coat. "Now, listen. On that road that don't exist, men ferry goods that don't exist neither. Irish goods goin' out, French ones comin' in. All kept in the belly o' Kilready Castle. Men have died to keep that secret, but I see no reason why you should be one of 'em."

Smuggling, just as Graves had suspected. Paris's heart began to gallop so hard he felt sure the ends of his cravat must be fluttering over it. Pray God if Mary noticed, she would think his response driven by fear. "Thank you for the warning, ma'am," he said with a catch in voice. "I want no part of any bad business that might go on in these parts."

Absently, he started to rise, uncertain what his next move ought to be. Though a bit of poking and prodding might provide a great deal of evidence that Dashfort was implicated in the smuggling ring, would exposing it, exposing him, ultimately wreak further havoc in Kilready?

"Sit, sir. Sit," she commanded, thumping her palm on the mattress for emphasis. "Have ye forgot about th' ghost?"

"I really don't—"

"God's truth. He exists, and I know it." She lifted one hand and laid it over her heart. Shining spots of pink and white speckled the skin of her forearm; one burn was fresh and purplish red. "Didn't I bring him into th' world?"

It took an inordinate amount of time for him to process her words. "You mean—?"

"My son. You've heard, I know, about my boy. An' you know who th' boy's da is, likewise."

Reluctantly, Paris nodded. "I know you were a servant at the castle, exploited by your master—"

"No." Her face grew hard. "Twasn't like that, no matter what folks think." A pause as she studied him. "You don't believe me, do you? But he was young an' handsome then, an' I…well, I wasn't always a washerwoman." Her voice softened a little as she spread her arms and turned her attention to their myriad injuries. No matter what she said, however, her willing participation in the affair did not make Dashfort less of a wretch. "He was mine long before he was hers," she insisted, referring he supposed to the late Lady Dashfort, "and she knew it, too. That's why she sent me away." Slowly, she shook her head. "When he went t' Lon'on, he never looked back... I didn't expect him t' marry me. But I never thought he'd leave me flat like he did. Well," she added after a moment with a shrug, "an' maybe he was grievin' too. Her Ladyship had just lost her babe, after all. Don't s'pose he ever knew when his other boy, my boy, was born."

Her eyes were glazed now, lost in memory. "I didn't think he'd live, my Tommy. A strange, sickly thing. Bore th' mark of our sin, he did." Paris's breath caught, though he should not have been surprised by such a misguided explanation for the boy's albinism. "He was only a few days old when Mr. Quin came t' take him from me. Promised t' see him well cared for. Oh, I shouldn't have let him go…" Her words broke off on a moan of anguish. How Paris wished he could offer some reassurance, but he could think of nothing but the grim cell in Kilmainham Gaol. "Not long after that," she continued when she had composed herself again, "the Kilready servants began to tell tales about th' ghost what first cried in th' nursery and then walked through th' halls and now wanders—"

"Along a certain path," Paris inserted, his understanding beginning to grow. Quin had seen an opportunity to use the child to prey on people's fears. In order to keep them away from his illicit activities. Perhaps even to keep the earl himself away. "But how do you—? Ah. *That's* why you became Kilready's washerwoman. It gives you an excuse to visit the castle."

"Once t' month. Since he was a babe. I see him, an' he sees me. But last week, sir, when I took the clean linen, he was gone. Vanished like the ghost they say he be." She spoke in a surprisingly matter-of-fact voice about the disappearance of her child. It seemed her arms were not the only part of her that had been toughened by scars.

"Why are you telling me this?" he asked softly, in the way he might prompt a witness to say more than she intended.

"Because there's somethin' else foul afoot at the castle, Mr. Trenton. My boy went missin' the same day as th' girl."

"The girl?"

"A month or so ago, an old friend of his Lordship's came to Kilready with his sister. An Englishman. They say 'is Lordship did hope to marry the girl."

"*Did* hope?" Paris echoed, reluctantly intrigued. "Does he have that hope no longer?"

"The girl didn't take a fancy to 'im, as I heard tell."

Perhaps the young lady in question had heard what had become of the previous Countess of Dashfort.

"And you think the two disappearances are related somehow?" A strange coincidence, certainly.

She shrugged. "Dunno. But I'd hate to see it be three." She gave him a knowing look as she rose and he followed suit. "Folks do say there's no snakes in Ireland," she said as she stepped once more to the door. "I say the last one's slitherin' about Kilready Castle."

"Does Lord Dashfort know his agent's reputation among his tenants?"

"I don't reckon he wants to know," she replied with a bitter laugh. "All those years in Lon'on, don' s'pose as he ever cared where th' rent money came from, only whether it came when it was supposed to. It means dangerous business for some o' the folks around here. But needs must, Mr. Trenton."

He nodded. *Needs must when the devil drives*... and he had very little doubt the sort of devil Dashfort employed. Sadly, the unscrupulous landowner's agent was a species of serpent that still thrived throughout the island.

Paris fished in the pocket of his greatcoat for his purse. "Wait. For the blacksmith," he said, laying a few coins on her outstretched palm. "And for you and your father." He poured out more than enough to cover his bill. "Do you read, ma'am?" he asked, as she let the coins run through her fingers like water, pooling into the palm of her other hand

"A little." She didn't look up. He'd send a simple note, once he'd returned to Dublin. To let them know what had become of the boy. Oh, how he hoped he would not be writing to report the lad's death.

It took but a moment to gather his things. In the lane he found his broken-down gig and the equally broken-down horse waiting for him. He could feel the eyes of the village on him as he swung onto the seat and slowly made his way up the hill to Kilready Castle.

He'd hunched in its shadows once before, trying and failing to stanch Henry's blood with his bare hands. As Paris rolled beneath the portcullis now, he glanced up at its teeth, surprisingly sharp and free of rust, having too recently been put to the castle' defense. Unsettled, he guided the horse to a stop and jumped from the gig. He swept his gaze around the courtyard. From here he could see nothing of what lay below, neither the village nor the foaming waters of the Irish Sea. Easy enough to forget on what Kilready's master depended for his—no, not for his survival. For his elegant charade as an almost-Englishman in London.

But the death of Lady Dashfort had put paid to that performance. The gossip columns had made much of the earl's Irishness, despite his repeated assertions of his English birth and his English education and his English residence. In the end, though a peer, Lord Dashfort had been a mere Irishman in English eyes, volatile and prone to violence. And when Paris thought of the bloodshed that had occurred on these grounds not a year ago, he wondered if they hadn't been right.

Lost in his thoughts, he did not immediately hear the little girl's squeal. Or rather, the sound did not register. Too familiar, too much a part of the noise that surrounded him daily. But of course this squeal could belong to neither Daphne nor Bell. In the moment it took for that realization to settle over him, a boy's voice added to the din of thundering hooves and rattling wheels.

"You there! Look out! I can't—!"

Paris tightened the grip on his horse's head, and the skirts of his greatcoat rippled as the dog cart and its occupants raced past. In a spray of gravel they managed to stop before crashing into the stable block.

"I'm sorry, sir," the boy said breathlessly as he jumped down and raised his hat, quite the little gentleman. He glanced up at the girl on the seat, the one who had squealed. His sister, Paris guessed. "We oughtn't to have been going so fast."

The girl's face bore no signs of chagrin. In fact, Paris recognized amusement twinkling in her eyes. The pair of them looked to be close in age to Daphne and Bell, the boy clearly the elder by a year or two, though slight of build. Both were fashionably and expensively dressed. And the boy spoke with an unmistakably English accent.

But all of those details were insignificant beside one glaring fact: The boy might have been Tommy Fagan's twin. Oh, this boy's hair was straw blond, rather than white, and his skin was fair in an ordinary way. The eyes, though, were the same hazel-brown, and the narrow features were unmistakable. It was like looking at a watercolor version of a familiar pencil sketch.

The commotion had drawn several hands to the door of the stable, though not one of them stepped out or spoke. Before Paris could think of what to say to the children, two men on horseback thundered into the courtyard. The boy fidgeted with the reins.

"What ho, my boy?" called the one in the lead, a man with the same blond hair and close-set, brownish eyes. He stopped before them, while the second man held well back, too distant for Paris to see anything of his features. "Didn't I warn you not to let Crispin have his head?"

"It won't happen again, sir," the boy vowed in a voice that wanted to waver.

The girl's smile curved wickedly as she shook her head, perhaps intending to underscore her brother's promise, though the gesture gave the impression of adding to their father's scold. Although she was still sitting primly on the seat, with her hands folded neatly in her lap, Paris wondered suddenly whether those hands hadn't in fact been holding the reins.

"Are you—?" The boy swallowed. "Are you harmed, sir?"

"Not at all," Paris reassured the boy. "But I daresay your father's advice is sound."

His words drew the attention of the man who could only be Lord Dashfort. "You are a stranger to Kilready, sir." He looked Paris up and down. "A gentleman, by your dress."

"The name's Trenton, my lord," he said with a bow. "I've come to speak with Mr. Quin."

He might not have known that Dashfort stiffened at his words if his mount hadn't tossed its head. The earl laid a steadying hand along the animal's neck. "What about?"

"I'm with the surveying party that passed through last week. I was delayed in the last village by a disagreement over a property boundary. I assure you I won't take much of his time. I would not wish to distract him from your lordship's more pressing business."

That answer seemed to soothe the ruffled the earl, who dismounted rather heavily and motioned for one of the stable hands to take his horse. "Come," he said, gesturing toward the castle. "I'll have a servant show you to his office."

The castle's massive door, oak studded with iron, swung inward seemingly of its own volition. As a result, he entered the castle unable quite to free his mind of Mary Fagan's haunting tale. The eerie effect was exacerbated by the condition of the entry hall, where little had been done to bring things into the present century. Tattered tapestries lined damp stone walls and the skeletal head and antlers of an Irish elk hung over an outsized hearth, giving the impression he had stepped into Ireland's past.

While the servant who'd opened the door took the earl's riding whip and gloves, the girl from the dog cart skipped into the hall, humming an unfamiliar tune. A few steps behind her came the other man, the brother of Lord Dashfort's intended, he supposed.

"Was there any post, Lord Setterby?" she paused to ask him. "Any news of your sister?"

Clearly annoyed by the question, Setterby gave only a brusque shake of his head.

To Paris's surprise, the girl turned to him next. "It's the strangest tale, Mr. Trenton. Several nights ago, Lord Setterby's sister—why I suppose you would say she took ill. Alexander and I saw her, right before she wandered out of the castle after dark." Something more than mischief flickered in the girl's eyes. "I think the ghost must've got her. Kilready is ever so haunted."

Though she smiled as she spoke, her demeanor chilled him. "I, er, I had heard that, yes," he managed to reply.

"You're Irish." Setterby spat the word like a mouthful of a bad vintage.

Well, Paris had not expected to continue to be mistaken for an Englishman here. He dipped his head in acknowledgment. "From Dublin, sir."

Dashfort turned and once more looked him up and down. "I was not aware the surveying party included any Irishmen."

"Almost a week," the girl continued pensively, oblivious to the men's voices. "I do hope nothing terrible has happened to her."

"Enough, Lady Eugenia," snapped Setterby.

The boy, Alexander, entered the hall at last. "Were you speaking of Miss Gorse?"

Miss Gorse?

Paris would have given a great deal to have been able to recall the sharp intake of breath that escaped him at the sound of that name.

Dashfort, thankfully, appeared not to have heard it. But Setterby fixed him with assessing eyes. Blue eyes, familiar in their striking shade. But far, far colder. "Is that name known to you, Trenton?"

Years of courtroom experience aided his attempt to maintain a cool façade in the face of the unexpected. "Only as a common shrub, my lord. Prickly. With yellow flowers, I believe."

Beneath that calm surface, scattered thoughts galloped through his head at a pace his borrowed horse could never hope to match. Rosamund had come from Kilready Castle? He no longer wondered at the state of her dress, her shoes, her very being. No surprise she had fainted at the end of that journey. Why, it had to be nearly twenty miles! What could have—?

But he knew the answer. The man responsible for her plight stood before him now. Or rather the *men* responsible, he amended silently, recalling his suspicions about her brother.

He could still hear Rosamund's trembling explanation of why she had left her previous "situation," as she'd called it. There had been two children, of an age with Daphne and Bell, she'd told him. Alexander and Eugenia, of course. Whose father had imagined himself entitled to certain liberties…

Paris crossed his hands behind his back, rather than trust himself not to grab Dashfort by the cravat and drive a fist into his face. A serving girl in a starched white cap—Mary Fagan's handiwork, he supposed—appeared before him. "Shall I take you to Mr. Quin, sir?"

Setterby continued to keep Paris pinned with a watchful gaze. He could not decide whether the man was satisfied by his reply—or rather, whether he believed it. Satisfaction was clearly not on order.

Dashfort, however, waved a dismissive hand, and Paris quickly attached himself to the maid to lead him from the room. As they walked along an open corridor that ran along the courtyard, he stopped and patted his coat. "Oh dear, I've left some important paperwork in my gig." A flicker of annoyance crossed the girl's face at the delay. Doubtless she had been called away from more important tasks. "If you'll just tell me which way I should go, I'm sure I can find Mr. Quin's office," he told her.

Once she'd pointed out the way, she hurried off in the opposite direction, leaving him alone. Quickly, he made his way to the stables, only to discover that some remarkably efficient groom had thought to unhitch his gig from the winded jade. The time it would take to make the horse ready would be more than enough time for Setterby's suspicions to form themselves into actions.

Setterby. The man's mount, a black stallion with a distinctive white blaze, stamped impatiently in a nearby stall, pricking its ears forward with interest. Still fresh; it would take more than a morning ride to wear out such a fine piece of horseflesh. And still saddled. Could Paris turn the stable hand's mistake to his advantage?

Offering a muttered and entirely made-up explanation to a nearby groom, he unlatched the door to the beast's stall and led him to a mounting block. *Horse theft.* He'd be lucky if he didn't end up swinging at the end of a rope beside Tommy Fagan. Nevertheless, before any protest could be raised, he hoisted himself into the saddle and was gone in a thunder of hooves.

He reached Merrion Square as afternoon turned to evening, having stopped at a posting inn to trade Setterby's horse for one less recognizable but also less swift. Fatigue dragged at his heels as he dismounted, tempering his relief. He'd made innumerable missteps. Lost his way. Perhaps even given himself up for lost. Now, however, Rosamund needed his help. His protection.

Was he capable of offering her anything at all worth having?

Much to his surprise, Molly met him at the door. "Thank God you've come home, Mr. Paris," she said, taking the hat he thrust into her outstretched hand.

"Where's Miss Gorse?" he demanded, making no attempt at pleasantries.

"Gone."

The word was a quick stab, a deceptively shallow wound. The sort one attempted to shake off as an inconsequential scratch. "Oh. I see." Of course she'd gone. He'd behaved very little better than Dashfort.

Well, perhaps the best thing to do now was to let her go. Find some way to forget. He pulled off his gloves, thrust them in the pocket of his greatcoat. "Did she—did she happen to leave any message?" Curse that tiny flicker of hope. He waited for Molly to speak again, to drive the knife deeper, to gouge out that cursed optimism and replace it with pain.

"I was in the kitchen with the girls when it happened. Fetchin' the tea tray. But Cook hadn't put the kettle on, you see. We had to wait for it to boil..." The pace of her tale reminded him of nothing so much as the wretched cart-horse he'd hired. "By the time we came upstairs again Miss Gorse had...well, she'd disappeared. No note," she said at last. "Nothin' at all."

Disappeared. Like Kilready's ghost. With a quick nod, Paris stepped past her. Rosamund had already proved herself a courageous, resourceful woman. How foolish of him to imagine she might need his help. And in any case, Molly's words were a timely reminder that he had Tommy's defense to mount, important work to be done. Amends to make. Revenge to take.

But first, perhaps, a drink...

His foot was on the stair when she spoke again. "Mr. Burke?"

The appellation settled over him, bearing with it the weight of responsibility and other qualities that were no part of him—not within this house, at any rate. He could not recall Molly ever addressing him as *Mr. Burke* before, not even in jest. And this was no joke. Her face, he saw with sudden alarm as he turned toward her, was creased with dread, aged ten years in a matter of days.

"What is it, Molly? Is there something else?"

"It's the girls..."

Oh, God. He hadn't even considered his sisters' devastation. One more loss for them to face.

"They figured out right quick that Miss Gorse had gone," Molly said. "Bell had tears in her eyes, as you might figure. But Daphne..." She shook her head; for the first time in his memory Molly was at a loss for words. "I told them like as not she'd only stepped into the park for a breath of air, though I knew in my heart it weren't so. I told them I'd go and have a look myself. When I went out, they were in the drawing room, playin' with that kitten an' drinkin' their tea. I swear I no more than took a turn around the square. When I came back, not a quarter of an hour later..."

She was twisting his hat around and around in her hands, mangling the brim, refusing to meet his eye.

"Molly?" This sudden transformation was not the work of days, he realized, but the terror of an hour, or even less.

At last she lifted her face. "When I came back, the girls had gone too."

Chapter 15

With money she could ill afford to spend, Rosamund paid for a private cabin on the *Claremont* packet, bound for Holyhead. She had to have some place to hide during this, the most dangerous leg of her journey. Dangerous because she would have no way to slip from her pursuers' grasp during the crossing, unless she chose to dive into the Irish Sea.

The cabin to which she was directed was considerably smaller than the one she had occupied on the voyage going the other way. Then, of course, she'd shared the space with a lady's maid, one hired expressly for the journey. Mrs. Sloane had refused to travel into the "savage kingdom," as she called it, and much to Rosamund's surprise, Charles had quickly dismissed the woman. Now, she better understood his decision. He had wanted her to have no familiar face but his own to turn to. No friend. Why, he'd even gone so far as to send the new maid on her way the moment they'd arrived at Kilready, lest she had developed some bond with Rosamund in the week they'd known one another.

One quick glance took in the entire cabin. The narrow bed was attached to one wall, with space beneath for her trunk, if she'd brought one. On the opposite wall stood a washstand and a chair, both fixed to the floor. If she'd tried, she might have been able to touch both walls at once.

But she didn't try. In truth, she didn't mind the tight space. It felt… secure, a stay against the wide world. A world in which Charles could be anywhere, watching her. A world in which she had nothing to her name but eleven shillings and sixpence, tied in a stolen handkerchief she treasured because it had belonged to Paris.

A wave of nausea washed over her and she sank onto the floor. Not seasickness. Not yet, anyway. They weren't under sail. She might instead have blamed the harbor stench, an unpleasant brew of salt, rotting fish, and tar. But the truth was, she was sick with fear. Until this moment, she had not dared to let herself think beyond the simple imperative of getting away from the place to which she would so easily be traced. Now, however, she had to face the enormity of her decision. Everything she had left behind. The uncertainty of her future. What would become of her once she was back on British soil?

Fighting the temptation to crawl beneath the bed and hide like a child, she instead drew her knees up to her chest and let her cheek rest upon them. She was weary, that was all. Wearied by the long walk from Merrion Square to the docks at Dunleary. If she rested for a bit, perhaps all would become clear to her. Perhaps… Her eyelids drooped and she began to drift into sleep. Why, perhaps she could become a governess in earnest…

A sharp rap on the cabin door roused her from something that had not yet chosen between dream and nightmare. She'd been in her bed in the Burke household. Paris had just gone from the room. The heat of his lips had not yet left hers. Now he was knocking to be let in again. To chide her further? To dismiss her? To kiss her again?

Would she open the door, or tell him to go away?

Her heart pounding, she managed to shake off the clutches of drowsiness and struggled to her feet, only to find the ship still steady beneath them. But the captain himself, praising the good weather and fine wind, had promised her they would set sail for Wales as soon as possible. The cabin had no window to tell her whether it was still afternoon or had turned to nightfall. No way of knowing whether she had slept soundly for an hour or merely dozed for a moment. Had there been some delay? Had Charles found her already, persuaded the captain to tarry at anchor until he could drag her ashore?

Bang-bang-bang. The thin door rattled beneath a second application of someone's knuckles. The person on the other side was unlikely to believe the cabin empty and go away if she did not answer. Refusing to let herself dwell in dreams, she drew back the bolt.

With a flick of the latch, the door swung wide to reveal the first lieutenant, smart in his uniform, a stern sort of frown etched between his brows. And next to him, one on either side, stood Daphne and Bell.

"Would you happen to know anything about these stowaways, ma'am? They claimed to be looking for a lady who answered your description. But these Irish urchins are notorious liars—I figure they saw you come aboard and concocted the tale on the spot."

"No," she breathed, the sound hardly forming a word at all. Nevertheless, the lieutenant took it for her answer. A denial. The girls winced as he tightened his grip on their shoulders, preparing to take them away.

"No," she repeated, her voice stronger. "They're not urchins." Though they *were* remarkably filthy and tattered. What must they have endured trying to find her, to follow her? "I know them. Oh, girls—why?"

The ship gave a great lurch.

"No," Rosamund said a third time. "They mustn't stay—"

But too late. The *Claremont* had cast off anchor and was finally underway.

The motion tossed the girls into the tiny cabin, overfilling it. While they clutched her around the waist and sobbed out an unintelligible explanation for their presence, Rosamund fished in her makeshift purse for coins to pay their passage, assuring the lieutenant that they would all make do in the crowded space. For what choice did they have? She certainly could not afford a larger one.

The girls continued incoherent until she managed to extract herself from their grasp and sink down to meet them at eye level. "Why—?" *Why did you follow me?* she had intended to demand.

But Bell spoke over her. "Why did you leave us?"

"Because I had to." She would keep her voice firm. She would not be moved to tears at the sight of theirs. "I was sorry to do it, but I—"

"You promised you would not go without saying goodbye."

"She lied," said Daphne simply. Rosamund realized the elder girl had already swiped her tears away and schooled her expression into indifference. "Just like Paris."

"No, not just like Par—like your brother. Who, by the way, will be frantic when he discovers you gone." Would he imagine she'd led his sisters astray? Or worse? "Does Molly know?"

Daphne merely looked away. Bell shook her head. "She wouldn't have let us out of her sight if she'd suspected what we were up to."

No, no, no. He would come after them, of course. Would her brother and Lord Dashfort accompany him? "There wasn't time to explain. I received distressing news and I had to get right away. I have to—to go home." Except she hadn't any home. *Oh, God.*

She sank back onto her heels. She was in danger of sliding all the way down to the floor and curling into a ball once more, but a sound stopped her. The tiniest, feeblest cry. Not the girls. Not even human.

"Surely you didn't—?" Her frantic gaze found a small basket clutched in Bell's grasp, unnoticed until that moment. Before she could finish her question, the basket shook, seemingly of its own volition, and its lid lifted just enough to give a glimpse of Eileen's pink nose and silvery whiskers.

Absurd, really. Laughable. So why were there tears coursing down Rosamund's face?

Curiously, the sight of her tears seemed to marshal the girls into action. Bell fished the kitten from the basket and held it out to Rosamund as a source of comfort. Daphne, always ready to demonstrate her status as the commonsensical elder sister, urged her into the chair and began to fan her face with her hand.

By the time some lower member of the ship's crew came about with water for the washstand and some very dry biscuits with tea, the three of them were piled in a giggling heap on the bed, using the ribbons of Rosamund's new bonnet to urge the kitten to chase and pounce.

"I'm sorry," she told the girls earnestly as she dipped Paris's handkerchief into the water to wipe their faces and hands. Her nonexistent linens were packed away in her nonexistent trunk. Thankfully, she no longer needed the handkerchief to hold her money; the two remaining coins fit perfectly well in the toe of her shoe. "I'm sorry I left without explaining why I had to go. I was—" But why hide it? People hid everything of value from children. "I was frightened."

"Of what, Miss Gorse?" Bell asked, trying to work out how to eat the hard biscuit with two missing teeth and another that was loose.

Rosamund shook her head. That she couldn't explain. She would not speak ill of their brother in front of them. She would give them no cause to imagine that any brother could be the cause of a sister's fear.

"People do remarkably silly things when they're frightened," remarked Daphne. She sat beside her sister on the edge of the bed with her feet dangling. Now and then, she swung them, forgetting perhaps her determination to be disapproving.

"Yes," Rosamund agreed. "Like running away without leaving a note."

"Or packing a bag," Daphne countered.

"Or packing a kitten instead!" chimed Bell.

More laughter. It held the hysteria at bay, but only just.

Thankfully the Irish Sea was not in a mood to dance one of its characteristic jigs. The *Claremont* sailed along smoothly, and neither Rosamund nor the girls showed any sign of seasickness.

It was late—very late, she guessed—when she persuaded the girls to try to rest. Fascinated by the cavern beneath the bed, the two of them camped there with the kitten, their pelisses pressed into service as pillows, with Rosamund's for a blanket.

She, meanwhile, took the narrow bed. Despite the hour and the lulling motion of the ship, sleep was a long time in coming. The girls giggled over their adventure while Rosamund's mind flitted from one dilemma to the next, incapable of landing on any solution.

* * * *

The *Claremont*, suffering from no such anxieties about its best course, landed without incident right where it ought on the following afternoon. When no other options presented themselves, Rosamund herded the girls off the ship and in the direction of a large posting inn, following the crowd of people who had made the identical voyage.

Eileen was once more securely in her basket, but that was all the order Rosamund had managed to impose. Their rumpled and travel-stained dresses were no better for having been slept in, and they had nothing to disguise their sorry state but equally wrinkled pelisses. The girls hadn't been wearing bonnets when they arrived, and she hadn't even a comb to fix their hair.

When the bedraggled little crew reached the hotel, Rosamund laid out her sixpence for a loaf of bread for the girls and paper and pen for herself. If she hurried, she could send word of the girls' whereabouts to Molly when the *Claremont* set out on her return.

Such a letter would have been challenging enough to write without the clamor of the public room, where a ruddy-cheeked serving girl had taken pity on them and given them leave to occupy a table, though they could afford to give her no custom in return. Rosamund had removed her bonnet and laid it in the center to disguise the table's emptiness and to shield her work from the girls' eyes.

More challenging still was the certain knowledge that every word she wrote would also be read by Paris. She labored over each stroke of the pen, careful not to waste the paper that had been so dear.

"Will this letter make it onto the packet yet today?" she asked the serving girl as she passed.

"Dunno, miss." The young woman glanced out the window with a practiced eye. "The wind does like to turn 'round about now. Why, look—the *Peregrine* can't hardly make way." Rosamund followed her gaze and was shocked to discover how abruptly the weather had changed. The sky was gray now, and in the distance, a flag whipped outward. She watched for a moment as a smaller ship, not a packet but a private vessel, fought the rising tide and the churning waves, struggling to reach the shore.

What would she to do if her letter could not be delivered for days? No help could get to them. Nor could the girls return to Dublin. But they had nowhere to stay here. Some escape she had plotted! Her only consolation, small though it was, lay in the certainty that if they could not leave Holyhead, neither could her brother arrive.

Pushing aside her half-written letter, she picked absently at a crust of bread the girls had left behind. She had no appetite. Carefully she wrapped the remaining mouthfuls in Paris's dingy handkerchief to save for later. Oh, what was she going to do?

The girls, thankfully, seemed oblivious to their plight. Daphne was busily engaged in studying the great variety of people coming and going at the bustling inn. Bell sat on the floor beneath the table with Eileen, whose *mer-r-rowls* were a mixture of satisfaction and ferocity as she triumphed over the head of a sturgeon almost as big as she. The serving girl had been kind enough to sneak that scrap out of the kitchen when she'd spotted the kitten poking her nose out of her basket prison.

Rosamund forced herself once more to her task. The letter might be an exercise in futility; nevertheless, it was her last, best hope—and besides, she had to focus on something, or she would break down and weep.

Three sentences, four. Perhaps the words would come a little more easily now. She would *not* think of him reading over Molly's shoulder. She would—

Daphne gasped. The sound, quiet but sharp, pierced Rosamund's consciousness. Probably the outrageous purple hat worn by the lady seated on the other side of the room. Rosamund had noticed it when they disembarked from the *Claremont*. She would *not* stall her progress to indulge her curiosity. She would—

Bell bounced up, jostling the table and sending her pen streaking across the page.

"I declare, girls, if I can't get this letter written, we'll—"

But they gave no sign of having heard her. Bell squealed and Daphne muttered, "I don't believe it." Finally, Rosamund could no longer resist finding out what had caused the stir.

When she looked up, Paris was standing just a few yards away.

The girls rushed forward and wrapped their arms around their brother, nearly knocking him off balance. They were no doubt peppering him with questions. But ordinary sounds seemed to have been sucked from the room, leaving behind a dull, disorienting roar. How had he managed to find them so quickly? And was he alone?

As he came closer, his gaze never left hers. Dark eyes, red-rimmed with fatigue. Dark beard—two days' growth, at least. While she watched, a welter of emotions sketched across his face. Anger, fear, relief. And—oh, yes. *Guilt.*

Well, why not? By coming here, he had ensured Charles would be able to track her down. And when her brother found her, he would make her feel the full force of his wrath. Afterward, she would find herself trapped in a miserable marriage with a wretched man who had one wife already in the grave.

With a shaking hand, she reached up and slapped his handsome face.

She knew she had been right about the guilt because he made not even the feeblest attempt to stop her from striking him. As if he knew he deserved whatever punishment she could mete out.

Afterward, she expected to feel satisfaction. Instead, a wave of regret washed over her. Her trembling fingers crept to her lips, holding back a sob. For just a moment, his sardonic mask had been lifted entirely. Now it was firmly back in place.

He wrapped one arm around Daphne's shoulders, laid his other hand on Bell's head. They were ogling him, waiting to see his reaction to their governess's shocking act. But he did not look at them. His eyes still had not left Rosamund's face. "Why, Miss Gorse," he said, with that familiar wry twist to his lips. "Fancy meeting you here."

"Don't be angry, Paris," begged Bell. Daphne made a frantic gesture to silence her, apparently more interested to see how the drama played out without interference.

"I might say the same, Mr. Burke," Rosamund replied. Oh, how she despised the way her voice shook. With relief. With…something that wasn't relief at all. "Molly told me you'd rather drown than cross the Irish Sea."

"Did she now?" Surprise flickered into his eyes, and he gave a weary laugh. "Well, I very nearly managed to do just that."

Bell sobbed and clutched him harder. "He just means the sea was a bit rough," Daphne both chided and reassured her. And then she glanced upward again, seeking confirmation. "Right?"

He looked at his sisters at last, shifting his grip to clutch Bell by the shoulders and reaching up to muss Daphne's hair. "Let's sit down, shall we?" he said, moving them toward the table. Rosamund noted that he hadn't answered Daphne's question.

The three Burkes settled themselves around one half of the table, the girls clinging to their brother. On the other side, Rosamund stood, uncertain. She ran one fingertip along the table's scarred edge. "You must have crossed on the *Peregrine*, Mr. Burke. Were you alone?"

He lifted his head. She could still see the red mark her palm had left. "*Alone*, Miss Gorse? Your confidence in my sailing abilities is quite extraordinary. I assure you, the ship was fully crewed, and the passengers—" She parted her lips to interrupt the flow of his raillery, but something about the look in his eye gave her pause. "I'm quite aware of your meaning, ma'am." He eased back in his chair and crossed one booted leg over the other. "Rest assured, there was no one of your acquaintance on board."

Rosamund released a shaking breath and let herself sink into a chair. *A reprieve*. Of one sort, anyway. Charles might be half a day's sail away from her, but she was once more just as desperate as she had been on the night she'd met Paris on the quay. The single shilling now hidden in her shoe made no difference at all.

Daphne, however, had been reminded of her annoyance with her brother. She had released her hold on him and was once more regarding him skeptically. "No one of her acquaintance? Why, there must've been dozens of people on that ship. How could you possibly know whether Miss Gorse was familiar with any of them? And anyway, I still want to know why she—"

"What's this?" With his free arm, Paris reached across to snatch up the half-finished letter. "Ah, I might've known you wouldn't disappear entirely without a note to—why—" A laugh burst from him. Humorless. Hurt. "To Molly. Of course."

Too late to stop him, Rosamund was forced to sit with her hands folded in her lap, watching as his eyes scanned the page, taking in her feeble attempt to explain why she had left, the predicament in which she had found herself when Daphne and Bell had followed her on board the *Claremont*.

He read it through twice, at least. Perhaps three times. The handful of words on the paper were otherwise insufficient to require such lengthy attention. At last he raised his gaze to hers. "I confess I have spent the better part of the last day puzzling over why you had chosen to involve my sisters in your flight." With a flick of his wrist he tossed the half-finished letter onto the table. "Knowing them as I do, the truth ought to have occurred to me sooner. Why, it could just as easily have been the case that they had absconded with you."

"*Par*-is," came the expected chorus of protest, followed by an almost unintelligible attempt to explain simultaneously their decision to try to find their governess.

He held up his hand. "Enough. Answer me these questions, one at a time, if you please," he said, looking between them. "Whose idea was it to follow Miss Gorse?"

"Daphne's," said Bell, and to Rosamund's surprise, the elder girl did not try to deny it. "But my idea to bring Eileen along," she added.

At that, he drew up his lips as if trying to contain a laugh. "And how did you determine where to look?"

"Lady Sydney was just setting out on her afternoon constitutional," explained Daphne, "and she said she thought she'd seen Miss Gorse walking south. So we went that way."

He looked both of them over carefully, taking note, Rosamund felt sure, of the dirt and the state of their clothes. "You came to no real harm on this adventure?"

"No, Paris," Daphne promised solemnly. "We were careful."

"No harm," echoed Bell. "Although…well, my legs and feet are tired."

"I should think so. Why, it must be nearly four miles from Merrion Square to Dunleary." His eyes darted toward Rosamund but did not rise to her face, as if he did not quite trust himself with what he might see there. "Such journeys are very hard on the shoes."

She feared for a moment that she might be the next subject of his interrogation. Instead, he freed his other hand from the circle of Bell's arms, retrieved the discarded sheet of foolscap, and took up the pen. With none of her own uncertainty or hesitation, he added several lines to the bottom of Rosamund's letter and swiftly signed his own name to the missive. She made no effort to read what he had written.

"You'll excuse me for just a moment," he said, moving as if to rise and dropping a kiss onto the top of Bell's head. She might still have resisted, but the kitten chose that moment to emerge from beneath the table and distracted her. Eileen licked her whiskers and staggered rather drunkenly toward Bell, thrown off balance by the sudden roundness of her belly.

Letter in hand, Paris strode from the table, pausing first to speak to the serving girl for a moment, then disappearing through the door that led into the inn. Before he had returned, a tray of food arrived: a steaming tureen of stew, more bread, even a pot of tea. The serving girl set it before them with a wink, and the two Burke sisters needed no other encouragement.

Rosamund held back for a moment. She oughtn't to take any more from him than she already had. Though she really couldn't remember when she'd last eaten. And as the delicious aromas rose from the table and wrapped themselves around her, she discovered she was quite hungry. Starving, in fact.

No sooner had she fallen on the food than Paris returned, just in time to see her shoveling stew into her mouth in the most unladylike fashion. Eileen had behaved with more decorum as she attacked the fish head on the dirty floor. She tried to restrain herself long enough to thank him, to invite him to join the repast. But the offer died as she licked a drop of stew from her lip and glanced around the table. The tureen had already been scraped bare, she realized, and the loaf of bread was now little more than scattered crumbs.

"Quite all right," he said, seating himself once more between his sisters. The corners of his mouth curved with that smile that wasn't quite a smile; this one, in fact, looked somehow sorrowful. "I will be perfectly satisfied with a cup of tea."

While they finished eating, he offered to regale them with his adventure. It was on the tip of her tongue to ask about Kilready. But he of course began at a later chapter of his story: his return to Dublin and Molly's shocking revelation. Then he told how he'd set out again immediately, uncertain where to look, and how he'd wasted time seeking here and there. "I did not have the good fortune to enquire first of Lady Sydney, you see," he added with a wink for Bell. "But I did have one advantage over you. I was on horseback. My feet aren't tired at all." Eventually, his enquiries had led him to the harbor—the two girls had caught the notice of several people—but he had arrived too late to board the *Claremont*. "Fortunately, the *Peregrine* was still at anchor and I was able to secure a place just as she was ready to sail. Though we very nearly had to turn back to Dublin when the wind shifted and the sea grew rough."

"Were you worried, Paris?"

He took a sip of his tea, then looked down at Daphne with his laughing expression. "And what, may I ask, would have been the use of worry?"

Rosamund, however, was not fooled. She had glimpsed the slightest tremor in his hand as he returned his cup to its saucer. And she could not help but wonder, oddly, whether her own brother had ever worried for her.

After they ate, the girls were quiet. Drowsy. Someone had pushed Rosamund's bonnet aside to make room for the food and even Eileen could do no more than bat half-heartedly at its strings, though they dangled invitingly over the edge of the table.

Absently, Paris pulled the ribbon away from the kitten and rubbed its frayed end between his thumb and forefinger, his gaze at first unseeing. Then, as the pale blue silk came into focus, the motion of his fingers stopped, and she watched his eyes travel over the bonnet to which the ribbon was attached. Another strange expression quirked across his features and was gone. The ribbon slithered from his grasp as he rose.

"Come."

At the sound of his voice, his sisters started as if from slumber. "Are we going h-h-home now?" asked Bell around an enormous yawn.

"Not tonight. We're staying here at the inn."

Daphne nodded drowsily and staggered to her feet, while Bell gathered Eileen in one hand and reached for Paris with the other. Only Rosamund did not move.

"Aren't you coming, Miss Gorse?" Daphne asked, impatient for bed.

Rosamund fixed her gaze on the table and the sad remnants of their feast. "I—"

"Yes, Miss Gorse. Mustn't dawdle."

Paris's voice. Despite its mocking tone, her pulse quickened. But no. She mustn't accept the offer. For a dozen reasons. A hundred.

She looked up and met his gaze.

She rose.

She grabbed her bonnet and followed.

Chapter 16

The room to which the chambermaid showed them was neat and pleasant, but small. A folding screen had been set up to partition the space further, into a sitting room that contained just one seat—an overstuffed chair with comfortably worn upholstery, placed beside the crackling hearth—and a bedroom that contained just one bed.

A hip bath and cans of steaming water stood on the bedroom side of the screen, and a pile of fresh linen lay on the bed itself.

"Your man told me your trunks got left behind when you sailed," the chambermaid said. "Pity those porters can't do a better job o' managin'. I scrounged a few night things for you, an' I'll take your dresses to sponge and press, if you'd like, ma'am."

Rosamund was still doing mental calculations. One room in which to undress and bathe and sleep. One room…for the four of them? She tried her best to hide her unease at this state of affairs. "I—er. Thank you," she said, though she'd hardly heard the girl. She gave another nervous glance around the room.

And discovered Paris was suddenly nowhere to be seen.

"'e went back down to the pub, ma'am," the chambermaid explained.

Of course. "All right, girls," Rosamund said, emboldened by his absence. She ushered the sleepyheads behind the screen and assisted them in undressing. After giving all three of their dresses to the waiting chambermaid who carried them away, she helped Daphne and Bell to quick baths and tucked them into bed. At last she stepped into the tub herself. The girls were sprawled on the bed and sound asleep before she had finished bathing. Eileen, curled beside Bell's head on the pillow, gave one flick of her ears, a sort of wave of dismissal, as if to dissuade Rosamund from disturbing them further.

After donning an old-fashioned nightgown—borrowed, ill-fitting clothes were nothing new to her now—she wrapped herself in an extra blanket, stepped around the screen, and went to sit before the fire to dry her damp hair. Her gratitude at having food and a place to sleep tonight could not erase her anxiety over the morrow, and despite her fatigue, sleep seemed unlikely to come soon. The Burkes would of course return to Dublin on the first available ship. But where would she go? What would she—?

At the creak of a hinge, she spun her head in alarm and discovered Paris standing in the doorway, his greatcoat slung over one arm.

"Am I too late to say goodnight?" He spoke low, but as always his voice had the curious power to travel across the room and slip under her skin.

She clutched the blanket tighter. "Your sisters are asleep."

"But you are not." He stepped fully into the room and gestured about him with the arm covered by his coat. "I apologize for this uncomfortable arrangement. It was the last room they had. I'll sit up in the pub tonight, of course. I only wanted to make sure you had everything you need."

She managed a nod.

"They assumed we were traveling as a family."

Understandable, and mostly correct. But did that mean…? She released the blanket and raised her hand to stroke one cheek. "Do I truly look old enough to be the girls' mother?" Had the trip left her as haggard as that?

A silent laugh lifted his chest. "I had expected you to express more horror at the thought of being mistaken for my wife." He turned back toward the door. "Good night, Miss Gorse."

"Wait."

He paused but did not immediately turn around.

Beneath the blanket, she twisted the tie of the nightgown around one finger. "I owe you an explanation, Mr. Burke."

As he turned, she saw surprise, or something like it, flit across his face. "No. At least, not tonight."

Would there be another opportunity? "Please."

Slowly—reluctantly?—he crossed to her. When he reached the fireplace, she rose, offering him the only chair. He shook his head. "I'll make do with the floor."

She could bear a great many things, as it turned out. But not that. She could not allow him to sit at her feet while she explained how and why she had lied. Why she had left. She lifted his greatcoat from his arm and laid it across the empty chair, then sank to her knees. "As will I."

As she arranged the blanket around her, he leaned back against the seat of the chair and stretched his legs out in front of him. Now that she had an audience, her courage flagged. "I—I'm not quite sure where to begin," she whispered, praying not to disturb the girls.

The flickering firelight gave his dark features a more than usually devilish cast. He crossed his booted legs at the ankles, his arms over his chest, settling in for a long tale. "In Berkshire, I should think."

He remembered. Of course he had remembered. "I was not born there, if that is the jest you mean to make," she replied, grateful for once to sound so prim. "I was born at Gorsemere Park, in Suffolk."

"Your father's house," he prompted.

"The traditional seat of the Viscounts Setterby, yes." It was not at all the story she had intended to tell. But perhaps it was best to begin at the beginning. "I have little memory of the place. My Papa died when I was not quite five. I have little memory of him, either." She focused on the fire, unwilling to see either pity or its absence on Paris's face. "My half-brother, Charles, now holds the title. You've met him, I think?"

"Yes. But how did you know?"

The question brought her gaze back to him. "A gentleman came to see you. A, uh, a Mr.—Greaves?"

"Graves." Before her eyes, his jaw turned to granite.

"He mentioned you'd gone to Kilready."

He nodded, a single dip of his head.

She could read nothing in the gesture—nothing more than confirmation of her worst fears, that was. She fought the impulse to glance over her shoulder, as if she expected to find her brother standing on the threshold. Instead, she drew a deep breath and continued. "Charles said Gorsemere was ramshackle, and there wasn't—isn't—money to repair it. He closed it up and settled in London. He moved Mama and me to another of the family properties, Tavisham Manor. In Berkshire." She was determined to make him understand that she hadn't lied about *everything*. "A modest little house, really, despite the name."

"Is your mother still living?"

Rosamund shook her head. "She died when I was thirteen. Of a fever she contracted while visiting among the cottagers, bringing them food. Charles said I must—I must learn from her example."

"Her generosity?"

Such a simple question. How often had Paris asked one like it in his capacity as barrister? How often had it brought a witness to tears? She could feel their salt stinging in the back of her eyes and her throat, and she swallowed against the sensation, pushing back against the memory of Charles's words, carried along on the tide. *It's too dangerous. You mustn't go among those people again. Think what happened to your mother.* "He only wanted to keep me safe," she insisted, more to herself than Paris. But was it true? If she had been safer, certainly the poor families who had counted on the support of the lady of the manor had been less so.

"He cared for you himself after that?"

"Oh no. He hired Mrs. Sloane to keep me company."

"And was she kind?"

"She..." Oh, she'd set out with every intention of being honest with Paris. Why did the truth suddenly seem so complicated? Charles was strict with himself, with everyone. Certainly it was no surprise he had hired a woman after his own principles. "She was not cruel."

The lines of fatigue in Paris's face settled into hardness, though he said only, "I'm glad to hear it."

"I don't suppose Charles exactly relished having the responsibility for a young girl," she quickly made excuse. "He visited Tavisham, on occasion." How silly to compare her feelings on those occasions to the delight on Daphne and Bell's faces whenever their brother walked into a room. "I had everything I truly needed."

Paris lifted one brow. "Did you?"

The crackle of the fire was loud in the stillness that followed his question. When she dropped her gaze, she discovered she'd once more tangled her fingers in the tie that gathered the neck of her nightgown. She released her grip and watched the ribbon unravel as swiftly as her illusions. "No," she whispered, the truth tearing at her mercilessly. *I didn't have love.*

She hadn't realized she was shuddering until Paris's arm came about her shoulders, drawing her against the firmness and warmth of his chest with one hand while the other tucked the blanket more securely around her. "He w-w-wanted me t-to w-wed his friend, Lord D-Dashfort," she managed to get out past trembling lips and chattering teeth.

"Shh," he murmured, passing a soothing hand over her hair.

But she needed to speak, to finish her story. "I think that's w-why he b-brought me t-t-to Ireland. S-so it would be harder for me to say n-n-no this t-t-time."

His hand stilled. "This time?"

She was hardly aware of having said those words, but hearing him repeat them, she knew they were true too. Why, it would take more than the fingers of one hand to count the friends Charles had brought to Tavisham in the last couple of years. To shoot, he had said. At the time, the frequent visits had baffled her; Charles had made no secret of his disdain for country life. But perhaps a part of her had always suspected that her brother wanted to relieve himself of the burden of caring for her. What better way than by marrying her off?

She didn't speak again until she was certain she could do so without stammering. "Yes," she said, holding herself up a little straighter, twisting in his half-embrace to face him. "But this time, I got away."

"You did." He nodded encouragement, and the firelight slipped over his raven hair and glittered in his beard.

But the words offered little comfort when she recalled what had happened since. "Oh, why did you do it? I could've explained." She fought to keep her voice from rising. "I was wrong to lie, but you had no cause to seek out my brother, to—"

"I didn't," he interrupted hastily, shifting closer to her once again, as if to offer further reassurance. "I had no idea I would find him in Kilready. The business that took me there had nothing to do with him. Or you. It had to do with a poor boy imprisoned in Dublin, whom I hope to defend from changes of theft."

She struggled to mask her surprise. It was not the sort of case with which she would have expected one of Dublin's top barristers to concern himself.

"I met Lord Dashfort quite by happenstance as I was preparing to return to Dublin," he continued. "He'd been out riding with his children, and another gentleman. Your brother, as I came to understand. The village was all atwitter with the story of the young woman who had refused the earl's offer of marriage. But I had no notion it was you. I would never have made the connection if Dashfort's son hadn't asked if there was any news about Miss Gorse." She felt more than heard his hesitation before he added, "I'm afraid I did a poor job of masking my astonishment when I heard your name." In his dark eyes, she once more glimpsed an unmistakable glimmer of guilt.

She froze. "Did my brother take note of your reaction? If he seeks you out to discover the reason for it…"

"I did not even give my real name. He has no way to find me. To find you."

She knew from experience that Charles would not be so easily thwarted. "You're right, of course. It's impossible," she lied, forcing a smile. Once more she raised her hand to Paris's face. Gently, this time. Beneath her cool touch, his skin burned as if with fever. "I'm sorry for striking you earlier. As your sisters will tell you, I've not been myself these last days.

I—I panicked. I expected any moment to see Lord Dashfort and my brother behind you."

His hand came up to hold hers in place. She relished the pleasing prickle of his beard against her palm. "You won't."

She had not always understood her brother. But she did now. She knew it was not a promise Paris could keep.

"I should go downstairs," he murmured, not releasing her hand.

After dredging up the ghosts of her past, and fearing what lay in her future, she couldn't bear to be left alone now. That tempting lock of hair had fallen over his brow. Her heart fluttered in her breast, an uncertain rhythm that made her lightheaded and breathless.

"Please," she whispered, leaning closer to him. "I'd feel safer if you stayed."

* * * *

Safer.

Paris supposed she meant it as a compliment. She still had no idea the danger he posed. The heartbreaking trust she'd shown in him tonight, trust he had in no way earned…

"Did he hurt you?" he demanded. "Dashfort, I mean." The damage her brother had done was evident.

She flinched. "No."

"When you first came to Merrion Square, you told me the gentleman had taken certain liberties—"

Her hand slipped away from his face, and her steady blue gaze with it. "He kissed me. Or tried to."

"Ah." As he feared, he'd behaved as badly as Dashfort. Or worse. "Perhaps I didn't deserve to be slapped tonight," he told her. "Last week, however…" Her chin jerked up again, but he kept speaking, forestalling her protest. "I shouldn't have kissed you. Forgive me." It was his turn to cut his gaze away. "And I suppose when my gifts arrived—intended, please believe me, only to make amends for my boorishness—you must have thought—" He shook his head. "No wonder you left."

"It would take more than a bonnet and a pair of shoes to drive me away," she said, sounding bemused. Perhaps even amused. Once more she held him prisoner with those eyes. "And also more than a kiss."

Swiftly, she leaned forward and pressed her lips to his.

This time, however, she wisely pulled away before he could kiss her back. "You taste sweet," she said, running her tongue over her lips. "Like tea."

"When I don't taste sour," he reminded her gruffly. "Like whiskey. What exactly is it you want, Rosamund?"

A nervous laugh rippled through her as she tipped her head to the side. Her hair tumbled over her shoulder, and the firelight transformed it into a cascade of gold that rivaled the beams of the midday sun. He wanted to lose himself in its depths, no matter if he got burned. Desperately, he tried to replace the image before him with the memory of her on a previous night, when she'd worn her hair in a prim, neat braid.

It made no difference at all.

"No one in my life has ever asked me that question," she marveled, her voice soft. "Except you."

No. Not *soft*. Prickly. Aristocratic. *English*, for God's sake.

"Then you ought to consider carefully before you answer it." His own voice was little more than a growl. "Go to bed, Rosamund." He jerked his chin toward the screen. "Over there."

"Have you ever tried to sleep in a bed with two young children and a kitten, Paris?"

It was an argument he knew he was unlikely to win, not least because he could think of no way to make the circumstances she described sound appealing. So he changed tactics. Leaning toward her, gentling his voice, he said, "You're in shock, I think, my dear. You don't want me."

She appeared to consider his words for a long moment. And when she at last nodded and said, "I think you're right," he told himself he had no cause to feel hurt. Then she added, "Right about the shock, I mean. I'm so cold. And I—I can't seem to… I need…" The room's shadows were deep, but he could nonetheless see the pain in her eyes.

"Aren't you the slightest bit worried I might be overcome with passion and ravish you?" he asked—intending the words as a teasing reminder that they were on the verge of dangerous territory here. A warning he promptly undercut by glancing toward the screen, behind which slept his sisters. Soundly, he hoped.

Her gaze followed his and the corners of her lips turned up. "On the floor of this shabby posting in? No. I trust nothing untoward will happen here tonight. But you did ask me what I wanted," she repeated, smoothing her palm over the hearthrug, "and my answer is—"

He reached out to brush a fingertip across her lips. "Shh. Save those words. Think longer on my question. One day you will realize you want something, someone other than…"

She looked up at him, unblinking. Unpersuaded.

He lifted away his hand. "All right," he whispered, resigned. "Lie down."

The better part of him hoped that when it came to it, her senses would return and she would refuse. But the rest of him wanted to roar with satisfaction when she smiled a wicked little smile of triumph and stretched out obligingly on the floor, one arm tucked beneath her head. He covered her with the blanket.

After banking the fire, he tugged off his boots and lay down beneath his greatcoat, farther away from the hearth and what he hoped might pass for a respectable distance from her. At least he'd be close at hand, if there were any trouble—

Every attempt at rationalizing his decision scattered when she scooted closer, closer, until the curve of her backside was pressed against his groin. This was an entirely different kind of trouble. He willed his heart to stop pounding, to stop driving blood into his cock, where it most emphatically was not needed.

"That's better," she muttered. "Warmer."

Much warmer. "Roisín," he sighed against her hair.

She stiffened slightly in his arms, then tested the unfamiliar word. "Roisín. What does it mean?"

"Little rose," he said simply, wondering whether she knew he'd borrowed the name from his sister's book.

"Oh." Her swift release of breath sounded disappointed. "It's just the same as 'Rosie.'"

He pulled her closer still. "Not to an Irishman."

She seemed to consider his reply for a moment before saying, "Goodnight, Paris."

He felt certain that the spark of desire burning inside him—in addition to the hard floor—would ensure he passed a damned uncomfortable few hours. But as soon as she spoke, a wave of relaxation swept over him. With his arms wrapped tightly around her, absorbing every rise and fall of her breast, he soon dropped into a deeper and easier sleep than he had known in months.

Chapter 17

Rosamund awoke with a shiver, alone on the cold hearth.

Panic fluttered through her chest before she could stop it. She still could not explain, even to herself, why she'd been so desperate to make Paris stay with her last night. Persuading him had taken every ounce of her courage and something else besides. Something she hadn't even known she possessed. Mrs. Sloane would have called them *feminine wiles*.

Perhaps she *had* been in shock. Would that explain—to say nothing of excuse—her erratic, improper behavior? Not just last night, but every night since she'd met him? Enjoying the intimacy of a midnight conversation. Relishing the feel of being held in his arms. She had so little experience making her own choices. Why, just look at the foolish ones she'd made! Kittens and sticks of barley sugar and…Paris. Sweet things that would inevitably grow up, melt away, turn bitter.

Then, in the faint morning light, she saw Paris's greatcoat still draped over the chair. He hadn't left her. Not yet.

She sat up, stretched stiff muscles, and rose. Behind the screen, Daphne and Bell slept on; Eileen was busily engaged in her morning ablutions, washing vigorously between spread pink toes. Pale sunlight pierced the thin curtains covering the window beside the bed, and when she peeked out, she could see rough water in the distance. Too rough? Would it be very poor form to pray that the ships would have to remain in the harbors of both Holyhead and Dunleary, so that her brother could not come after her, and Paris could not leave? Oh, she felt like a ship, buffeted by winds of uncertainty, not knowing whether she most wanted an anchor or a sail.

Quickly, she splashed water on her face and managed to pin up her hair. The chambermaid must have slipped in before dawn and returned their clothes, considerably fresher than they had been. Once she was dressed, she went to the hearth, folded the blanket under which she'd slept, and then stepped behind the screen again, intending to lay it on the foot of the bed.

This time Bell was awake. "G'morning, Miss Gorse," she murmured sleepily, reaching for the kitten with half-open eyes. Then she exclaimed and sat bolt upright. "Oh!" Startled, Eileen arched her back and turned into puff of white fur. Bell grinned as she tried to soothe her. "Oh, it *is* a good morning, isn't it Miss Gorse?"

The commotion woke Daphne at last. "What're you on about, Bellis Burke?" she groaned.

"*You* know, Daph," she said, nudging her sister and giving her a significant look that seemed to be directed at Rosamund as well.

"Oh. Oh, yes." Daphne smiled too, though her expression bordered on sly. "Good morning, Miss Gorse."

One did not need to be a governess to recognize when children were up to something. At a loss to know what it might be—perhaps they were simply exuberant at remembering they'd been reunited with their brother—Rosamund shrugged and wished them good morning in return.

"Now, out of bed, you two, and dress yourselves, quick as a wink."

"What's the hurry, Miss Gorse?" asked Daphne. Definitely sly.

"Ladies do not *hurry*, Daphne," she answered, mustering her primmest voice. "They are, however, prompt and prepared to greet the day."

Eileen nudged her hand to be petted, so Rosamund plucked the kitten from the tumbled bed and carried her to hearth to keep her from being a distraction to the girls while they dressed. Listening to the sisters prod and annoy one another produced an unexpected twinge of melancholy. The certainty of a sibling's affection, the security of family, seemed so remote as to be a dream.

Before they had finished dressing, Paris came in, clean shaven and wearing a fresh cravat. "And how are my sisters this fine morning?" he called from the doorway. "Well rested?"

"Oh, yes," replied Bell from behind the screen. "But aren't you going to ask Miss Gorse how she slept?"

His eyes sought and found her standing near the fireplace, and he winked. She remembered suddenly how he had called her Roisín. *Rosie*. She had never imagined the name could give her anything but pain. But when spoken in that suggestive, Irish way of his… Her answering blush seemed to begin in her toes. "I daresay she must have slept poorly indeed, with you two for her bedfellows."

"Don't forget Eileen," retorted Daphne, and the two girls giggled rather conspiratorially before making their appearance.

He ushered them downstairs to the inn's dining room, a considerably quieter and pleasanter room than the pub. Paris sat beside Bell, who was sneaking bits of coddled egg and kippers into Eileen's basket. Rosamund sat across the table, beside Daphne. They looked for all the world like the little family their hosts believed them to be.

The charm of that image exerted a dangerous pull. This was not her family, could never be her family. Charles was still her guardian, and he would never permit it.

A young man came into the dining room and announced in a surprisingly deep voice, "The *Claremont* is aweigh. The *Industry* has hailed the shore. If you're Dublin-bound, make ready to board."

The words caused a slight stir among the other diners. Two gentlemen rose and left the room. "Come, girls," Rosamund said briskly, not looking at their brother. "Finish up now." Despite Paris's reassurances, Rosamund still feared Charles and Lord Dashfort might well be aboard that ship.

Paris, however, continued to eat at a leisurely pace.

Daphne watched him for a moment. "Aren't we going back to Dublin today?"

He glanced at Rosamund before answering. "I thought, so long as we'd come this far, we'd all go to London instead." *All.* Her heart caught. "Miss Gorse has affairs to which she must tend, and you two must be missing Mama and Papa."

"And Cami and Erica and Galen. Oh, truly, Paris?" squealed Bell as she jumped up and threw her arms about his neck.

One long-fingered hand covered the back of her head. "Truly."

"London," Daphne repeated, a hint of awe in her voice. "Is that where you'll do it then?"

"Do...what?" A puzzled frown appeared on his brow.

Bell looked up at him and shook her head in a mock scold. "Oh, Paris. Marry Miss Gorse, silly."

Rosamund watched the color leave his face, while feeling her own rise. They were saved from having to offer any immediate response, however, by the discovery that Eileen's basket lay empty on its side on the seat of Bell's abandoned chair.

Precious moments ticked by while they debated where to search for the escaped kitten. "She was just here," insisted Bell, starting forlornly into the basket, while Daphne tried to claim that none of this would have happened if she had been put in charge. Rosamund glanced toward the windows, her mind as choppy as the gray water.

What on earth had given Daphne that idea that she and Paris were going to marry?

How much time before the passengers from the *Industry* came ashore?

Leaving Daphne and Bell to bicker not-so-quietly with one another, she hurried about the dining room, searching for a little fluff of white among the forest of legs, both furniture and human. An occasional glimpse of something gave her hope, but it was always only a handkerchief or a napkin that had fallen to the floor or, once, a lady's fur muff lying on a chair.

At a shout from the kitchen, she jerked upright, nearly striking her head on the corner of a table. Paris, who was closer, went to investigate. Moments later, following a few alarming *bangs* that sounded like cast iron cookware colliding with the flagstone floor, and a cry of something that might have been pain, Paris emerged, rumpled and with a scratch down one cheek, holding Eileen by the scruff of her neck. Eileen carried within her tightly clamped jaws a lifeless mouse.

The girls, at once proud and horrified, ran toward the two of them. Eileen, evidently fearful that her prize was to be taken from her, growled loudly enough for Rosamund to hear from several yards away.

"I wouldn't come any closer if I were you," Paris advised, reaching up with his free hand to gingerly brush the scratch on his cheek, then studying the smear of blood on his fingertips. "She's quite determined to keep it."

Determined, indeed. The mouse was fully grown and almost half the kitten's size, but Eileen had triumphed over it nonetheless. "Good girl," Bell offered, a trifle tentatively, while Daphne nodded and clutched the empty basket to her chest.

"The cook offered me half a crown to leave her here to catch pests in the kitchen," Paris said, one dark brow cocked. "I won't say I wasn't tempted." His sisters gasped in alarm.

Amusement and annoyance warring on his face, he jerked his chin toward the exit, the kitten still firmly within his grasp. In the inn yard, he managed—Rosamund was never quite sure how—to snatch the mouse from the kitten's mouth, dropping Eileen into Daphne's basket with one hand and flinging the carcass into the ditch with the other. "Sorry, puss," he answered her hiss of protest, "but no disemboweling rodents in the coach. Come, girls. Up you go."

The carriage Paris had hired stood before them, and in its traces, four high-stepping chestnuts stamped and pranced, almost as eager to be underway as Rosamund was. At least, until she recalled the quizzing that awaited her from Daphne and Bell. Her only hope was that they might have forgotten in all the commotion over the kitten. And she considered it far more likely that Charles had given up the chase.

Paris helped his sisters in first, then turned to her and held out a hand to assist her. His injured cheek, the same one she had slapped the night before, was pink again. This close, she could see three shallower wounds surrounding the angry scratch down his cheek, one groove for each of Eileen's unsheathed claws. Poor man.

Steeling herself not to react to his touch, she let him help her into the carriage and found the girls already seated side by side on the backward-facing bench. With a pang of uncertainty, she seated herself opposite the young inquisitors, leaving room beside her for their brother. As soon as he had closed the door behind himself, Daphne released the kitten from her basket prison. The driver chirruped to the horses and the carriage wheels began to roll. As Rosamund watched the tumbling gray water of the Irish Sea recede from view, a little sigh of relief escaped her.

Opposite her, Bell too was looking out the window. The changing scenery did not hold her attention for long, however. Abruptly, she turned away from the glass. "Do the others know?"

"Know what?" her brother asked.

"About the wedding."

Without looking at Paris, Rosamund squared herself on the bench and said with as much firmness as she could muster, "Whatever can have given you the notion that your brother and I are getting married?" She blamed that ridiculous book of flower poetry for putting the idea in the girl's head.

Bell was frowning now. She disliked being told she was wrong. "Daphne told me. Woke me from a sound sleep and whispered it in my ear. Didn't you?" She twisted sharply, seeking confirmation from her sister.

For just a moment, with all eyes upon her, Daphne looked frightened and perhaps a tiny bit chagrined. But her customary boldness soon returned. "The firelight shone through the screen last night," she explained. "It was better than a magic lantern. I saw you kiss." Her eyes darted from her brother to Rosamund and back again, taking in their reactions to her accusation. "I even saw you lie down together. And Miss Gorse never came to bed." Her chin jutted upward in defiance. "I—I know you think I'm still a child. But I'm not a simpleton. I know that means you have to get married."

* * * *

Paris had risen that morning believing the most difficult thing he would have to do that day would be to ask for help from Eamon Graves. Well, second most difficult, actually. First, he'd had to make himself leave Rosamund, warm and sleepy on the hearth.

He had not considered the particular difficulties to be posed by his sharp-eyed younger sister. If pressed, he would've been willing to swear he was incapable of being surprised by his siblings' antics. But he was certainly surprised now.

Surprised most of all by the strong, sudden impulse to drop to one knee in the middle of the carriage floor and ask Rosamund Gorse to make him the happiest of men.

Instead he shook his head in disbelief, refusing to let himself look toward her, fearful that at the sight of her, he might not be able to stop himself. Surely, he could come up with some explanation for what had transpired? After all, he was reputed to be skilled at argument, able to mount a cogent defense.

"That sounds like quite some dream, Daph," he said quickly, and laughed.

"Dream?" The word burst from her, propelled by outrage. "It wasn't a—"

He held up a hand. "Look, now. I can't say where Miss Gorse slept. I certainly wouldn't blame her if she found the prospect of sharing that bed less than inviting, what with Bell's cold feet and your snoring."

Bell attempted unsuccessfully to muffle her giggle. Daphne turned red. "Paris! I don't—"

"I can assure you, however, that *I* was in the pub all night, playing piquet with the captain of the *Claremont*. He took me for five shillings."

Thankfully, he was in no position to have the truth of this story denied. He had definitely gambled last night. And he had, in fact, given the captain five shillings, along with the letter he'd been struggling since dawn to write.

Daphne blushed a deeper red, the shade of humiliation, and dropped her gaze to the floor. Guilt chilled him. He reached out a hand and laid it on Daphne's knee. "Let's forget about it, shall we?" Still, he did not look at Rosamund. "No damage done."

He hoped.

The girls, however, were not inclined to forget. "Don't you *want* to get married, Miss Gorse?" Bell asked, not five minutes later.

Beside him, Rosamund shifted uncomfortably and cleared her throat. "Why, er…yes," she answered after a moment. "I would quite like a home and a family of my own someday." Was that a note of longing in her voice? Hadn't she seen how much trouble family could cause?

"Don't you have any brothers or sisters?" Daphne asked, aghast.

"I have one brother, considerably my elder."

"Like Paris, then."

"My brother and I are separated by about the same number of years as you and your brother, yes," Rosamund agreed. "But I believe they are quite unalike in other respects."

Was it true, however? Everything she'd told him last night indicated that her brother was controlling and manipulative. Was he any better? The deception being perpetrated on his sisters was entirely his doing. Every bit of it, from Miss Gorse's installation as governess in their household to the present awkward conversation. Further proof his siblings ought never to trust him to do the responsible thing.

"Well, cheer up, Miss Gorse," said Daphne. "If our sister Erica could find not one, but *two* gentlemen willing to marry her, you shouldn't lack for offers."

"Girls," he warned. He wished it were possible to release Eileen again to distract his sisters. But of course the cat was already out of the basket.

As he spoke Rosamund tugged the ribbons of her bonnet away from Eileen's eager claws and straightened the loops of blue silk into a neat bow beneath one ear. At this angle, he could not tell whether the ribbon matched her eyes, as he'd hoped when he chose it.

"After all," continued Bell, undaunted, "you're very pretty." He could not prevent the rough grunt of agreement that rose in his throat. "And not *quite* on the shelf."

Rosamund only laughed.

He prayed that would be the end of it. Bell, however, still wasn't ready to give up. "You could marry Paris even if you don't *have* to," she suggested. "He can be quite charming when he chooses."

"Bell!" he scolded.

"But alas," Daphne added, rolling her eyes and sending a glance of commiseration toward Rosamund, "he does not often choose."

"Why, thank you, dear sister." He let himself slump and scowled a bit. "I'm sadly outnumbered here. Perhaps I'll just sit with the driver instead."

"Oh, Paris, don't be silly." Bell giggled. "It's starting to rain."

"I'd still be better off. How's a fellow to defend himself when it's three—no, four—against one?" Eileen, having been denied the amusement of Rosamund's ribbons, was now attempting to make herself a comfortable nest right below his breastbone. She had evidently forgiven him for thwarting her conquest. Her tiny paws kneaded and plucked, snagging his silk waistcoat.

Rosamund turned just enough that she could fix him with a steady gaze. No, the bonnet's ribbon didn't match her eyes. Nothing could match that extraordinary shade of blue. "Do you account me among your attackers, Mr. Burke?"

She was sitting ramrod straight, and he found something about her posture unexpectedly alluring. Perhaps it was the recent confirmation of the softness that hid beneath its rigidity, the teasing notes that lurked within her sternest voice. He found himself wishing he might have the opportunity to change her mind about the efficacy of a good tongue-lashing.

Displacing the kitten, he reached across to take up Rosamund's hand and was rewarded by a gasp that was not all disapproval. "Perhaps you're right, Bell," he said, darting a glance toward his sister before focusing on Rosamund's delicate features. "Perhaps I ought to propose, just to teach our Miss Gorse a lesson."

His sisters gave a rare, unified squeal of surprise and delight.

Rosamund smoothly eased her fingers from his grasp. "I should exercise caution if I were you, Mr. Burke." She was all prickly, prim governess now. Aloof and cool, she suddenly made him wonder whether the memory of holding her in his arms wasn't a dream, after all. Then a defiant spark lit her eyes. "I might just say yes."

Chapter 18

When he had agreed to undertake this journey, Paris had imagined himself fully prepared to face its torments. The general awkwardness and discomfort of travel, exacerbated by sharing a coach for nearly three hundred miles with his two youngest sisters. His family arrayed before him in a disapproving line at the journey's end.

He hadn't fully considered the particular sort of torture involved in sharing that journey with Rosamund, however.

A thousand meaningless, incidental touches to be endured. The clasp of hands or the cupping of an elbow every time he helped her into or out of the coach. Inside the coach, the nudge of shoulders or brush of legs. Then, of course, there were the nights. He'd made certain there could be no repeat of the temptation at the inn in Holyhead. For four nights, he'd arranged a room for Rosamund and the girls, while he had sat up in the pub, even when he might have had a bed to himself.

But he hadn't yet found a public room bench or an ancient oak settle hard enough to keep him from thinking of her.

Sitting up nights provided a ready excuse to sleep, or at least to feign sleep, during the day, which would have absolved him of listening to the girls' chatter. But he had rediscovered a kind of pleasure in his youngest sisters' company. They were bright and amusing and cleverer than he had realized. Besides, he did not want to miss a glimpse of Rosamund's smile or the sound of her laugh. He even enjoyed her ill-fated attempts to get his sisters to absorb occasional knowledge about geography or the history of the places through which they passed.

Yes, *torment* was the word for it, worse now as they neared the end of the journey. The girls had long since given over teasing him about marrying

Miss Gorse. But the carriage still seemed to echo with Rosamund's words. *I might just say yes.* He wanted her in a way that he had not wanted anything for a very long time. Perhaps ever. Yet he could not quite convince himself that he deserved happiness. And he knew she did not deserve misery.

When the carriage stopped for what would likely be the last change of horses before reaching their destination, he said to Rosamund as she descended, "Might I have a word with you, Miss Gorse?"

As usual, her fingers lay across his palm as he handed her down from the coach. This time, he let his grip tighten. Neither incidental nor meaningless. She did not pull away.

"Looks a respectable place," he announced as he glanced around the inn yard. "Perhaps it would be best to dine here. While we're waiting, we can stretch our legs." Not once in his life had he been enthusiastic to arrive in London, and this time was no exception. He nodded toward a path leading into the center of a small village, on the edge of which stood the posting inn.

The girls, eager for even a moment's freedom from the coach, did not need to be prompted a second time. Rosamund let him thread her arm through his and hold it there. "We can walk and talk, Miss Gorse. Let the girls run ahead." As they strolled along behind them, he told her, "I wrote to my family and told them to expect us by tonight."

Above them, the tree limbs were still bare, though dotted with the promise of leaves; the air was sharp with the scent of new growth pushing aside the old. She breathed deep before responding. "We will all be glad to be done with our journey, I'm sure."

Once his sisters were out of earshot, almost out of sight, he asked, "When we reach London, what then?" An awkward foray into uncovering the deepest desires of her heart.

"I suppose I will try again to do what I intended to do in Dublin: hire a lawyer, someone who can help me challenge my brother's guardianship."

He stopped walking, the better to take in what she'd said. "You mean, when I met you on the King's Inns Quay…"

"That's right, Mr. Burke. Ironic, isn't it? You've brought me all this way, when I'd already found just the man I wanted." And with that, her fingers released his arm, one by one, and she dropped her hand to her side.

Good. She ought not to rely on him. He could not be the one she needed.

She seemed to know it, too. "You intend to return to Dublin, I assume. The case that took you to Kilready sounds desperate indeed."

Would she—could anyone—understand these feeble attempts to make amends for his past mistakes?

"My father is an excellent lawyer," he assured her. "And my brothers-in-law are powerful and well-connected men, with experience on both the field of battle and the field of honor. More than capable of standing up to your brother. They will know what is due a viscount's daughter."

Her head dipped in a sort of nod. "Then I must hope I can enlist them to my cause. Though I fear there's nothing anyone can do. More than anything, I want to be able to return to my home in Berkshire and see that all is well taken care of." The brim of her bonnet hid her expression from his gaze, though if he leaned forward slightly, he could see her soft, trembling lips. "But Tavisham isn't really *my* home, is it? And little as some of its people have, I have nothing to add. Nothing to offer them at all."

Had her father left nothing for her maintenance, made no provision for her dowry? Was that why her brother was so determined to see her wed Dashfort?

They walked a few steps more in silence before she said, "I suppose I shall have to take a post as a lady's companion instead. Or perhaps a…" She swallowed the word on a quiet gasp.

"A governess?" he finished for her.

"At least I now have some experience. Oh, I am sorry for deceiving you and your sisters," she confessed in a rush. "I convinced myself that my charade would do no real harm. And," she added after the slightest hesitation, "I knew it was the very last place my brother would think to look."

No, Setterby had some other misery in mind for her. But Paris's search for someone to care for his sisters had taught him how poorly the world treated the impoverished gentlewomen responsible for girls' upbringing and education. It could be lonely, difficult, even demeaning work. On one hand, Rosamund already seemed inured to the isolation. He had no doubt she could survive it. But survival…well, sometimes, it was a punishment all its own. Daily, she would be surrounded by someone else's family, taunted by what she might never have, like a mirage appearing to one dying of thirst in a desert.

"You are good with children," he murmured. So far removed from their earlier banter, what else could he tell her? That her presence in his home had dusted off old memories and teased laughter into his veins and made him remember that once, his family had been his sanctuary, his joy? That he wanted, somehow, to make her part of it, though she was English and needed something not within his power to give?

She made no reference to his mock proposal, nor gave any indication that she either expected or would welcome a real one. "You are kind to say so. Very few will be as eager to learn as your sisters, I'm afraid."

They rounded a bend in the path and the girls came into view once more, walking on the low stone wall surrounding some sort of monument, arms extended to keep their balance. The kitten was perched on Bell's shoulder, tail in the air.

He shook his head at the sight. "Or as eager to risk their necks."

Beside him, Rosamund mustered a quiet laugh.

As they approached the center of the village, the girls spotted them. Holding hands, with Eileen tucked securely in the bend of Bell's free arm, they jumped off the low ledge and came running across the hard packed dirt of the roadway that passed through the little town.

Their impending interruption prompted Rosamund to turn toward him and lift her face to his. The startling blue of her eyes was still marred by clouds of uncertainty, though he knew now the part of herself that she had been hiding behind them. Or thought he did.

"I cannot hope to repay your kindness in bringing me all this way," she said.

"I could not do otherwise, Miss Gorse."

"Indeed, you could. Some in your position most certainly would."

She had known so few kindnesses, his Roisín. He wanted to reach out for her hand, to hold it in his, to share one last time the touch they both craved. But he would have to make do with words. "I do not always do what is right. My mistakes have caused real harm—especially to my family. But I think even Daphne and Bell would be willing to admit I am not so far gone as to abandon a young woman, penniless, hundreds of miles from anyone who could offer real help."

For a moment, she said nothing in reply. When at last she parted her lips to speak, he was not entirely sure what to expect.

He could not have anticipated what came next.

"Your *mistakes*..." She seemed to be mulling over the possible meanings of the word. "Your involvement with the United Irishmen, do you mean?"

He managed, only just, to prevent a sharp intake of breath. "That is a matter best not discussed in public, Miss Gorse." He tried to keep his voice light, relaxed. "Nor in private, to be quite honest. Molly told you, I gather?"

She shook her head. "Daphne and Bell."

He hadn't even realized his littlest sisters knew. But then, it had always been nigh on impossible to keep a secret in that house. If his private business had stayed private, Galen would never have found out, would never have gotten involved, would never have...

"Come on, Paris." Bell grabbed his hand, the one that had started to reach for Rosamund, and began to pull him back in the direction of the inn. "I'm starving."

"How far are we from London?" demanded Daphne.

"If all goes well, we should be there by teatime." There would be a great deal of fuss over their arrival. Worry about their health and clothes and whether the kitten had fleas. Already he found himself wishing for an excuse to hold himself apart from it. Perhaps this had all been a dreadful mistake.

"Ooh! Look at that, Miss Gorse." Daphne pointed toward an elegant equipage thundering into the inn yard, sweat flying from its quartet of prime goers and from the brow of the coachman as well. A crested carriage, he saw when it had slowed enough to be more than a blur of black and gold.

Rosamund's fingers bit into his upper arm. "*No.*"

Her whisper ought not to have been audible above the pounding hooves and rattling wheels and jangling harness. But he heard it, nonetheless. Or felt it, perhaps, as if in spite of his best efforts, she'd become a part of him.

With her other hand she snagged Daphne and dragged them all backward, into the meager cover of the trail. "No. Oh no," she was muttering, her eyes never leaving the carriage.

Even without recognizing the crest on its doors or hearing any explanation from Rosamund, he could guess that the coach held her brother. Confirmation was shortly supplied when Setterby opened the door and descended, followed closely by Dashfort. Rosamund was reduced to a low, anxious moan at the sight of the two men.

"What is it, Miss Gorse? Who are those—?" His arm slipped free from Rosamund's grasp as his hand shot out to muffle the rest of his sister's words. Bell's tiny fingers dug into his other palm and Eileen gave a squeak of protest as the girl clutched her closer.

Despite the spectacle he felt certain the four of them must make, neither Dashfort nor Setterby glanced their way as they strode across the inn yard. How had Setterby found them so quickly? Followed them so precisely? With so little to guide him, how could he possibly—?

The coachman reached behind to toss down a satchel from the roof of the carriage. Similar, but not identical to the one Paris had carried with him to Kilready. The one he had left behind in his hired gig, labeled with a calling card bearing the address of his old Henrietta Street lodgings. From Kilready Castle, it would have been an insignificant detour, a few moments' diversion, on the way to discovering his family home and the identity of his sisters' governess.

If not for the unforgiving waters of the Irish Sea, the two men would have found them before now. Thanks entirely to his carelessness.

Frozen in her crouched position, Rosamund watched them through wary, hunted eyes as they disappeared into the inn's public room. She'd feared just this moment, and Paris had imagined it impossible.

An hostler came from the stables, struggling under the weight of a yoke across his shoulders, bearing buckets of water for Setterby's horses. They were to be rested, not changed. In other words, there would be no interval in which that carriage would be rendered immobile and he, Rosamund, and his sisters could get away in their own, which stood a few yards away, with fresh horses already hitched.

But Setterby's coachman was distracted—someone from the inn had brought him a pint—and the postilion had wandered off to water the shrubbery. Now or never. With a sharp look for Daphne, whose wide-eyed nod showed she understood his wordless command, he lifted his hand from her mouth to clasp Rosamund by the elbow and urge her to rise.

She started and turned to look at him in abject terror. Her brother might be to blame for the fear in her eyes. But this? This was Paris's fault. He'd led Setterby right to her.

"Walk toward our carriage," he ordered them, his voice low. "Do not dally, but do not seem to hurry, either. Draw no attention."

They were almost past Setterby's carriage when Eileen, who'd grown larger and stronger in the course of a week, managed to squirm free of Bell's stranglehold and darted away. His heart stuttered, but he nudged his youngest sister forward. Rescuing the kitten could mean losing Rosamund. "For Miss Gorse's sake," he whispered, "we must go on." Tears sprang to Bell's eyes and her lower lip wobbled, but she clamped it between her teeth and gave one quick nod. *Brave*, Rosamund had called her. How had he never realized it himself?

Just before Eileen scampered beneath the terrible hooves of Setterby's beasts, the coachman reached out a hand and snatched her up. "Wot's this?" The burly man looked about him; there was no escaping his gaze. How long before he realized he was staring right at the very party of four he sought: a fair-haired Englishwoman, a dark-haired Irishman, and two young girls?

But the man showed no sign of interest, no suspicion. Was it possible? Had neither Setterby nor Dashfort described to his coachman the people they trailed? "Yourn?" the man asked, holding out Eileen. The tiny kitten was nearly lost in the man's enormous hand.

Paris gave the other three a gentle push toward their carriage and turned back. “Yes, thank you.” Just to be safe, he swallowed his pride and erased every trace of Dublin from his voice, speaking the King’s English as if he’d been born to it. “My daughter”—after all, they’d passed as a married couple with children before on this trip—“would have been devastated to lose her.”

“I got a girl, meself. Hate to see ’er cry.” The coachman chuckled and handed over the little troublemaker. “Some cats is right skittish around ’osses. Tell your little one she’d best get a bit o’ string if’n she means t’ keep ’er.”

“I’ll do that, sirrah. Thank you.” With his free hand, Paris touched the brim of his hat, turned, and walked calmly to his waiting coach. Five strides, three, two…

With a nod to his driver, he swung into the carriage, and the wheels were rolling before he had collapsed onto the forward-facing seat beside Rosamund. Both Bell and Daphne had tears streaming down their faces as they took the kitten from him, fussing over her and petting her and scolding her.

Rosamund, however, made not a sound. If she wept, she did so silently. Her face was turned toward the window as she watched the road behind them, her spine so rigid he knew instinctively that if he dared to touch her now, she would simply snap in two. If she weren’t already broken.

Could he get her to safety in time? Or was it already too late?

Chapter 19

When they reached the outskirts of London, Rosamund allowed herself to turn away from the window and slide back on the seat. No point in looking behind her when the road was clogged with coaches of every variety and horses beyond number. Any one of them might have been conveying Charles in his relentless pursuit.

Still, she held every muscle clenched to the point of pain, afraid of collapsing in a shuddering, sobbing heap. She'd let herself imagine, for a few hours, a few days at most, that her brother had given up. He didn't really care what became of *her* after all. She'd never forget his chilling words to Lord Dashfort: *Rosamund will be yours to deal with. However you see fit.*

All those years, she'd been nothing to him. Nothing more than a means to an end.

But it was the end that mattered to Charles. And for that very reason she had known, deep down, that he wouldn't let her escape.

Although Paris going to Kilready had made it easier to trace her first to Dublin, then to England, and now to London, it had been by no means impossible before. The metropolis might have promised some anonymity, but Paris's family was her only security now, and they had not exactly lived shy, retiring lives. Even Rosamund, living in near total isolation in Berkshire, had heard of his famous sister, the novelist, and her notorious husband, whose home they were soon to reach. It might take Charles another day to uncover the connection between Paris Burke and Lady Ashborough. No more. *What then?*

Despite her best efforts, a shudder escaped at last, rattling through her shoulders, down her spine, along every limb. Thanks to the heavier traffic, the carriage happened not to be in motion at that moment, so there was no disguising it as another of the endless jostles and jolts of travel, wood and iron wheels over rutted roads or unforgiving bricks. She gripped the edge of the seat to keep herself from sliding onto the floor as the tremor passed out of her body, like lightning striking the ground.

No one saw. Bell and Daphne were looking out opposite windows in open-mouthed awe punctuated by occasional squeals of astonishment or delight. Even Eileen stood watching with her paws on the window frame, her basket prison once more abandoned.

Paris too kept his gaze fixed on some point beyond the glass, though his posture was that of a man whose thoughts were far away. He showed no sign of having felt Rosamund's jerky movement, though it had surely shaken the bench they shared. The cushions of even the most well-appointed carriages were never as plush after several days as they seemed at first.

Then his hand, which had been lying on the seat between them, moved. Slowly, he crossed the inches between them—a journey somehow longer and more perilous than the one they had just undertaken—and covered her gloved fingers with the gentle pressure of his own.

Daphne, having turned in response to her sister's command to observe something marvelous out the opposite window, watched it happen. Rosamund expected an exclamation, a tart remark. The girl's lips curved, but to Rosamund's surprise, their expression was neither sly nor cynical. It was pleasure that turned up her lips. Happiness. And oh, yes, just a hint of triumph.

Another shiver was building, somewhere in the vicinity of Rosamund's ribcage. Her heart, perhaps, though she refused to think in such nonsensical terms. Hearts beat, fast or slow. They did not ache, neither with joy nor sorrow. They certainly did not quiver with anticipation, with awareness that in a moment, something had changed.

She wanted to linger on the edge of that sensation, to hold onto it, fearful that any movement might cause the fragile connection between them to collapse. But once she'd given in to her body's determination to tremble—with fear, and with something that, inexplicably, wasn't fear at all—she seemed to have lost all control. Again, the tremor passed through her, along her arm and into her hand.

Paris tightened his grip. "We're coming into Mayfair now. Not much farther to Finch House."

Without craning her neck or shifting her position, she could watch the scenery outside the windows change. The houses grew larger, the streets wider and quieter. She might now, if she looked, be able to sort out one carriage from the next, to determine how closely Charles followed. Only Paris's touch kept her from moving, from torturing herself.

"Cami lives *here?*" Bell's question held a mixture of awe and worry. She stroked Eileen's fur with vigor, like a mother cat trying to make her baby look respectable. The kitten tolerated the attention for a few moments before crouching and springing with a wobble from Bell's lap to Paris's, her favored spot. The slightest grimace flickered across his face as her claws sank through his woolen breeches.

"Yes," he said as the carriage rolled to a stop on one of the tree-lined streets of Grosvenor Square. "Just here."

Liveried footmen came down the steps of the townhouse to help them from the carriage. Unceremoniously, Paris plucked Eileen from his leg with his free hand and nodded for Daphne to open to the basket. Once the kitten had been secured, he opened the door and stepped down to help Rosamund out, all without releasing her hand, his touch light but still a source of strength.

Her feet on the ground, she scanned the street. Out of the corner of one eye, she saw a man, not in livery, perhaps not even a servant, approach the carriage to speak to the driver. Instinctively, she sought to raise the alarm, but Paris handed her off to a footman before she could speak.

Realizing that to linger in the open might be dangerous if Charles were in fact close behind them, she hurried toward the stairs instead. The house itself was five stories tall and nearly as wide—to call it *imposing* would hardly do it justice. The home of one of the wealthiest and most powerful men in England. Surely even Charles might quail a bit at the thought of knocking at its front door, to say nothing of attempting to enter uninvited.

Behind her, she could hear the bustle of the girls clambering out of the carriage, squabbling over who would carry the kitten's basket, speculating eagerly over what their mother might say about Eileen and whether Cami would allow an animal in the house. The normality of it all brought a small smile to her lips. She cast a furtive glance over one shoulder and saw Paris speaking to the stranger; nothing about his posture indicated that the man was a threat. Perhaps he had been right when he had promised all would be well. Her fingers tingled with the remembered warmth of his touch.

And then she also remembered his determination to return to Dublin at the first opportunity. Perhaps that touch had been his way of saying good-bye.

This time, the violent shudder that rattled through her caused her to stumble on the second to last step. All at once the door opened and the girls rushed past her to enter the house. She might have lost her balance entirely if Paris had not materialized at her side and set one hand under her elbow to keep her on her feet. "No need to be nervous," he insisted, though his own gaze was fixed on the cavernous entry hall and she thought she heard a note of uncertainty in his voice.

An old and suitably creaky butler bowed them in. "Mr. Burke, I gather. You are expected. I'll show you upstairs."

The girls' voices ricocheted between the marble floors and a high coved ceiling painted with scenes from some mythological battle. Rosamund did not try to sort out which battle. At the moment, the real ones she faced were more than sufficient to occupy her mind.

With Paris's hand still on her arm, she followed the butler. The girls fell in behind, muttering irritably about the slow pace the man set. They stopped before a tall set of doors, which a footman opened. The butler stepped inside. "Mr. Burke. Miss Gorse. Miss Daphne Burke. And Miss—"

Bell, seeing no need to wait for an introduction to her own family, charged into the room, Eileen's basket in hand, and was greeted with a deep "*Woof!*" that seemed to vibrate throughout the house.

"Now, Elf. Behave." A gentleman's voice, fairly bursting with amusement. "And you must be Bell. What's that you've got?"

Though she could not yet see into the room, Rosamund could hear Bell's stammering answer. "A k-kitten. Her name's Eileen."

"Ah. Well, perhaps we'd best send Elf down to the garden until proper introductions can be made. Philpot?"

Framed in the doorway, the butler's shoulders sank. "Yes, my lord." He disappeared into the room and reemerged with one thin hand on the collar of an English mastiff whose head reached the man's waist. A less effective stay against the dog's obvious strength and energy, Rosamund could hardly imagine. The dog snuffed both her and Paris in passing, then thumped obligingly down the staircase, ignoring Daphne who had pressed herself against the wall.

In spite of herself, Rosamund sucked in a little gasp of surprise. But genuine bafflement had settled over Paris's features, and he muttered, "Cami has a dog?"

"I guess we should show ourselves in, now we've been announced," said Daphne and crossed the threshold.

Paris and Rosamund followed. The drawing room was large and elegantly furnished. Tall windows at front and back, framed by gold draperies, cast late afternoon light across blue and bronze papered walls. But what Rosamund noticed first were the people, a roomful of them, all approaching at once with exclamations of welcome and relief, laughter over the imagined altercation between dog and cat, questions that were fated to go unheard and unanswered. Irish voices and English ones. A flash of startlingly red hair. She hardly knew where to look.

Overwhelming, yes, because so far beyond her experience. And yet the warmth in the room drew her, drove back the chill of fear and loneliness. She wanted to step right into the middle of it, like one stepped into the comfort of a familiar embrace. She would have done, if not for the pressure of Paris's fingertips just above her elbow.

He was hanging back, everything about him shuttered like a house battened down for a storm. Dread was etched into his face. He seemed to lack the power to take another step, and Rosamund found herself wondering whether he had grasped her hand in the carriage not to reassure her but to seek reassurance.

A woman with dark hair and spectacles struggled to rise from her chair, one hand on a belly swollen with child, and made her way toward them. "You must be Miss Gorse. Welcome to Finch House. I'm—"

"Lady Ashborough." Paris spoke as if the name belonged to a stranger.

The lady sent him a sharp glance. She shared Paris's raven hair, but her eyes were a brilliant shade of emerald green. "Camellia," she finished, turning back to Rosamund. "Paris's elder sister."

Rosamund, feeling all the awkwardness of the sibling reunion, blurted out, "I've read your book."

A fashionably-dressed gentleman glided over to their circle. "Many thanks, ma'am. My wife's eager readers help keep us in dog food." A wink creased the corner of his eye, and he bowed. "Ashborough, at your service." When Rosamund rose from her answering curtsy, he held out an arm to her. "Allow me to make the introductions."

Paris still had not released her. "No time for pleasantries," he said shortly. His voice cut through the chatter and commanded the room to attention. "This is Miss Gorse."

"Why's everyone so interested in our governess?" Bell was standing in the center of the room, showing off Eileen to a woman with flaming red hair streamed down her back, kneeling on the floor before her: her sister Erica, Rosamund could easily guess. The Duchess of Raynham. There was something hoydenish about her—at least, that's what Mrs. Sloane would have said. Rosamund, having never met either a hoyden or a duchess, liked Erica on sight.

Without lifting her eyes from the kitten, and yet giving the impression she saw a great deal, Erica said, "I don't think she's your governess anymore, Bell."

At those words, Paris abruptly let go of her arm, and the space between them, a few inches at most, felt suddenly vast. "Miss Gorse needs your help." He laid a curious stress on the word *your*, as if to exclude himself. His gaze had been traveling the room as he spoke, but something brought him up short. Squaring his shoulders, he gave a crisp nod. "If you'll excuse me." Before anyone could reply, he disappeared through the still open door.

"Ordinarily, we pretend Paris improves on acquaintance," said the duchess. "But you must already know the truth, Miss Gorse." Rosamund could not keep herself from starting at the remark. Erica gave an exasperated sigh—Rosamund knew, now, where Daphne had learned it. "I suppose someone should go after him," she said, and when no one else either agreed or offered, she sighed again and rose.

"Wait, Erica." The man who spoke had dark eyes, but his once black hair had been transformed over time to the shade of polished pewter. Paris's father, undoubtedly. There was more of Ireland in his voice than in his son's, but Rosamund had no difficult in determining who had taught Paris to speak in a way that made people listen.

He withdrew a folded paper from inside his coat. "See that he gets this."

"Yes, Papa," the duchess said, taking the letter and following her brother out.

When she had gone, Rosamund felt every eye in the room upon her. She hardly dared to step forward, though she knew she must. Once she could muster the strength, she moved to the center of the room. To Bell and Daphne, who were looking at her with expressions of hurt and betrayal.

"Not our governess?" Daphne spoke first, not just her face but her entire body pinched and wary.

"I owe you an apology, Daphne. And you too, Bell," she said, shifting her gaze from one to the other. "The truth is, I never was your governess."

Bell tipped her head to the side. "Of course you were. You built us a schoolroom and you taught us loads."

"It was only ever a temporary post." Rosamund tucked a soft brown curl behind the girl's ear. "Only until you were reunited with your parents."

"But what about Paris?" Daphne folded her thin arms across her chest, withdrawing even further into herself. "I saw you—" Heat rushed into Rosamund's cheeks, but she made no attempt to stop the girl from speaking. "In the carriage. I saw him hold your hand."

This time, Rosamund would not deny it, though she could only guess what his family must think. "Yes, he did. I am very grateful to him for bringing me all this way and for trying to comfort me when I was frightened.

I scarcely deserve such kindness. You see, I deceived your brother. When I learned he was in search of a governess, I let him believe I was she."

"You lied?" Bell inched closer to her sister.

Daphne appeared to consider this revelation for a moment. "I think…I think perhaps she felt she had to," she explained to Bell. "Remember what she told us in the ship? And remember those men? That's why she was frightened. That's why she left us. Isn't that right, Miss Gorse?" With earnest eyes, she looked up, seeking confirmation.

Rosamund could only nod. Laying a hand on Daphne's shoulder, she faced the others. "I hope all of you can forgive my duplicitousness. Although I wish it were in my power to contradict Mr. Burke's claim, I'm afraid he spoke the truth. I am very much in need of assistance. My brother, Lord Setterby, is no more than a few hours from London. We crossed paths on the road, though I do not think he saw us. And Lord Dashfort, the man he insists I marry, is traveling with him."

A gentleman came forward, tall and sharp featured, with tawny hair. He moved with confidence, the sort of man used to taking charge. "Raynham, ma'am." His bow was stiff but not unfriendly, features too harsh to be handsome. "A pleasure to meet you. You must be fatigued after your journey. Won't you sit down?"

He gestured toward the sofa and the empty seat beside a woman of fifty-something, with dark blond hair—or perhaps light brown, shaded with gray. Paris's mother, she supposed. She had hazel eyes, more green than brown, though they lacked the gem-like intensity of her eldest daughter's.

"An excellent idea," proclaimed Lady Ashborough, who looked on the verge of collapse herself. Well, not *collapse*. It would be difficult to image her susceptible to such weakness. But it was easy enough to see how she might topple forward and end up like a trapped tortoise, unable to right herself again. With one hand on her back and another on her husband's arm, she made her way to a chair and gingerly lowered herself into it.

Raynham remained standing. "If I may, ma'am," he said, addressing his words to Mrs. Burke, at present fussing over Daphne and Bell, who had followed Rosamund to the sofa. "I know how eager you must be to spend time with your youngest daughters. But the conversation of adults cannot be entertaining to them." Then, to Rosamund's surprise, he unbent, lowering himself to look Daphne and Bell in the eye. "My sister, Lady Viviane, has asked if you might keep her company this evening, at my stepmother's house."

Though Rosamund recognized the move was intended to ensure the girls' safety, she expected some resistance to the offer. But the duke had a way of speaking that made refusal difficult. With a quick glance at one another, they nodded.

"May we bring Eileen?" Bell asked.

He smiled. "I suspect my sister would never forgive me if I said no." He rose. "If you'll wait for me on the landing, we can be on our way in five minutes." After kissing their parents and their sister, the girls went to the door.

The knot that had begun to form in Rosamund's stomach swelled, rising into her throat. Absurd to feel alone, for the room was still half full of people. But they were strangers. Paris had gone and now Daphne and Bell were leaving. For a week, she had allowed herself to live the ridiculous lie that they were—could be—*her* family. This, however, was their real family, and now she had no connection to it, beyond her desperation and their charity, both of which she wished to be able to deny.

Once the girls were gone, the duke turned to address Rosamund again. "I believe it will be best for you to stay with me and my wife, Miss Gorse. Every step between you and Setterby that can be lengthened or redirected is to our advantage."

Our. Could he understand the comfort that single word brought? The knowledge that she was not alone. And yet, discomfort lingered. Because it seemed clear the word did not comprise Paris.

"My secretary, Mr. Remington, will accompany you to Laurens House whenever you are ready."

"*Secretary*?" Amusement curved Lord Ashborough's lips. "Not that I doubt Remy's ability to write a neat hand. But I expected a somewhat flashier title for his new post. *Aide-de-camp*, perhaps."

"I wonder which of us you intend to skewer with that remark," Raynham replied, also amused, she decided, though she had not been sure of it at first. The two very different men, linked by their two very different wives, though sisters, appeared to have reached a somewhat uncomfortable accommodation.

"Myself, of course," answered Ashborough with another smile, before growing serious. "Remy gave the coachman clear instructions?"

"Naturally."

"What—what sort of instructions?" Rosamund dared to ask. He must have been the man she'd noticed on the street.

"Though Burke's letter was full of reassurances about your earlier escape, I nonetheless anticipated Setterby might be searching for you," Raynham explained. "Mr. Remington merely offered your driver an… incentive to return from whence he'd come by a different route. To forget his passengers and where he delivered them. In cases like this, you see, I prefer a bit of insurance to prevent loose lips."

Just how much experience could a duke have with *cases like this*? "But my brother already knows—"

"Too much, yes. But rest assured. You shall have nothing to fear from him. We are prepared to meet him in your place, whenever he arrives." A nod of his head made clear that *we* referred to him and Lord Ashborough. She was less certain what was meant by their willingness to *meet* her brother. A conversation? A duel? "If you wish it."

Did she wish it…whatever *it* might be? There was an appeal in avoiding another confrontation with Charles. A separate appeal in telling her brother just what she thought of what he had done, and what he was trying to do.

Paris's mother reached for her hand and patted it reassuringly. "Thank you," Rosamund managed, looking from one gentleman to the other. The duke bowed and was gone.

"May I ask about the character of this Lord Dashfort?" asked Mr. Burke.

"He's the one whose wife died last spring, isn't he? She took a tumble over a balcony railing after the servants had heard them arguing." As Lady Ashborough related the story, she exuded a sort of veiled irritation. No doubt an author who had dared to compose such a tale would have found the plot decried as unrealistic by the reviewers. "An accident, it was said, though no one in the ton believed it. I remember Aunt Merrick delightedly reporting how often the man received the cut direct at any event he dared to attend. Eventually he was driven out of town, back to his Irish estate. The only punishment he received, as I recall."

"Yes." The lump in Rosamund's throat had expanded to the point she could barely force words around it. "He is eager to remarry so that his children may have a mother's care."

"Hmm." Mr. Burke cupped his chin in one hand and tapped a deliberative finger against his lips. "A compelling cause, I'm sure. To Lord Dashfort, at least. Though one might expect your brother to express some qualms about giving his sister to a man so careless with wives."

A laugh stirred in Rosamund's chest, thankfully blocked from escape by the lump in her throat. *Feminine hysterics*, Charles would have called her reaction. He had no qualms where she was concerned, no feelings at all.

"He never wanted the responsibility of my guardianship." Rosamund forced herself to say aloud the truth that had been haunting her for years. "He wants to be rid of me."

At those hoarse words, Mrs. Burke's grip on Rosamund's hand tightened almost painfully. "Hmm," said Mr. Burke, tapping his finger against his mouth to punctuate the sound. She tried to decide whether he found her explanation reasonable, or if the sound indicated skepticism. The whole company waited, but he offered nothing more.

"Then he is a fool, Miss Gorse," pronounced Camellia with a strange expression on her face. "But brothers sometimes *are* fools." She reached beneath her spectacles to pinch the bridge of her nose. "Gabriel, ring for tea, please."

"I'm afraid we haven't time, dear," began her husband.

Camellia stopped him with a raised finger, reminding Rosamund rather abruptly that she was the eldest of the siblings and accustomed to being in charge. "Yes, yes. You want to hurry Miss Gorse away. Never mind that the poor woman is hungry and travel weary and frightened. Let her have a cup of tea."

Lord Ashborough nodded and went to the bellpull. Critics of Lady Ashborough's book often speculated about the degree to which the authoress had managed to tame her husband, who was accounted to have been a scoundrel. Rosamund believed she knew the answer.

When the maid arrived, Lady Ashborough said, "The tea tray, please. And be so kind as to tell my brother and sister, wherever they may be hiding, to join us."

The maid curtsied. "Yes, my lady." The young woman disappeared into the corridor and returned before a full minute had passed. "Begging your pardon, my lady," the maid said. "But Mr. Philpot says that Her Grace and Mr. Burke left the house a quarter of an hour ago and didn't say when they'd be back."

Camellia looked as if it required all her reserves of patience not to snap at someone. "I should have been the one to talk to him."

"Absolutely not," her mother and Lord Ashborough said together, their voices a mixture of worry and alarm—whether for Camellia's sake or Paris's, she couldn't be sure.

The fingers of Rosamund's free hand dug into the arm of the sofa. She had known he was reluctant to come to London. His words at the last posting inn. The tight grasp of his hand in the carriage at the moment of their arrival. His sudden retreat. She hadn't understood, however, what fueled his reluctance. She realized now the bitterest irony: The very thing she wanted most was the thing he was trying to escape. Pain had awaited him here, pain felt on all sides. Both his parents and his siblings were irritated by his behavior, obviously. But beneath their irritation, she sensed concern. Fear. What had happened to drive this wedge between Paris and his family?

And by seeking assistance from them, would she be the cause of driving it deeper?

"Forget the tea, Mary," Lord Ashborough said. "Forgive me, Miss Gorse, but my wife needs to lie down." With a start, Rosamund realized that tears had begun to leak from beneath the rims of Lady Ashborough's spectacles.

"I never intended to be the cause of so much trouble—" Rosamund began, rising.

Mrs. Burke, who had also come to her feet, took her hand and patted it again. "You've nothing to apologize for, dear. We're grateful you've brought Paris back to us."

Then the three of them left the room, the marquess and his mother-in-law on either side of Camellia, who was vigorously waving off their attempts to fuss over her.

Rosamund had nearly forgotten Mr. Burke until he spoke behind her.

"Please forgive Gabriel, Miss Gorse. I'm afraid impending fatherhood has him rather on edge." His wry laugh reminded her of Paris's. "He is usually a most charming host, but I suppose no one is at their best when they're worried about what the next day will bring."

To that, she could readily agree.

With a wave of his hand he invited her to sit down once more on the sofa. "Put yourself at ease, my dear," he insisted as he took the place beside her. "The matter with your brother is well in hand."

She wanted desperately to believe that was true, and it was difficult not to have faith in Mr. Burke, who spoke with assurance and smiled in a fatherly way.

"Tell me," he said, clearly trying to distract her, "what sort of pupils did you find my young daughters?"

"A credit to their first teacher," she answered honestly. "Clever and bright. Astute observers." Though lately, what they'd been observing was the growing attraction between Paris and Rosamund. *Do you think my brother handsome, miss? I saw him hold your hand. I saw you kiss.* What would their father think of those lessons?

He laughed, clearly pleased by her praise of his methods. "I'm delighted to hear it. I've made a fair few missteps in my time. But that is how we learn, eh? Trial and error. Children especially must be allowed to make their own mistakes—and be forgiven for making them."

Mr. Burke's child-rearing practices certainly had nothing in common with Charles's.

"Take my elder son, for example," he continued. "I have been tempted to rail at him many times in his life. If I'd thought it would do even a bit of good, I would have done it in a heartbeat. But no one could be harder on Paris than he is on himself. He's burdened himself with an enormous load of guilt for things far beyond his control."

Mistakes, Paris had called the incidents that ate at him, the same word his father had used. Had he learned from them? He'd certainly suffered for them. "And I've only added to his burden," she whispered.

Mr. Burke shook his head. "Oh, I do not mean to minimize your struggles," he said quickly when she started to protest. "Or even his role in exacerbating them. Paris can be, er, difficult." With that, he rose and paced a few steps away. "For almost a year, he's been hiding from those who love him. I feared we'd lost him. Now, he's come back to us. Something's changed, certainly. And I think I know what." He turned to look at her, his dark eyes knowing yet pained. "My son cares for you. Enough to brave a most difficult reunion." The slightest hesitation. "Am I right in thinking you care for him too?"

Mr. Burke was as astute an observer as his daughters. Or nearly so. *Care* was such a—a cautious word to describe her feelings for Paris. *Love*, then? She knew so little of love…just enough to know that it would be foolish in the extreme to have fallen in love with a man who tried to hide his own pain behind a sardonic, charming smile.

Well, Charles had often called her a little fool. Perhaps he hadn't always been wrong.

Somehow, she managed to nod. "But every time I think we've reached an understanding, he…" She glanced toward the door through which Paris had exited.

"I see." With a thoughtful nod, he returned to the seat beside her. "I can't say I'm surprised. I was just as hard-headed once and nearly lost the love of my life. You see, when I met Mrs. Burke, I was a poor law student with decidedly modest prospects. She was the daughter of an earl. Her father threatened to disown her if I persisted in my suit. I was ready to concede defeat, even over her protests. I believed she was too good for the likes of me."

She thought of the way Paris held himself apart from her. Everything he'd said. *You're English. My sisters' governess. A viscount's daughter.* Every label he'd chosen placed her somehow beyond his reach. Above his touch.

"What happened to change your mind?"

"She, er…" Uncertainty, and more than a little embarrassment, flickered across Mr. Burke's face. "She tricked her maid, sneaked into my rooms, and, er, made her wishes in the matter quite clear."

Mr. Burke's meaning was equally clear. Heat swept into Rosamund's cheeks.

"And did—did her father disown her for what she'd done?" she asked. Despite Mr. Burke's assurances, fear of Charles loomed large. And not just fear for herself. He had the power to make Paris's life miserable too.

"Oh, yes. Only after he died was she able to reconcile with her brother. She still will not answer to 'Lady Anne,' though it is her rightful title."

It was a sort of warning, Rosamund supposed. Things surely had not always been easy. But perhaps nothing worth having ever was. "If I may be so bold, sir," she said, "I believe I understand why a lady would be more than content to be Mrs. Burke."

At that, Mr. Burke fairly beamed.

But would his son be so easily persuaded?

Chapter 20

Paris was out the door and onto the street without considering where he meant to go. Perhaps it didn't matter. Anywhere he would not see the stricken, angry, disappointed faces of his family, the ones he'd failed more times than he could count. All that mattered now was that he'd done what he'd set out to do. Daphne and Bell were once more safe in their parents' care. Rosamund would get the help she needed. And he would get…away.

He'd not gone far before he heard the sound of someone following him. Some bit of madness made him hope it might be Rosamund, but he ruthlessly snuffed out the thought—he might want her, but she was too smart to take such a foolish risk for him. He'd put her in enough danger already.

Whoever was following moved swiftly to catch up. He slowed his steps. He'd acted childishly enough already.

"Lovely afternoon for a walk, really." Erica fell in beside him, wearing neither bonnet nor pelisse nor gloves. After six months of marriage, she exhibited no outward signs of change, though her husband, the Duke of Raynham, was by Cami's description a stern and orderly gentleman, a true high-stickler. In short, everything Erica was not. "But I suppose that's not why you left. It's a lot, isn't it? All of us in one room…"

"Not *all* of us." He hadn't realized how much of his dread—his hope—had been focused on looking his brother in the eye, until he'd scanned the sea of faces and seen that Galen was not among them.

"Galen wanted desperately to be here when you arrived. But Papa forbade it."

Of course. His father had always been adept at managing conflicts among the six of them.

"He insisted that Galen stay at school, or else he wouldn't be prepared for examinations at the start of Easter term. Galen tried to argue—something about the true test of a great poet," Erica went on with a shrug. "But you can't win an argument with Papa."

"No, indeed." He'd wondered from time to time why his father had never completed the necessary terms to become a barrister. He would have been formidable in a courtroom, impossible to rattle.

She looped an arm through his, easily matching his pace with her athletic stride. "Where are you guiding me, dear sister?" he asked.

"Not far. Curzon Street. With Mama and Papa at Cami's, I thought you might rather stay with me."

A reprieve. A kindness he did not deserve. And damn but if his first thought was not to wonder where Rosamund would sleep.

"It will be a short stay," he told his sister. "I intend to return to Dublin as soon as possible. Tomorrow, if I can manage it. An important case."

Surprise flickered into her expression, but she nodded. "Papa mentioned how hard you've been working of late."

He couldn't bear what sounded suspiciously like praise. "I have. But I see now I was a fool to think I could ever make amends." The confession came out as a whisper, hardly audible over the noise of even the quiet Mayfair streets.

She heard him, though. "Amends?" Pausing in the middle of a crossing, she fixed him with a stare. "Amends for what?"

Erica did not merely march to her own beat. She danced her own steps to music no one else ever heard. In childhood, she had been the earliest source of his discontent, the annoying, interrupting, pestering little sister with whom he'd thought he had nothing in common. Except, of course, Henry Edgeworth.

Quickly he dragged her out of the street. "Let's not have you run down by some dandy in a high perch phaeton. I don't need yet another stain on my conscience."

"*Another...?*" She stared up at him, sudden comprehension in her eyes. "Oh. I should have known..."

He expected her to rail at him on the spot. Instead, they walked the next two blocks in stony silence. But at soon as the butler had shown them into Laurens House—a double-front brownstone that might have passed for unassuming beside the extravagance of Finch House—she turned on him with that familiar flash of fire in her eyes and said, "How dare you?"

He let himself be half-led, half-pushed into a nearby salon. The footman's face betrayed not one whit of surprise as he pulled the door closed behind the duchess.

With four fingers planted against Paris's chest, she gave him an easy shove onto a brocaded sofa. He supposed he ought to be grateful it wasn't the floor. He might have resisted her—though a life spent half outdoors had made her surprisingly strong. But he was tired, and he knew he'd had this coming for a very long time. "How dare I what?"

"Make all of this—*any* of this—about you?" Her arm flailed out in a wide arc; if he had not leaned back, she would have struck him across the face. He tried to convince himself it would not have been deliberate. "Henry and Galen and… *A Thiarna Dia*," she muttered, borrowing one of Molly's favored Gaelic epithets. "The failure of the uprising does not rest on your shoulders."

He could not help but wince. "Not on mine alone, no. But I have my share to bear. Whose fault was it that Henry and Galen got involved? Whose fault that Galen will be a cripple for the rest of his life and Henry—? *God*, Erica." He drove his fist into the cushion beside him, wanting pain and feeling nothing. "Henry's dead. I was supposed to be there with him. But because I was careless and let Galen out of my sight, I had to rescue my little brother first. And when I finally got to Henry…" He could feel the tremors start deep within him as the memory rose like a gory specter. "I wish I could tell you his last words were of you. But I don't know what they were. I was too late. Afterward, I sat in our kitchen with his blood on my hands—his actual blood—and heard you tell me that I was the reason for your misery."

Erica flopped down beside him and circled his balled fist with her hands. "In more than twenty years you'd never listened to me. Why did you have to start then?" Chidingly, she shook her head. "I was frightened. Furious. With you. With…the universe. I adored Henry. I begged him not to risk his life."

"While I urged him on." He shook his head. "Can you forgive me?"

"No. I can't." When he would have pulled away, Erica's fingertips dug into his knuckles. "Don't you see? I can't forgive you because I don't *blame* you. Henry believed in the cause of a free Ireland. He died for it. Don't diminish his death by making it about something else—by making it about you."

"Even though he—?" He bit off the words. The truth that was not his to tell.

"Loved you?" she finished in a whisper. "I didn't realize you knew."

Guilt will destroy you, people said. If only it were true. If only the guilt and the grief he felt had been capable of truly devouring him. Then surely, surely he wouldn't still feel this much pain…

He managed to nod. "Yet I would have let you marry him—let him marry you—"

Out of the corner of his eye, he saw her toss her head. "That's just what I mean, Paris. *Let* him? *Let* me? You take responsibility for things that have very little to do with you. You assume you know best. Henry was honest with me. He genuinely wanted my happiness. I accepted his proposal knowing he desired men. Knowing that, for a time, he fancied you—despite the fact that you're a selfish ass, as he used to say."

He flinched at the truth of those words, then absurdly found himself fighting a laugh. Henry would indeed have said just that. Erica smiled too through the tears welling in her eyes. Her voice was softer when she continued. "That doesn't mean he let you exploit his love. It doesn't mean he didn't love Ireland too."

Oh, there was balm in her words, and he wanted desperately to be soothed by it. Healed by it. But surely, surely, the wound was too deep…

"I'm your brother, Erica. The eldest son. I was…I was supposed to watch over you. Take care of you. And Galen and Daphne and Bell, too. Instead, Cami had to come all the way from London, with that—that English devil, and—"

"Are you referring to her *husband*?" Abruptly, Erica released his hand. Her voice held a very Cami-ish note, and if she too had worn spectacles, she would have been peering over them disapprovingly.

"Her husband *now*." He made no effort to keep the sneer from his voice. He'd tolerate the man, for both his sister's and Rosamund's sake, but he didn't have to like him. "I suppose we can be grateful he married her at all."

For a moment, his sister simply stared at him. "What are you implying, dear brother?"

Heat spread above his collar. "I think you know. Cami's been wed just seven months. Yet she looks as if she's going to bring that rake's child into the world tomorrow."

Twice she parted her lips to answer him, then stopped the words from coming—an uncommon response from the sister who had always been inclined to speak first and think later. "Do you know what I think?" she said at last. "I think your hatred for Lord Ashborough has nothing to do with him being a rake. Or an Englishman. I think you hate him because he had the audacity to save you—at a moment when you weren't sure you wanted to be saved."

He let his gaze wander the room, though he could take in nothing of its finery. His mind had returned to that night in the kitchen at Merrion Square, Ashborough risking his neck to help an enemy—because Cami, the woman he loved, had asked it of him.

When had Erica grown so wise?

"It's not about you, Paris," Erica said again, as if she intended to go on saying it until he believed her. "Our sister is incandescently happy. It would be hard to imagine a more perfect match. She's found a man as clever as she is. He supports her writing unconditionally." With one fingernail, she traced the flower pattern beneath her hand. "And as to the other…well, I'm sure you know as well as I what might happen between a man and woman on a long journey by carriage." He was grateful not to have to meet her eye. "But the fact of the matter is, Cami's as big as a barn not because the baby is coming too early for propriety's sake, but because there are two babies." She paused. "Gabriel's beside himself with worry about it. His mother died in childbirth."

Fear stabbed through Paris, along with guilt at his selfishness, his callousness. Close in age, close in temperament, he and Cami had always been prone either to squabble or to conspire. A year ago—less—he'd insulted her about Ashborough's intentions. Thinking to divide them from one another, he'd separated himself from her instead. He'd cut off his nose to spite his face, as the saying went. And as a result, he'd been missing her as he'd miss a part of himself.

But he was here now. Did he mean to squander this chance? If he did, and something happened to Cami, it might mean he'd go on missing her forever…

He put an arm around Erica's shoulders. She was frightened too, he realized. She'd never had much luck at hiding her feelings, though she tried, even now, to muster a smile. "I should think he would have learned by now that nothing will stop our Cam," he reassured her. "She'd survive anything for the pleasure of saying 'I told you so' to the person who said she wouldn't."

The curve of Erica's lips strengthened. "She would, wouldn't she?"

Then, because Erica never could sit still for long, she freed herself, leaped to her feet, and strode to the window overlooking the garden. She might be the Duchess of Raynham, but she was still a little wild thing at heart.

Which reminded him… "Whatever became of that hedgehog you found and kept as a pet?" he asked.

She turned away from the window with a puzzled expression at the turn in the conversation. "Henry persuaded me to let it go. He said it deserved its freedom. I figured he knew a thing or two about that."

Paris let himself marvel at her for a moment. Had he imagined her unchanged? In some ways, perhaps. But the Erica he'd thought he knew would have gotten flustered in the attempt to take him to task and looked to Cami to set him straight instead. Today, Erica had managed just fine on her own. She still radiated energy—perhaps the difference now was that she made no attempt to hide it. Somewhere in the last few months, she had discovered its power and now expected others to recognize its value.

And he supposed her husband might have something to do with that discovery.

"I hope, Erica," he said gently, "that you are incandescently happy too."

She turned back toward the window and nodded with an eagerness that spoke what words could not. "You'll get along well with Tristan," she insisted after a moment. "You're very much alike."

Paris made a soft, scoffing noise. What could an Irish barrister and unrepentant rebel possibly have in common with an English duke and officer of the British army?

"You're both so determined to do the honorable thing. To see justice done."

That was how his sister saw him? Even now? He didn't deserve her faith. Anyone's faith…

For a long moment, she said nothing more. Then, "Had you heard he's taking me to the West Indies?"

"Yes." In the letter announcing their sister's impending marriage, Cami had also explained that Raynham did not intend to resign his officer's commission in favor of the title he'd inherited, but rather had agreed to an assignment that would take him to a place rife with disease and disorder. Paris wanted to caution Erica against going, to urge her to think of the dangers. But he thought of what she'd just told him. Perhaps he was finally beginning to understand that people had to make their own choices. And that some risks were worth taking. He rose and went to stand beside her, looking down at the garden just beginning to come to life. "Think of the botanical specimens you'll bring home."

She leaned her head against his shoulder. "Thank you, Paris." After a moment, she said, "Tell me about Miss Gorse."

The request caught him off guard. "You might have heard all you wished, questioned her to your heart's content, if you'd stayed put in Cami's drawing room."

"It was not she I wished to question."

He hadn't the strength for an interrogation. "She's a young woman of respectable birth whose brother has tried to ruin her life. I'm sure you'll get along famously," he added, a trifle more sharply that he had intended.

"Indeed, I hope we will." She tipped up her chin enough for him to see her topaz eyes, bright with mischief. "It would be a shame if we did not."

"Don't," he breathed. He couldn't bear the implication in her teasing words. "She and I… It would be a dreadful mistake. I've made so many—you see? I—I couldn't even be bothered to find Daphne and Bell a proper governess."

She sighed and turned to face him, laying her palm against his chest. "You still don't understand, do you? You've been looking everywhere for forgiveness. But first you've got to forgive yourself. Your family loves you. And," she added with a significant look, "I don't think they're the only ones."

Where was the balm he had found in her words earlier? He didn't think his heart had ever felt so raw. "Love? I don't—"

"No," she agreed readily, "You don't. You don't get to decide when it comes. And you don't get to decide what it looks like—not for me. Not for Henry. Not even, dear brother"—a soft, sly smile curved her lips—"for yourself."

The future he'd once dared to imagine for himself certainly had never included anyone like Rosamund. But that future was gone. He recalled Erica's wise words about forgiveness. Did he—did he dare to let himself dream of a different one?

With a gentle push, his sister slipped past him. "Now, I have to get ready to attend a lecture. A Mr. Geoffrey Beals, former ship's surgeon in the West Indies, is speaking this evening about his findings pertaining to yellow fever. I wish to learn all I can before I go." At the doorway, she paused. "One of the footmen will show you to your room. You'll have the house practically to yourself."

When she was gone, he leaned his aching head against the cool glass. A house to himself. Quiet in which to sort his troubled thoughts. He'd never needed it more.

Nor wanted it less.

Chapter 21

When the last servant left the bedchamber, taking with him the empty supper tray, Paris let himself sink into the bath that had been set before the crackling fire—not an ordinary hip bath, but a real tub, filled with steaming water up to his chest. Clean clothes awaited him in the dressing room, and a well-stropped razor and shaving soap lay atop the washstand. Unimaginable luxuries after the past week's discomforts. Perhaps having a duke for a brother-in-law had its advantages after all.

He'd heard Raynham arrive, an hour or more ago. A bustle of activity, doors opening and closing somewhere down the corridor. Voices, muffled by well-built walls. Then, half an hour later, Erica and her husband had gone out to attend that lecture. A deep stillness had settled over the house, the sort of stillness he'd once craved. Lately, however, quiet prompted reflection, and he did not want to think—not about his family, nor Erica's sharp reprimands. Certainly not about Rosamund.

Not that he ever really stopped thinking about her. Her strength and her courage. The armor of thorns, beneath which hid something so soft and delicate and… A groan shuddered through him. He'd told himself again and again this past week to be content with having kissed her and slept with her in his arms. There could be nothing more. But what if Erica were right? What if he took just one more chance and let himself…

Beneath the water, his hand slicked over his hardened cock. Just one stroke. Or two. Something to take the edge off his madness. *You don't want this,* he'd told her. *You don't want me.* Almost convulsively, his grip tightened and pleasure stabbed through his groin. *Yes-s-s. No.* She *didn't* want him. *Couldn't* want him. His head tipped back against the rim of the copper tub as his legs grew taut. He wouldn't let her…

It was up to him…

"Paris?"

His whole body jerked at the sound and his head snapped upright to locate the speaker. Rosamund stood in the doorway, wearing a pale silk dressing gown, her hair hanging free, dark gold and still damp from her own bath.

Based on the blush staining her cheeks, he must've let loose an oath or two, though he could not remember a time when intelligible words had been more remote from his consciousness. Or perhaps she blushed for another reason. It would not be difficult for even the most innocent young lady to figure out he was doing more than having a wash.

Fighting the impulse to sink beneath the surface of the water entirely, he laid an arm on either edge of the tub instead and pushed himself more upright. After clearing his throat twice he managed to say, with absurd formality, "Miss Gorse."

Chidingly, she shook her head, and took a step closer.

"*Rosamund...*" In his head, it had been a warning. On his lips, it became an invitation.

Two steps more. "Your sister told me I'd find you here."

"Ah. I thought—" He ran a hand through his wet hair. "I expected you'd be staying with Cam."

Eyes wide with something he could only call pretend innocence, she shook her head. "Mm, no. Mr. Remington brought me here." Another step closer and she'd be able to peer right into the tub.

Her boldness didn't entirely surprise him. After all, he'd seen signs of it from the beginning: in the woman who'd fled Kilready Castle in the dead of night, in the woman who'd faced him across that attic schoolroom, in the woman who'd pressed her lips, and her body, to his.

"Why are you here?" He'd meant his voice to sound stern. Instead, he sounded desperate. This spark between them…it mustn't reignite.

"I have a question."

"And I'll be happy to answer it. Just—just go out and I'll meet you in the library in a quarter of an hour." Time to dry off and dress. Time to get his desire under control.

She shook her head. "I'd rather not wait. I've been thinking about that night in Wales, you see, beside the fire…"

Beneath the water, his cock bobbed in agreement. He'd been thinking about it too.

"You asked me what I wanted. My answer hasn't changed." As she spoke, she closed the remaining distance between them. No hiding the state he was in now. But her steady gaze hadn't left his face. "And I wondered, if I asked you the same question, what would you say?"

You. In my arms. Not just tonight. Every night, for the rest of my life.

"I would say that sometimes we want things we shouldn't."

"*Shouldn't?*" One golden brown brow arched. "I thought you were a rebel, Mr. Burke."

Did she think to—to *tease* him with that? He snagged her by the wrist, his touch far from gentle. She needed to understand. "Do you know what you're saying, Rosamund? Do you know what that means?" *Do you know what I've done?*

She did not flinch at his touch. Or at his harsh words. With her free hand, she lifted the hem of her dressing gown a few inches and knelt beside him. "I do. It means taking risks. Making sacrifices for something that truly matters. Something you believe in with your whole heart."

Her voice was earnest, her gaze unwavering. Was she truly prepared to take this risk…for him?

"Ah, Roisín," he whispered, releasing her. "Don't say any more. I can't…"

"Can't what? Can't hold me in your arms?"

"Not again. Not without making love to you." *There.* Surely she'd come to her senses now and go scampering back to her own chamber.

She didn't. She matter-of-factly picked up a washcloth, dipped it into the water, and began to scrub a bar of soap across it. "Good. Because kissing you, lying all night in your arms… It left me with such an ache. And I know you can make it better."

He was powerless to protest as she laid the hot, soapy cloth across his chest and began to bathe him, her fingertips tracing his collarbone and the curve of his muscles, stirring the dusting of hair along his breastbone. Then upward, across his shoulder, the back of his neck. He wanted to close his eyes and absorb the sensations, wanted to watch every movement of her hand and take in every detail of her face. Her lashes swept down, veiling her eyes, and her lips parted without making a sound. God, but she was perfection, with her pink-stained cheeks and her rose-scented hair and her…

"*Rosamund.*"

He had no idea what he'd been going to say next, but she stopped further speech with the tip of her finger. It tasted of soap, and still he wanted to draw it between his lips. "Don't say we shouldn't. Don't say we can't. Tonight may be all we have. Tomorrow could change everything."

It will, he vowed silently. Tomorrow, he would find a way to protect her from her brother. Find a way to turn this one night into forever.

"Oh, Paris," she sobbed. "I've been allowed to make so few choices in my life. Don't tell me I'm making the wrong one now. Or if I am, let me make it anyway." She lifted her finger away. "Please."

If there was a man alive strong enough to say no to that, Paris hadn't met him.

As he turned toward her, water sloshed out of the tub and onto the floor, wetting her dressing gown and making it quite clear she wore nothing beneath it. Lifting one hand, he cupped the side of her head and drew her close for a kiss. Her lips parted eagerly, but he did not immediately press his advantage. She deserved the utmost care, the sweetest caresses. He brushed his mouth across hers, softly at first, taking in each curve and line. Then firmer, more demanding, devouring her little gasps of pleasure, more tantalizing than the richest feast.

When he let her have her breath again, she whispered, "This is the most improper thing I've ever done."

"Ah, my sweet Roisín." He bent to nuzzle beneath her ear and knew by the kick of her pulse beneath his lips that she liked that bit of Irish lilt in his voice. "You're just getting started."

But the bath water was growing cold. "I think we ought to make ourselves more comfortable."

"Drier too," she said, reaching for the stack of towels on a low stool closer to the fire.

A rough, knowing laugh burst from him. "I wouldn't go so far as that."

Whether she understood the meaning of his words, he couldn't be certain. She'd hidden herself behind an outstretched towel, held up so he could step out of the bath behind it. He stood, let the water run down his arms and back, then took the towel from her hands to dry his face and hair. When he tossed the towel aside, he discovered she'd overcome her momentary shyness. Her gaze was fixed on his half-hard cock.

"I, er…" She couldn't seem to make herself look away, even as he stepped from the tub and began to dry the rest of his body with another towel. "I, uh, don't… Why, I should think *that* would make things ache *worse*," she finally blurted out.

A proper reply to such a statement required some thought. Feeble though the gesture might be, he wrapped the towel around his waist and secured it as tightly as he could, hoping the cool, damp linen would exert a calming influence. When he was done, he stepped closer and dipped his head to meet her eyes. "It could," he said honestly. "If I were careless. Or a cad. But I want only your pleasure, love. Which, let me be perfectly clear, can be ensured without any reference to…*that*."

Her blush deepened. "But I understood—that is, from what Mrs. Sloane told me, you have to…"

"Hang Mrs. Sloane." Doubtless the woman had regaled her with some horror story. He'd heard a few himself. "I don't *have* to do anything." He reached for her hand. "And I *want* to do only what you wish."

Her eyes were so incredibly blue. Every cloud had been driven off. "I want you to kiss me."

"Gladly, love."

He claimed her lips, let himself taste her at last, teasing her tongue with his until she caught the rhythm, the playful dance, the flicks and licks and strokes that set them both ablaze. Driving his finger into her golden hair, he kept her a willing prisoner to his mouth as he dragged his lips over her jaw to her ear, ever watchful for her response. A suckle here, a nip there—which sensations produced a sigh of pleasure, which a gasp of delight?

Her own hands were not idle, traveling across his shoulders, down his chest, then rising to bury themselves in his hair, pinning him as he had pinned her so that she could kiss him back. While his mouth trailed over her throat, she rubbed the palm of her hand along his jaw, against the grain of his beard. Five days since he'd last tamed it. "You look the veriest rogue," she teased. She liked that too. He could hear it in her voice, feel it in the thrum of her pulse.

He pulled away just far enough to trace his fingertips along the curve he'd been kissing. "I ought to shave. It's too rough against your skin. Every place I want to kiss you is so soft, so tender." She tipped her chin back as he stroked down her neck. "Here. And between your breasts." His fingertips slipped lower, into the hollow of her breastbone. "And most especially between your thighs."

Her chest rose with a sharp intake of breath. "You want to kiss—?"

"Your sweet quim?" He was determined to match her boldness. He couldn't let this chance go by. He dropped his hand lower still, tugging loose the tie of her dressing gown. "God, yes. Surest way I know to help you with that ache. Climb onto the bed and I'll show you."

For just a moment, she was too stunned to comply. But before he had a chance to reassure her, she slipped from his embrace. Her dressing gown slid over her shoulders and onto the floor as she scampered to the giant four poster and sat on its edge.

He'd cradled her in his arms the night they'd met. He thought he had some familiarity with her body. But what could have prepared him for the reality? The small high breasts with pale pink nipples. The surprisingly generous hips and thighs, and that thatch of curls a few shades darker than the hair on her head.

But first and last, he saw her eyes, flared with passion. Eager despite her innocence. Trusting.

She was watching him too, watching his face as he drank in her beauty. She sat leaning back on her arms, her lower legs dangling over the high mattress. This gift…he knew he didn't deserve it. But she was bestowing it upon him anyway. Slowly, she parted her legs, inviting him. He tossed aside his towel and went to her.

It would be an exaggeration to say he'd formulated any sort of plan, though he could not deny having dreamed of touching her. His hands trembled as he set them at her waist and kissed her thoroughly before sinking to his knees.

Ought he to have paused to pay tribute to her lovely breasts, or to stroke the curve of her waist? Every inch of her demanded his devotion. But this, *this* was the shrine at which he longed to worship. He traced the back of his knuckles up and down her silken inner thigh, drew in the sharp tang of her arousal. "Here, love?" he whispered, slipping one fingertip into her wetness. "Is this where it aches? Shall I kiss it and make it better?"

"Yes-s-s." Barely a hiss of sound. "Please."

Obligingly, he touched his tongue to the place his finger had found, tasted the spice of her. Her hips bucked. Holding her open to him, he kissed her thighs, the delicate crease of skin where her legs joined her body, the top of her mound, before setting his mouth to her in earnest, lashing her with his tongue and then taking her nub between his lips. Moaning, she clawed at the bed linens, and he imagined the stinging pleasure of those nails set to his back.

Then she was muffling her cries against a pillow, coming long before he'd had his fill of her. He might never have his fill of her. It was like awakening from a dream to find it had come true, and by God, he wasn't going to let it slip away from him again.

Almost reluctantly, he picked up the discarded towel to wipe his face, then rose from the floor and lay down beside her on the bed. The linen was cool against his overheated skin. She was still struggling to catch her breath. "I—I didn't—know. Oh!"

As she curled against him, he wrapped an arm around her. "I'll wager there's quite a few lessons I could teach our governess."

She gave a breathless, incredulous laugh. "Really?"

"Do you doubt me?"

A dangerous question. One small hand came up to rest against his chest, carving out space between them. "Sometimes, yes." Oh, those eyes, clear as a summer sky. Honest. "But not tonight." She nuzzled closer again, set her lips to his ear. "Now, tell me how I can soothe your ache."

His body fairly throbbed with need. But when she spoke those words, his first thought was for another ache entirely: the pangs of grief and guilt that had been filling his chest and fogging his mind since last May.

Gently, he probed the edges of that familiar pain. Still tender. But not unbearably so. He'd been certain that opening his heart to another would only make matters worse. What if…what if giving in to his desire, his feelings for Rosamund, was actually the path toward healing?

"I think, maybe, you already have," he said, and smiled when a frown of incomprehension wrinkled her brow. "But if you insist…" He rolled onto his back, lifting one arm to cradle his head, a posture that only highlighted his aroused state. "Do just as you please, love."

"What if I do nothing at all?" Hoisting herself up on one elbow, she looked down at him, a glimmer of mischief in her eyes, her hair falling around them like a curtain of gold silk.

"Don't think I haven't enjoyed myself already tonight," he said, trying to keep both disappointment and desperation from his voice.

"Oh, yes. I know. Why, when I first came in, it looked as if you were…"

"Taking matters into my own hands?" he suggested with a naughty grin, half for the delight of seeing her blush.

She ran a fingertip through the hair on his chest. "Will you show me?"

It was his turn to flush. "Show you how I—?" Until she'd entered his life, he'd never been at a loss for words.

She snagged her lower lip between her teeth and nodded.

Though he'd never performed that particular trick for an audience, his cock was only too ready for him to oblige her. He swept his hand over his flesh, up and down, before settling to a firmer grip. He couldn't deny it felt good—he couldn't remember ever being this hard. From beneath lowered lashes, he looked at her, wondering if she liked what she saw.

But she wasn't watching the movement of his hand. She was watching his face, earnestly searching for something. "I'm sorry," she whispered, leaning closer. "Sorry I hid from you. But you've been hiding too. Please, Paris. Show me."

"Show you…?" He managed somehow to grind out the question. Or was it a question? He knew what she wanted from him.

Everything.

And what would she think when he gave it to her, when she saw his weakness, when everything he'd kept hidden spilled from him in a torrent?

Her cool hand slid over his belly and came to rest around his fist. Quickly he shifted so that she was touching him and he was guiding her, harder, faster. The telltale spasm began in his cods and spread upward, driving a groan out of his chest. Her greedy gaze alternated now between her hand and his face. "Yes," she whispered. He could not control the rictus of desire as it contorted his features, and she saw it all, the indescribable expression that only a man's lover ever glimpsed, utter vulnerability, a grimace of pleasure-pain, his lips parted on a muffled cry as he spent.

Heedless of the mess, she leaned over him and pressed her lips to his temple to catch a single tear that had leaked from beneath his lashes. "Thank you," she breathed against his skin. "I needed to see you. All of you."

After that, what other secrets could be worth keeping?

"I love you, sweet Roisín," he murmured as he drifted to sleep.

Chapter 22

Rosamund woke in her own bed with a smile on her face. Not just because of what had happened last night, though her body still thrummed with remembered pleasure. And not entirely because of the last words he'd said. She didn't know whether she ought to put much stock in that confession, under the circumstances. She certainly hadn't expected it. But now that she had it, she was going to hold onto it.

She was going to make him see that he deserved happiness as much as she did.

Stretching, she sat up as the maid came in with hot water and wished her good morning. It *would* be good. She had something now that no one, not even Charles, could take from her.

"G'mornin', Miss Gorse." The young woman curtsied. "Her Grace sent me to help you dress."

This, of course, meant borrowing more from Paris's sister's wardrobe. But the Duchess of Raynham's clothes were considerably more lavish, both in style and quality, than plain Erica Burke's had been. Rosamund chose a morning gown of fawn-colored poplin with a narrow stripe of pink, and with the maid's skillful pinning, the dress looked as if it had been made for her.

"Pretty as a picture," pronounced the maid. "Now, if you'll sit down at the dressing table, I can help with your hair." Rosamund, who was still in a mood to indulge herself, complied eagerly. The maid picked up a brush in one hand and section of hair in the other. "Goodness me, ma'am. What's happened to your neck? Oh dear, and here on your cheek, too."

Rosamund peered into the mirror at the mottled pink skin to which the maid pointed and remembered the pleasing burn of Paris's rough beard. She flushed, turning her face redder still.

"Well, Her Grace keeps a pot o' cream for rashes and things," the maid reassured her and went back to fussing over her hair. "She makes it herself, in the stillroom at Hawesdale. From flower petals and the like. Seems she's always getting' her hands into something she shouldn't."

Once her hair was arranged, the sweetly scented lotion was found and applied. Not everywhere, of course; Rosamund was rather enjoying the more private reminders of Paris's touch.

What had been his first thought upon waking up this morning? He'd fallen into such a deep sleep last night, she hadn't been able to rouse him. Hadn't been able to tell him what was in her heart. Though she'd been tempted to sleep beside him, it would have been inviting discovery. Instead she'd cleaned things up as best she could, managed to cover him with sheets and blankets though he'd still been lying crosswise on the bed, and sneaked back to her own chamber.

Would she see him at breakfast this morning? And if so, how did lovers keep from blushing whenever they laid eyes on one another?

She needn't have worried. The breakfast parlor, a bright and airy room at the rear of the house overlooking the garden, contained only the duke and duchess and a pair of footmen, one on either end of a long sideboard filled with chafing dishes. Raynham laid aside his newspaper and rose when she entered. "Good morning, ma'am."

"I hope you slept well, Miss Gorse," said the duchess, smiling. Rosamund could not decide whether the words hinted at knowledge of anything that might have interfered with her rest.

"Thank you, yes." The unvarnished truth. She couldn't remember when she'd felt more relaxed, despite the worries that plagued her. "And the lecture—was it all you'd hoped?"

"Oh, indeed. Very informative. I'm hoping to supplement Mr. Beals's research by examining the local botanical remedies for these tropical fevers. People do tend to underestimate the power of plants and flowers."

"They underestimate the power of lady botanists, too," said her husband, whose eyes were once more focused on his paper. "At their peril."

Erica's eyes flashed and then softened as she looked toward her husband with what Rosamund could only describe as a private smile. "Let me get you a plate, Miss Gorse," she said, remembering herself and rising.

"I can serve myself. You've done so much already."

"Nonsense. I've never been one for sitting still. Eggs? A bit of toast?"

A footman poured a cup of steaming chocolate and set it down at the empty place at the table. Rosamund realized suddenly that no fourth place had been set. "Your brother does not join us this morning?"

Erica gave a dismissive wave of her hand. "He was up at dawn. Might've gone for a ride with Raynham, but no. He insisted he had work to do. I daresay he's arranging for his return to Dublin." Her voice dropped, but Rosamund could've sworn she heard the duchess mutter, "Eejit."

"Oh. Yes, of course." Rosamund did not realize she had grabbed her fork at the wrong end until she felt the tines prick deep into the soft flesh of her palm. He couldn't really be leaving her, not after last night?

As soon as the old doubt rose, she scuttled it. It was true that on each of the prior occasions when they'd shared an intimate moment—that first kiss, the inn in Wales—she'd woken to discover him gone. But he'd always come back to her. She had to trust that he would do so again.

Just then, a commotion in the corridor drew everyone's attention, and without any announcement, the Dowager Duchess of Raynham entered the room, with her daughter, Daphne, and Bell in tow. Raynham's stepmother was an elegant, fair haired woman, surely not forty years of age, who moved with the grace one expected of a duchess. Her daughter, dark haired and sallow, looked to be a little older than Daphne.

"Good morning, all," the dowager duchess said, kissing both her stepson and her daughter-in-law on the cheek. "I hadn't thought to call quite so early, but…" She gestured at the three girls huddled near the door, who giggled rather conspiratorially. "Daphne and Bellis were adamant that Viviane meet the famous Miss Gorse first thing."

Stunned, Rosamund curtsied to the duchess and was nearly knocked over by Daphne and Bell, whose arms encircled her waist as she rose. "This is a pleasant surprise. I expected you to have forgotten all about me by now."

"Oh, Miss Gorse," Daphne chided. "How could we? We wouldn't be in London if it weren't for you. Paris never would've brought us otherwise."

"And we wouldn't have Eileen if it weren't for you, either," added Bell.

"Bell rescued the kitten," she reminded them, as she greeted Lady Viviane and they all moved toward the table.

"But you rescued Paris," said Erica, in a voice only for Rosamund's ears.

Mr. Burke had said much the same only the day before. Instinctively, she parted her lips to deny it. She was the one in need of rescue. She was hardly in a position to be rescuing others.

But the noise level in the room had risen tremendously, drowning out any reply she might make: voices and laughter and the clatter of silver and china as one of the footmen set three more places at the table. She hardly noticed when Mr. Remington entered with a letter for the duke.

"Miss Gorse." Raynham's voice, though entirely unlike Paris's, had its own way of slicing through the chaos and commanding attention. She might almost wish that every head in the room had not turned to look when he spoke.

"Yes, Your Grace?"

"A note from Ashborough." He gestured with the piece of paper in his hand. "As we feared, your brother has arrived in town. It seems he does not know everything, however. He wrote this morning to enquire whether any member of Mr. Burke's extended family might tell him where you were to be found."

Rosamund released a shaky breath. "And?" Bell, still standing beside her, gripped her hand. She wanted the answer to that question herself.

"Our next step depends at great deal on you, Miss Gorse. As you may or may not know, Ashborough acquired a vast fortune playing cards. I'm given to understand he's quite adept at what gamesters call bluffing."

She could not quite decide whether the Duke of Raynham was making a joke. "Do you mean to say he would lie? For me?"

Raynham gave a single nod. "If you wish it."

A temporary reprieve, at best. She shook her head. Lies were no way to live. And she could not continue to rely on others. She wanted this matter done, once and for all. "Yesterday, you indicated a willingness to meet with my brother."

"Of course. I am at your command, Miss Gorse."

"Write to him, please. Arrange to see him as soon as possible. This afternoon, if it can be done."

He nodded again. "Setterby will not trouble you after today." The slightest flick of his hand sent a footman scurrying for pen and ink. "You may entrust the matter entirely to Ashborough and me."

She lifted her chin and straightened her spine and said in her most governesslike voice, "No." Last night had given her a taste of her own power. Whatever came of it, she meant to go on making her own choices. She was done running from her brother. "I will be coming with you, Your Grace."

A chorus of concerned gasps rose around her, and out of the corner of her eye, she could see a flash of red as Erica shook her head. But she kept her gaze focused on the duke. A flicker of surprise—or was it approval?—crossed his otherwise impassive expression and was gone before she could even be sure she what she had seen. He bowed and tossed the letter onto the table. "As you wish."

* * * *

They arrived at Finch House shortly before one o'clock, a considerably larger party than Rosamund had imagined. Daphne and Bell wished to see their parents; Erica had agreed to accompany them. The Dowager Duchess intended to call on Lady Ashborough, which meant of course that Lady Viviane had come too. And surely Eileen was secreted in the basket dangling from Daphne's arm. Rosamund knew she ought to take comfort in the fact that everyone, even strangers, had rallied around her in this hour of need.

And she might have, if only *everyone* had included Paris. Why had he hidden himself away again?

Philpot bowed them in and led them to the same drawing room as the day before. Lord Ashborough rose to greet them. "Making our morning calls, are we? I'm sorry to say that my wife finds herself in some discomfort this morning and has decided to keep to her bed. Her mother is with her now, and Mr. Burke has gone out to fetch the physician. Just in case."

Despite the lightness of his voice, worry lined his handsome face. Rosamund recalled Bell describing her sister as being "in expectation of a happy event"; never before had she understood how pallid and ridiculous a euphemism it was for the anxiety and anticipation surrounding childbirth.

"I'll go to her, if I may," said the Dowager Duchess. "I may be of some assistance."

Erica announced an impromptu plan to take the girls on a nature walk through the garden at the center of Grosvenor Square. Once she had rummaged through her sister's escritoire for paper and pencils, and taken Elf's leash in hand, the four of them—five if one counted the dog, and six if Rosamund's surmise about the kitten was correct—set out. Rosamund wondered whether the duchess knew what she had in store for herself for the next hour.

Then, of course, only she and Lord Ashborough and the Duke of Raynham remained. "You mustn't trouble yourself about me," she insisted to the anxious marquess.

He managed a smile, though it lacked yesterday's carefree charm. "To be quite honest, Miss Gorse, I welcome the distraction. I fear I might just run mad if left to my own devices."

For once, he did not seem to be exaggerating for humorous effect.

"All right, then," said Raynham. "Your brother is due on the hour, Miss Gorse, and his letter suggests that Dashfort will accompany him. We have some thoughts about how to proceed, but what did you have in mind?"

She knew from Daphne and Bell that Raynham was a military officer. For a moment, she considered deferring to his judgment. But she did have one advantage: she knew the enemy they were to face.

"My brother has great disdain for those without power, myself included."

"He is a bully, you mean."

"I did not always understand that to be the case." She nodded. "But yes. And because of it, he likewise has great esteem for gentlemen such as yourselves. He will want you to think him clever."

"I know the sort, ma'am," said Lord Ashborough. "They're easy enough for a player with some skill to pluck."

She recalled what the duke had said about Lord Ashborough's gambling days. If he'd made his own fortune, other men must have lost theirs. And just once, she would like to see Charles be the loser.

"I wish you to frustrate him. Aggravate him. Make him angry enough to reveal what I have never been able to determine: why he has tried to do this to me."

"But surely he will not speak in front of you," the duke pointed out.

"Is there a room where I might stay hidden, yet overhear your conversation?"

"My study adjoins the library downstairs," said Lord Ashborough. "If the door between them is left ajar, you will hear rather more than one could wish, I fear."

"I have heard a great deal already, my lord. But today, when the moment is right, I have something to say."

Raynham nodded his understanding, and the three of them went to await their callers.

The single chime of the longcase clock was still vibrating through the room when Philpot knocked. "The Earl of Dashfort and Viscount Setterby to see you, milord, Your Grace."

She could hear the creak of chairs when Raynham and Ashborough rose, the muffled sound of two sets of booted footsteps, Lord Dashfort and her brother, crossing the plush Turkey carpet. Her vivid imagination had no difficult conjuring faces.

"I thank you for your assistance, gentlemen." Charles's voice sent a shudder through her, and she gripped the side of the wooden chair on which she sat to stop herself from leaping to her feet. "May I present Lord Dashfort, my sister's betrothed."

"Gentlemen."

There was a general rustle, the scrape of chairs as the gentlemen seated themselves. Lord Ashborough offered refreshments and was refused. Then an awkward silence fell.

"I understand you have a sister, Duke." Charles spoke first, in a wheedling, obsequious tone she had never heard him use. "I hope she is no trouble to you, as mine has been, so regrettably, to me."

Raynham was quick to quash his hopes. "A spirited sister is hardly reason for condolence, Setterby. And my sister has naught to do with your visit."

"Of course, Duke. My apologies." Quickly, he changed tactics. "Your letter, Lord Ashborough, gave me to understand that Mr. Burke is here. I wish to speak with him. I'm quite sure he knows where my sister may be found."

"Here?" Lord Ashborough drawled in his deep voice. "By no means. I said I believed Burke to have recently arrived in town." A clearly dismissive laugh. She recalled what Raynham had said about his skill at bluffing. "I daresay no one has ever before mistaken me for my brother's keeper."

Even at this distance she could hear her brother's sharp intake of breath. And she felt certain that Lord Dashfort's querulous "Setterby?" would only add to his frustration. *Good.*

"I own I find it strange that your sister would not keep her promise to Lord, er—Dipfoot, was it?" asked Lord Ashborough. "Did she have some objection to the match?"

"Though I've done my best to check it, I'll own she has an obstinate streak."

"I say," Lord Dashfort chimed in. "I don't think I like the sound of that."

Charles was quick to soothe him. "In the right hands, as I've told you, I'm confident she can be brought to heel."

"Forgive me, Setterby." Lord Ashborough again, sounding bored. "I thought this matter concerned your sister? Yet you would appear to be discussing a horse, or perhaps, er, some sort of dog?"

That brought Charles to his feet. She heard his bootheels strike the floor. "Damn it all. You know quite well what I mean." She could picture the little globs of spittle forming at the corners of his mouth. "Surely, among gentlemen, we can speak of the jilts as we like."

"I am quite familiar with how *gentlemen* speak of *ladies*. Whether they are present or not." Raynham's voice was solid ice transformed into sound. By suggesting her brother was something other than a gentleman, he seemed to want to provoke a response beyond mere conversation. *A challenge?* No—she couldn't have a man's death on her conscience.

"Come, Dashfort," Charles ground out. "This is obviously a waste of precious time. Time we might better put to use tracking down Rosamund."

She stood, unable any longer to keep still.

"Really, Setterby," the earl protested. "It seems an awful lot of trouble. The more I think on it, the less inclined I am to believe that your sister and I will suit. I haven't any wish for another difficult wife. Perhaps it would be best if you just returned what I gave you."

Charles cleared his throat. "That won't be possible."

Dashfort stood. "I say. I can't afford to—"

"Oh dear." She crept close enough to the door to see Ashborough tip back in his chair. He was observing the conversation between her brother and Lord Dashfort like a spectator at a badly-acted play. "Sounds like someone intends to renege on a debt of honor. Tut-tut, Setterby. Badly done."

"Stay the hell out of my affairs, Ashborough."

"Gladly. Get the hell out of my house."

Her brother was all cold fury. She thought for a moment that he really would leave. But Lord Ashborough had a keen instinct for just how far a man could be pushed. Charles rocked back on his heels and folded his arms across his chest. "Not without my sister."

"No." As she pushed into the room, four heads swiveled in unison. For just a moment, her resolve faltered. Old habits—even bad ones, like deference and obedience to her heartless brother—were not easy to break. Charles would have lunged toward her, but Raynham rose and stepped between them. She continued speaking as if there'd been no interruption. "And if you try to force me, I'll—I'll tell everyone I saw a ghost at Kilready Castle."

He'd so often tried to make her believe what wasn't true or forget what was. But she suspected that whatever perverse value she held for him would be sorely diminished if the world thought her mad.

Dashfort looked stunned. "You what?"

"You dare to threaten me with some nonsense from a gothic novel? Well, keep it up and you'll soon find yourself living in one. The day you turn one and twenty, I'll wash my hands of you," Charles snarled. "You've got nothing to your name—why, I'd wager even that dress is borrowed. If you won't marry Dashfort, how do you mean to survive?"

She willed her spine straighter. "I'll work. I'll find a post as a governess—"

"A governess? You'll be lucky to find work as a scullery maid when I'm through. You'll have nothing, *nothing*!"

The hinge on the door leading into the library from the corridor creaked as it swung inward. She realized now that it must never have been shut tight after her brother and Lord Dashfort had been shown in.

Paris stepped into the room. He did not look at her. His dark eyes were fixed squarely on her brother. Despite his rather rumpled clothes and unshaven jaw and mussed hair—he'd been running his hands through it again—he commanded perfect attention when he spoke, as he always did.

"That's a lie, Lord Setterby. And you know it as well as I."

Chapter 23

Paris forced himself not to look at Rosamund, though she was all he saw.

"Burke." Setterby spat out his name and Paris nearly smiled. Anger was easy to manipulate. "You dare to show your face after what you've done?"

He did laugh then. "And what sin is it you suppose I've committed, my lord?" The viscount could have no idea.

"You abducted my sister."

"What patent nonsense is that, Charles?" Her voice sliced the thick air between them. "You've been the one attempting to violate my will."

Paris couldn't have scripted a more perfect opening. He reached into his breast pocket and withdrew the paper Erica had given him the day before. He'd forgotten all about it until the early hours of the morning, when he'd awoken alone and needed some diversion to keep himself from seeking out Rosamund.

He stepped forward. "Speaking of wills…"

Setterby, who had turned toward his sister, spun around again, his face a startling shade of puce. "How's that?"

"This is a copy of the Last Will and Testament of Charles Gorse, Ninth Viscount Setterby," he said, holding up the folded parchment. "Your father, yes?"

Some of the color left the man's face. His eyes, ordinarily so like Rosamund's, were hard as slate. "Of course."

"Which of us, sir, will have the pleasure of telling your sister what it contains?"

Ashborough gave a theatrical gasp. "Oh, dear. The plot thickens. My wife will be sorry to have missed this. She might write it into her next book."

Annoyance flickered across Setterby's countenance. "So glad to furnish amusement, Ashborough. As to the will, it's all legal flourishes, dry as dust. My chit of a sister can have no interest in, nor comprehension of, such a document."

Paris could see Rosamund's lips part as she prepared to challenge her brother, so he continued smoothly, "The law does indeed have its peculiar forms. Shall I translate it for her, Setterby? Or will you?"

"There's nothing to explain." Setterby gave a dismissive wave of one hand. "My father's will named me her sole guardian. What else about that paper can concern her?"

"I suspect she might feel some interest in other portions of it. Her inheritance, for example."

Rosamund gasped, as he had expected. Equally expected was Lord Dashfort's impassivity. Of course he'd known. Only Rosamund had been kept in the dark.

"As her guardian, I have been tasked with managing my sister's affairs. The details are nothing with which she need be bothered."

"From what I know of Miss Gorse, I suspect she would not be at all bothered to learn that her father left her Tavisham Manor."

He half expected her to faint. Or, at the very least, to sink into the chair by which she stood. Instead she charged forward and whirled to face her brother. "Charles." Her voice was sharp, accusatory. "Is this true?"

Setterby shifted ominously, with clear intent to grab her by the arm. Instead he found his own arm pinned by Raynham. "You seem to have no proper notion of how ladies are to be treated, Setterby. I should very much enjoy an opportunity to teach you."

"Is that a challenge, Duke?" Setterby wrested himself free. "You all heard him. Can I count on you to serve as my second, Dashfort?"

The earl's narrow eyes widened as much as they were able and he stepped back from the fray. "I say, Setterby. *I* heard nothing of the sort."

"I'll remember your bravery, Dashfort," Setterby sneered, shrugging his shoulders and tugging his coat sleeve into place. "And as to you, dear sister, I should expect to see your gratitude, not your condemnation. A word of thanks for how I've managed Tavisham to advantage all these years—"

"*Your* advantage," Paris pointed out. "I spent the morning doing a bit of digging and managed to learn a few items of note. For instance: The terms of your guardianship require you to manage the estate in your ward's best interest—"

"Which I have done. It's a small property, no more than a few farms. Hardly enough to pay her dressmaker's bill."

"You were the one who insisted on the lavish gowns," Rosamund said, her voice shaking. "You insisted on parading me about like a—a—"

"An heiress," supplied Paris, more than a little fearful of the word she might choose instead. "You once told me, Miss Gorse, that you regretted having deceived me. It seems you were the one being deceived."

"*Heiress*," scoffed Setterby. "Do you dare to suggest that I have wronged my sister by using her small inheritance to find her a respectable husband? She has no other dowry."

"Why could I not be allowed to choose for myself?"

"Because your brother wished to choose for you," said Raynham darkly.

"And what of that?" argued Setterby. "Is that not part of my duty as her guardian and her only family still living?"

Ashborough crossed his arms behind his back and spoke in his driest voice. "Such selflessness."

"Alas, not *quite* selfless, I'm afraid." Paris tapped the parchment against his palm. "It would seem he planned from the beginning how Tavisham might best be used as a bargaining chip. I spoke just this morning with two gentlemen whom he approached last year, who could not meet his terms: Tavisham Manor and his fair sister, in exchange for—"

"Money." Rosamund still faced her brother; Paris could see no more than the stiffening of her spine. "It wasn't enough to humiliate me, to belittle me. Why, all this time you've been trying to—to *sell* me. To marry me off to the highest bidder."

"It's done as often as not," Setterby insisted, leaping to his own defense. "What are dowries and jointures, after all? Marriage, my girl, is entirely an economic matter. If you'd done as you were told, you'd have been well-settled by now."

"If I'd done as I'd been told, I'd be in misery right now."

Dashfort gave an awkward cough, which had the unfortunate effect of drawing Paris's attention. "It does sound as though Dashfort was willing to pay whatever price your brother asked," Paris said. "But it seems the transaction was not entirely about money."

She glanced over her shoulder at him, and it was very nearly his undoing to see the worry and pain flooding her eyes. "What, then?"

"You said it yourself not an hour ago, Miss Gorse," said Raynham. "Power."

Paris nodded. "Tavisham is what's known as a pocket borough. Which means that this particular 'small property,' as your brother describes it, exercises rather an outsized influence on matters of great importance. Its owner effectively chooses a Member of Parliament and cannot be gainsaid.

Your brother has exerted his pull over the election in the years since your father died, and it seems he hoped to marry you off to a man who would continue to be subject to his authority, to vote in the way he sees fit."

Setterby sputtered but did not deny the claim. "Well, what of it? Would you have the country governed by just any fools?"

Rosamund ignored him. "But if it's all to do with a seat in the British parliament, why should Lord Dashfort care? He's already a peer."

"An Irish peer," Paris said as he dragged his gaze from Rosamund to the earl. "Here, I must indulge in a little speculation. I believe it comes down to this: Lord Dashfort has demonstrated a great wish to legitimize his claim to be an Englishman. An hereditary English estate would have helped him, or at least his son, achieve just that. It may also be that there are matters expected to come before Parliament in which he wished to have some voice. Perhaps he even foresaw a time when he might want the seat for himself. If the Act of Union is passed, the Irish parliament will be dissolved, and there's no guarantee he'll be given a seat in the British House of Lords. His title will be worth little enough then."

During Paris's speech, Dashfort had been moving unobtrusively toward the door of the library. With surprising lightness, Ashborough stepped into his path. "Don't leave at intermission, my good man. I myself cannot wait to see the final act." Dashfort winced.

"You shall have a great deal of difficulty proving I've done anything wrong in my management of Tavisham or my sister's care," Setterby said with a jeer of defiance. "Surely, Burke, you will not deny that the law allows a guardian to act as he sees fit."

"The *law* may have very little to say on the matter," Raynham said loftily, every inch a duke, "but I believe you'll find there are still consequences for a man who mistreats his ward."

Setterby seemed to consider those words a long moment, and Paris found himself holding his breath. Every criminal had a breaking point. How far would Setterby go to save his own neck?

The man's shoulders dropped, only a fraction of an inch. But it was enough. His tone, when he spoke, was almost submissive. Wheedling. "Perhaps you gentlemen would be interested to learn how Dashfort acquired the funds with which he intended to pay me?"

Dashfort, who seemed to require a moment to grasp the implications of Setterby's words, nodded along until Raynham's dark gaze shifted to him. "I say, Setterby," he squeaked. "We were at school together. You don't mean to turn on me?"

"Oh," said Ashborough gleefully, "I think he does."

"It's that decrepit old castle." Setterby shook his head disparagingly. "Someday it'll fall right into the sea. But for now, men run their boats right into its dungeon. Makes it easy to get around the British tariffs on goods from both France and Ireland."

Raynham folded his arms across his chest. "I've got an associate at Whitehall who's always glad to hear any tips about smuggling along the Irish coast."

"It was never *my* doing," Dashfort insisted. "The smuggling. Why, I was hundreds of miles away for the last ten years."

"And you received no profit from it, I suppose?" Paris glanced toward Setterby and back again. "Paid no bribes?"

"I—" Dashfort shook his head, more in dismay than denial. "My late wife was determined to live in England, despite the expense. She hated Ireland, and for a time, she persuaded me to hate it too. To hate myself. I told my agent to find the money somehow. I—I didn't let myself consider what that might mean." His voice grew quieter still, and guilt suffused his face. "Still, it was never enough. Last year, I told her we would have to return to Kilready, and we…we argued, as everyone knows. Or pretends to know. She was hysterical. I—I didn't push her," he insisted, his gaze lost in the memory of that day. "She stumbled and fell before I could reach her. But it's still my fault that the mother of my children is dead."

After a moment, Paris said quietly, "I will not tell you that you can make amends." A week ago, he'd set out on a quest, animated by two parts guilt and one part desire to avenge poor Henry. Now, however, he saw matters differently. What he sought now was a way forward. For those who had no voice. And for himself. "But there is something you can do. You can make sure your agent pays for the suffering he inflicted on others."

"Quin? Was there really so much harm in what he did? A bit of this for a bit of that…"

"The harm," Paris explained, an icy edge to his voice, "is to your son."

Dashfort looked baffled. "Alexander?"

"Tommy Fagan. The poor child of your former maid, locked in a cell in Kilmainham for theft. He suffers from a condition called albinism—no color in his skin or hair. Quin's been using the boy in his scheme, to frighten intruders—"

"Kilready's ghost," breathed Rosamund.

Paris nodded. Dashfort shivered.

"But if you can muster no sympathy for him," continued Paris, "then by all means, think of Alexander, who must someday hope to make an honest living from his Irish estate, if you haven't ruined it first, with your rackrenting and your absenteeism. Give him tenants who can earn their bread, rather than steal it, and I daresay he won't find himself facing a rebellion."

Abashed, Dashfort nodded. "The boy—Tommy. You can arrange his release?"

"No, my lord. But you can—in exchange for your testimony against Quin in the smuggling case. I shall send an express to an associate of mine regarding the matter, but you must return to Dublin as soon as possible to speak on Tommy's behalf. The court will listen."

"Yes, of course," he agreed, more readily than Paris could have hoped. "I'll leave tomorrow. And once I'm there, I—I'll stay. I'll try to repair the damage I've done at Kilready. All of it. You have my word." That announcement was met by stunned silence. "Forgive me, Miss Gorse," he added with a bow in her direction and a sharp glance at Setterby. "Your brother used our old friendship—and my grief—to make me believe…" He shook his head, unable to complete the sentence. "I should have known better than to listen to him." This time when Dashfort left the room, Ashborough made no move to stop him.

After a few moments, Rosamund asked, "What happens to Charles?"

Setterby still seethed nearby, kept quiet and in his place by the force of Raynham's glare. "I suppose you'd be satisfied to see one of your friends here run me through?"

"On the contrary, Charles." Rosamund's eyes were wide with horror. "I never wished you ill. But you cannot continue to manage my life."

"The terms of the will dictate that Tavisham Manor is yours when you reach your majority," Paris explained.

"Why, that's in less than a fortnight. I suppose that was your great hurry to find me and marry me off to Lord Dashfort?" she demanded of her brother, who could not deny the accusation.

"There are innumerable ways to make a man pay his debts," Ashborough said. "I propose a written and signed confession—a sort of note of hand, if you will. To be called in at any time Miss Gorse feels necessary. The right word in the proper ear about your behavior, and you'll be ruined, Setterby. Look what a little gossip has done to your friend Dashfort. That required no swords, no pistols, no courts of law."

"Damn you all," Setterby muttered. But his shoulders sank a notch lower in defeat.

"Come," Raynham said, gesturing toward the study where Rosamund had hidden. "We'll find paper and pen in here, I trust. Ashborough has other matters to which he must attend." With a grateful nod, Ashborough left the room. "I may not have his experience with notes of hand, but I'm quite good at getting confessions."

Raynham closed the door behind them, and suddenly, Paris was alone with Rosamund.

"That was quite an entrance," she said. "I was a little afraid you'd left for Dublin without saying goodbye, even after…"

"About last night…" he began.

"Yes?"

"I've been thinking." He stepped toward her, stretched out his hands for hers. "About the past. And the future. When you said I'd been hiding, you were right."

"From your family?"

"From the mistakes I'd made—many of which involved them. It was foolish of me. If I hadn't already begun to see how foolish, Erica made sure I knew." He smiled and brushed his thumb across her knuckles. "And this trip has shown me I can't go on hiding from the people I love."

"Your family."

He did not know how to read the look in her eyes. "And you. Ah, Roisín," he whispered, stepping closer still. "I don't know how it happened. I wanted a governess to escape the responsibility of caring for my family. Instead, you gave them back to me. I was lost. But now I know what I want." Gathering his courage, he dropped onto one knee. Years of experience had taught him never to ask a question to which he didn't already know the answer. But he was determined to do it anyway. "Rosamund Gorse, will you be my bride?"

His heart raced as a welter of emotions crossed her face. Words started to her lips and were withdrawn. Finally, she set them in that prim little line he'd grown to love. "On the way to London, Mr. Burke, you told me that you believed your brothers-in-law could solve my problems. Without diminishing the important contributions of Lord Ashborough and the Duke of Raynham to today's proceedings, I'd like the record to reflect that I was right all along. I needed a lawyer, didn't I? I needed—*need*—you."

"Is that—is that a *yes*, love?"

Again, she hesitated. "I love you, Paris. I love Tavisham, too, though I never thought I'd see it again. Oh, I thought I was so clever, wanting to make all my own choices. But now I don't know how to choose"

He'd known as soon as he read the will that her inheritance could be the end of his hopes. In a matter of weeks, she would be quite independent. If she wished, eventually, for marriage and a family, the landed daughter of a viscount could do far better than a Dublin barrister.

But persuasion was his stock in trade. "Then don't. You've read my sister's book?" he asked. Rosamund nodded, a trifle warily. "So you know that at the end, the heroine proposes her own act of union, so to speak. Between an English gentleman and Irish lady. I despised it when I first read it. It was giving up, I thought. Giving in. But lately, I've begun to think Cami might have been right. Union might be a way forward, though I don't say it will be perfect, or easy."

"I suppose there's no reason to think it couldn't work just as well the other way around, an Irish gentleman and an English lady?" Her teasing smile gave him hope. "Could you be happy at Tavisham, Paris?"

He was sure of only one thing. "I cannot be happy anywhere without you. But I've got to go back to Dublin, first," he warned, "to see things settled there."

Her smile grew into something marvelously wicked. "When you return, I've got a job for you."

"Oh?"

"I've recently discovered I've got a parliamentary seat in my pocket," she said, patting her hip.

He laughed at first, but her eyes were serious. *An M.P.?* A huge responsibility—was he ready to face it? Once he'd dreamed of serving his country thus, but he thought that dream had died with all the rest. Now a new future opened before him. He might do more for Ireland at Westminster than he ever could have at home.

He tilted his head to the side and tried to muster a bit of his old savage mood. "Well, now," he growled. "I'm not quite sure how I feel about being your pet Irishman."

At that, she laughed and freed one hand to brush the hair from his eyes. And then she was in his arms and kissing him and there were only the two of them in all the world. A perfect union, indeed.

For a moment, at least. Somewhere in the house a door slammed and a moment later, a dog the size of a small pony ran into the room, being chased by a tiny white kitten. Behind them Bell squealed and Daphne said, "I *knew* it, Miss Gorse. I knew you were going to marry my brother." Erica smiled a knowing smile.

Soon after that, his father appeared in the doorway. "Worked it all out, eh?"

Rosamund freed herself from Paris's arms to go to him. "Oh, Mr. Burke. I owe you my thanks. You were the one who found the will—that was the paper you asked your daughter to give to Paris, wasn't it? That was what you meant yesterday when you assured me the matter was well in hand."

His father shrugged away her gratitude. "It wasn't much, really. When I got Paris's letter, I called in a favor from an old Oxford chum. And when I saw what was in the will, I knew your brother didn't have a leg to stand on."

Paris thought for a moment. "What if Erica had forgotten to give it to me? Or I had neglected to read it?" What if, in other words, he'd failed Rosamund too?

His father smiled. "Ask your clever governess."

Rosamund tipped her head, considering her answer. "Based on what I know of your sisters' education, I'd say your father trusts his children's ability to sort things out for themselves. And from what I've seen, that trust is not misplaced."

"Never yet," his father agreed. "But I confess I kept a second copy of the will," he added with a knowing wink, patting his breast pocket. "Just in case you got, er, distracted."

Paris threw back his head and started to laugh, but stopped abruptly when Ashborough staggered into the room looking dazed. Despite the presence of ladies, he sank into the nearest chair and dropped his head into his hands.

"Is Cami all right?" Erica demanded.

Without lifting his head, he nodded. "Camellia is amazing." The words were slightly muffled, but his state of shock was clear. "And I—I'm a father. Of two beautiful little girls."

Paris let out a low whistle. "More Burke women, eh?" Though he had the utmost faith in Cami's ability to reform this particular rake, daughters would surely seal the deal.

His father nodded sagely, his thoughts apparently traveling a similar line. He made his way to the sideboard, poured two fingers of brandy, and took them to his stunned son-in-law. "Well, today goes to prove what I always say: Men may make the laws, but justice is a woman."

Everyone, even Ashborough, laughed. Paris's eyes sought and found Rosamund, who was laughing too. Her usual prickliness had, at least for the moment, disappeared. He watched her amused gaze dart from one member of his family to another, stopping at last on Elf, who was trying to hide beneath a too-small chair while Eileen stalked across the room with her tail in the air.

He crossed to Rosamund's side and leaned down to murmur in her ear. "This is family, love. Being surrounded by utter chaos most of the time. You're sure it's what you want?"

She turned, took his chin between the fingers of one hand, and brushed his hair back with the other so he could not hide from her devastating blue eyes. The governess had come back in full force, thank God.

But she could not disguise the quirk of pleasure on her lips as she at last said, "Yes."

Chapter 24

As she stepped out into the sunshine of a lovely morning in mid-May, ghosts were the last thing on Rosamund's mind, despite the nearby churchyard.

She was, at that moment, wondering whether the large basket of flowers Daphne and Bell had been persuaded to carry up the aisle of the church would also contain a kitten; whether Elf had already chewed through the stout rope with which Mr. Whitt, the village blacksmith, had tied her to an anvil; and whether Mrs. Riggs, Tavisham Manor's cook, had kept her promise to stay on through the wedding breakfast, despite the discovery that the affair was to be attended by a "real live duke." "Really, Mrs. Riggs," she'd overheard the vicar's wife saying, "I hear tell the marquess is the one you have to watch out for"—which of course, hadn't helped matters a bit.

Beneath a charming wrought-iron trellis hanging with ivy, Mr. Burke stood waiting to walk her down the aisle. While Paris had been busy in Dublin, and Mrs. Burke occupied with her new granddaughters, he had come to Tavisham to help Rosamund order affairs there. He'd sat beside her as she listened to her tenants and made note of their needs. He'd read through leases and explained their terms with patience. He'd helped her figure out how to make it all run smoothly—for, as it turned out, Tavisham was not quite as small a property as her brother had claimed, and when better managed would provide the young couple with a comfortable income without continuing to drain the farmers who worked its lands.

"Did you sleep well, my dear?" Mr. Burke asked, holding out an arm to guide her down the rough path to the church door.

She'd stayed with the vicar and his wife last night, for every room at Tavisham Manor was taken: by the Duke and Duchess of Raynham, Lord and Lady Ashborough and Phoebe and Chloe, and Mr. and Mrs. Burke and Daphne and Bell. Paris and Galen, who'd been scheduled to arrive from Oxford last evening, had been forced to put up at the inn in the next village.

"I did," she told him, though she was almost embarrassed to admit it. Should a bride be nervous on the night before her wedding? Or maybe it was tonight she was supposed to be nervous. But she wasn't nervous about *that*, either. Not after the agony of spending six long weeks apart.

And almost before she realized it, they were entering the little stone church, filled to overflowing with the good people of Tavisham and her family-to-be. Her eyes went immediately to the chancel. To Paris, standing there, handsome as ever, in a green coat and a dull gold waistcoat. His sharp profile was turned toward Galen, whose auburn hair curled over his collar and gave him the air of a poet. They were laughing quietly together, some private joke between brothers.

Before silence fell over the company, before anyone had even realized she was there, Paris looked up and found her. How had she ever imagined she could hide anything of herself from those dark, knowing eyes? But he couldn't hide from her, either. A look of awe spread over his face, and then he smiled. Just the open, genuine smile she had always longed to see.

She wanted to run to him. Thank God for Mr. Burke, who kept her steady. She drew a deep breath, straightened her spine, and walked slowly and deliberately into her future.

Afterward, she could remember only snatches. The way Paris's fingers trembled as he lifted the delicate veil of Irish lace she'd pinned to the bonnet he'd given her. The breathless moment when the vicar asked if there were any objections—and was met with silence. Nothing from Charles, who'd gone skulking back to Suffolk. Not even the cry of a hungry baby. And the swell of love when the vicar had pronounced them man and wife, and she and Paris had turned to face their cheering, smiling, sobbing family, and Eileen had shot like a bolt of lightning down the aisle. Thankfully, Elf had not been at liberty to give chase.

Rosamund couldn't have told a soul what was served at the wedding breakfast, but the Duke of Raynham praised the lightness of the sponge cake and she made a mental note to give Mrs. Riggs a raise. Phoebe and Chloe, dark-haired and easy-going, were passed from hand to hand and lap to lap. Rosamund thought her heart might stop when she caught a glimpse of Paris at the far end of the table, a baby in each arm, debating with the Marquess of Ashborough over the merits of some piece of legislation soon to come before the House of Lords.

When the meal was finished, Galen got stiffly to his feet and raised his glass.

"To the union of two souls. To the joining of two kingdoms. To the Burkes."

A rousing chorus of "Hear, hear!" went up from the company. From out of nowhere, her husband was at her side asking for a kiss. And whether it was the toast or the kiss that had been the signal for a general remove, she couldn't say, but afterward, the party began quickly to scatter.

Lord and Lady Ashborough and the babies were the first to go, heading a parade of three coaches that included Mr. and Mrs. Burke and their youngest daughters, who would stay a while at Stoke Abbey, Lord Ashborough's ancestral estate in Shropshire, before going on to Wales and then home. It had been essential, confided the Duchess of Raynham, for her to see her mother off and not the other way around. For Erica and the duke were now on their way to Bristol, where they would meet Mr. Remington and board the naval vessel that would take them to the West Indies, a voyage over which the family had already shed its share of anxious tears. "We'll be back in a year," she insisted to her brother as she waved from their coach.

Borrowing a bit of the duke's calm certainty that the trip would be a success, Rosamund squeezed Erica's hand and said, "Bring me something lovely for my garden."

Galen was the last to go, "but not without a kiss for my new sister," he cried before climbing into his gig. She had been told a bit about what had come between the brothers, but she saw no evidence of it now as they exchanged a few low, laughing words.

"Don't forget this," she said, handing up his walking stick.

"Ah, yes. He wouldn't want to be without that," said Paris with a wink. "I hear the ladies find it dashing."

When Galen's gig was out of sight, Paris took her hand in his, and they walked in silence along the gravel drive. She tried to think of something to say, but his frequent letters from Dublin had already answered every question that came to mind. Tommy Fagan had been released from prison and returned to his mother, on whom Lord Dashfort had settled a sizable sum and a pleasant cottage on the edge of the village. The earl had also hired bricklayers to close up the secret passage into Kilready's dungeon, and hired Mr. Graves's younger brother to tutor his children. She sincerely hoped that, over time, Alexander and Eugenia would recover from the trauma of losing their mother and come to love the country that was now theirs.

Too soon, they stood before Tavisham Manor. She'd hardly grown accustomed to thinking of it as *her* house, and now it was *his*, according to the law. She glanced up at him, her husband, whose eyes were taking in the squat stone building as if he were seeing it for the first time. Stillness had settled over everything. A flicker of uncertainty crossed his face, and she thought of the enormous adjustments this match would also require of him. He looked down at her and smiled. "Will you show me around our home?"

Our.

As the dining and drawing rooms must already be familiar to him from their earlier celebration, she began on the opposite side of the wide central staircase, with her least favorite room. At Mr. Burke's encouragement, she had ordered the walls repainted a soft rose color and the furniture recovered with cheery patterns, but it was still rather too easy to picture Mrs. Sloane seated at the large work table or pretending to doze on the sofa, like a watchful old bulldog waiting to sound the alarm at any sign of mischief.

Even now, Rosamund could not quite bring herself to cross the threshold. Nevertheless, she had already had her books and her needlework moved into the room; this was the lady's parlor and it would be her proper place as the lady of the manor. From the doorway, Paris's dark eyes took in every detail, though he made no comment.

Adjacent to that room, though not adjoining it, was the library, with its stout oak desk and dark paneled walls lined with bookshelves. She loved its masculine warmth, the deep leather chairs and the welcoming window nook, where she had often hidden herself to read for hours. But she loved Paris more, and when he'd sent two trunks of books and papers from Dublin, she'd placed them in this room with her own hands, eager to show him that he'd at last have a gentleman's study of his own. "When the door is closed, you'll have all the quiet you could want," she told him as they stepped inside.

Again, he took it all in without speaking. Then, releasing her hand, he walked out the door, returning a moment later with his arms loaded: plump floral cushions, her workbasket, and a stack of novels. "There's such a thing as too much quiet," he said, as he distributed her things about the room. "I didn't come here to be alone."

"I love you." The words rushed from her, and her own eagerness caught her off guard. She'd not spoken them before, though they were true and had been for quite some time.

His eyes danced with wry humor. She felt certain he was about to tease her. To say, "I know." And it would be fair enough, for he'd known her, known her heart, even when she had been trying desperately to hide it from him.

But then his expression softened, and he took her hands in his and leaned in to kiss her cheek. "I don't deserve it," he whispered against her ear. "But I shall endeavor to be worthy of you, my dear. Now," he said, straightening, "what about the upstairs?"

"It's just bedchambers."

"Yes."

The heat of her blush would have taken the chill off the house, if any had remained. He threaded her arm through his and together they climbed to the floor above, which contained another four rooms. Rosamund had always been relegated to the smallest of them, which overlooked the privy. The master's suite—or at least, the room which Charles had commanded whenever he had deigned to visit—had an expansive view of the gardens at the back of the house. This room she was ready to reclaim.

Her fingers trembled only slightly as she opened the door and they stepped inside. Mrs. Coats, the housekeeper, had made everything fresh after last night's visitors—the crisp white bed linens had already been turned down, and the two large windows had been left open to invite the spring breeze. "This is where we'll be tonight," she explained, and blushed again.

Paris nudged the door shut with the toe of his boot. "Must we wait?"

Sunlight filled the room, filtered through the bright green leaves of a spreading oak tree just outside. "But it's broad afternoon!" No cover of darkness to cloak them, no softening haze of candle or hearth.

He lifted one hand to trace the curve of her heated cheek. "There's no shame in it, Mrs. Burke."

Mrs. Burke. She'd never grow tired of hearing it, though she supposed a part of her might always be prickly Miss Gorse.

He'd sensed her hesitation. "But it's just as you please." The same words of reassurance he'd spoken that night at Laurens House. The promise that the choice would always be hers.

Twisting, she brought herself against him and reached up for a swift kiss. Yes, he'd see every inch of her in this sun dappled room. But she would see every inch of him, too. "Oh, Paris. I've missed you so."

"I've missed you too." He spoke between kisses, as if he needed to learn her lips all over again. One strong arm curled around her waist, one hand cradled her head. "Do you need me to call your maid to help you undress?"

"I haven't a maid," she confessed breathlessly. Sally, who swept and dusted and made up the fires, would doubtless find it odd to be summoned at this hour. "I can manage."

He caught up her hands and kissed them. "Let me." With nimble, careful fingers, he unpinned her new dress of china blue muslin and slipped it from her, then gently turned her away from him to unlace her stays. When they fell away, he swept his hands up her arms and over her hips, taking in every lightly-clad curve with an appreciative murmur.

Not to be undone, she turned and slid her palms over his chest, pausing to feel the pounding of his heart. Hungrily, she pushed his coat over his shoulders and let it join her gown on the floor, then set to work on the too many buttons of his gold waistcoat. At her hiss of frustration, he took up the task and made swift work of it, while she proceeded to tug his shirttails free from the band of his breeches.

"Here," he grunted, bending and lifting her in his arms. "I forgot about the threshold bit. This will have to do." Softly, he laid her in the center of the bed before removing her shoes and stockings. Now, only her embroidered cambric shift shielded her from his dark gaze.

When he leaned his backside against the mattress to shed his boots, she knelt and reached around to unwind his cravat, then slid her hands down to the buttons of his fall. "I've been thinking about that night at your sister's," she whispered into his ear before nipping at his earlobe. "And I wondered…"

"Yes?" he hissed as the first button slipped free with a soft *pop*.

"Can a lady"—*pop-pop*—"please a gentleman"—*pop-pop*—"as you"—*pop-pop-pop*—"pleased me?"

His breeches slid to his ankles and he kicked free of them before turning to face her. "I believe I'm supposed to say that a *gentleman* would never ask a *lady*—to say nothing of his *wife*—to perform such a lewd, lascivious act." With every few words, he prowled closer, and she scooted backward beneath the force of his gaze, until she lay beneath him, pinned to the mattress by his welcome weight and delicious heat.

"But *you* didn't ask," she pointed out. She'd never felt so marvelously naughty in all her life. "*I* did."

He lowered his mouth to hers, withholding the promised pleasure of his lips to say, "Then by all means." She opened herself to his plundering kiss, clinging desperately to fistfuls of his shirt and canting her hips to meet his.

By degrees, he gentled the pressure of his mouth, eased his weight from her. "But not just now," he whispered, pressing his lips to her forehead. "I want—ah, love. Will you let me come inside you?" The tiniest flutter of nervousness traveled from her chest to her belly. Had he felt it? Softly, he kissed her again. "I'll be so gentle, love. I just need—"

"Yes," she whispered back. "I need it too."

His previous frenzy all but forgotten, he rose from the bed to shed the rest of his clothes, and she greedily studied the lean planes of his body.

Then he urged her once more onto her knees so he could lift her shift over her head. In that moment of blindness, she heard his sharp intake of breath. At last, she laid down and he came beside her, nothing between them now.

"You're perfection," he said, his gaze roving over her. "I'm almost afraid to touch you."

"Don't be. I…" She didn't have words for her desire.

But he understood her, all the same. His fingertips began their slow erotic journey in the hollow at the base of her throat. She watched the progress of his hand, mesmerized, as he brought her skin to life with his touch. Brushed the pad of his thumb back and forth across the tips of her pink-peach nipples until she whimpered. Trailed sparks over the curve of her belly and into the honey-brown curls between her legs. Light, playful touches, so different from the sensations that had brought her to a swift peak once before. Eagerly, she parted her legs, welcoming the glide of his fingers between her folds as he teased her nub, hearing her own wetness as he dipped a finger into her, slipping from one sensitive spot to the other, until she thought she might go mad with the pleasure of it.

As his hand explored her, his manhood nudged repeatedly against her thigh, hot and more than a little forbidding. But when he levered himself onto one arm and came over her, distracting her with soft, sweet kisses, she forgot to be nervous. He fitted himself to her with such care, entered her with such easy, gentle thrusts, that she felt no pain, just the agreeable ache of being stretched and filled at last. And all the while his clever thumb continued to work its magic on that little pearl. She pressed her knuckles to her mouth to stifle her panting cries.

"No." It was almost a growl, and his eyes were fierce. Feverish. "Not this time. I want to hear you. I want to see you." He thrust deeper, and her answering gasp escaped, mocking her feeble effort to muffle the sound. Giving up, giving in, she reached up to brush the hair from his damp brow instead. "Come to me, Roisín," he pleaded.

She couldn't deny him, couldn't deny herself. Pleasure burst, then rolled over her in waves as his seed flooded her womb with heat.

Afterward, he rolled onto his back and she curled against his side. They lay, breathless, tangled in the sheets. She luxuriated in the rise and fall of his chest, the rhythm of his heart as it returned to a steadier pace. In all her wildest imaginings, she had never dreamed of such deep contentment, the certainty that their union would be stronger than the fragile pieces from which it had been made. Because she'd wanted a man who was good and loving and just, and she'd found him in an Irish rebel. Because she was prim and proper and English, and he was her perfect rogue.

A few minutes later, his palm began to rub circles over her bottom. "Oh." To her amazement, her need surged again in response to his touch and she pressed herself eagerly against his hard thigh. "You were so quiet, I assumed you'd fallen asleep," she said as she glanced up at his face.

But it wasn't drowsiness that made his eyes heavy-lidded and warm. "It's broad afternoon, Mrs. Burke," he teased, smiling down at her. "And I'm not one bit tired. What say we make a little more noise?"

Epilogue

December 24, 1800

"Babies," Daphne declared loftily as she peered over the edge of the crib, "are boring."

"When they aren't crying," Bell agreed. "Or stinky."

Arthur James Rowan Laurens, Marquess of Hawes, raised one tiny fist at his young aunts and scrunched up his face. His father swooped in to forestall the inevitable eruption. "Or hungry," Tristan said, settling the baby in his mother's arms.

Though the Duke of Raynham had lost the sunburnt color he'd first sported upon his return from the West Indies several months ago, Erica's face was still more freckled than ever. Her husband didn't seem to mind, however. He dropped a kiss on the ones scattered across the bridge of her nose as the baby began to emit greedy smacking noises.

"Come," said Paris, shepherding his youngest sisters from the room before they began to complain again.

"If I were you," Erica spoke after them, "I'd use this time to build my arsenal. Because once I've laid Arthur down for his nap, the snowball fight to end all snowball fights will begin." Her voice had a newly soft, maternal note to it Paris hardly recognized, but the words themselves could belong to no one but his middle sister.

"I don't see why they couldn't have at least chosen one of the names from the list we sent her," Daphne complained as he closed the door behind them.

"It's traditional to give the heir a family name," Paris explained. "Rowan to honor our papa, and Arthur James in memory of Tristan's father." The late duke had been an avid student of the Arthurian legends. Paris suspected, however, that the baby's first name was equally a nod to Arthur Remington,

Tristan's secretary, who had demonstrated yet another surprising set of skills when the little marquess had insisted on making his appearance before the *Seaflower* could dock in Liverpool.

Daphne considered the matter, then shrugged. "Well, that means all the best ones are left. You and Rosamund can have your pick."

"If the baby is a girl," he pointed out. The list of names Daphne and Bell had labored over was predictably one-sided.

Bell frowned. "What else would she be?"

Paris laughed. In truth, he wanted a daughter—despite having grown up surrounded by sisters. Or perhaps because of it.

Cami met them at the bottom of the stairs holding a dark-haired toddler by either hand. The girls were dusted in white. Not snow, as he'd first thought, but flour. "Oh, there you are," she said, sounding relieved. "Eileen chased Elf into the kitchen again, and surprised Mrs. Riggs in the middle of rolling out piecrust. Did I—?" There was flour in Cami's hair too. "Did I hear something about you girls going outside?" she asked hopefully.

At almost two years of age, Lady Phoebe and Lady Chloe Finch, in addition to the decided advantage of being girls, could perform all sorts of tricks that boring babies could not. They ran and played pat-a-cake and babbled words that sounded suspiciously like "Daphne" and "Bell." Or near enough that the young aunts were gratified by the attempt.

"Let's make snow angels," suggested Bell as she took one of the twins by the hand and the four trundled off to get into their wraps.

"Take Elf with you," Cami called after them, sinking into the first chair she found, which happened to be in Paris's study.

Since Paris and Rosamund's marriage, the Burke family had continued to grow, while Tavisham Manor—a modest little house, just as Rosamund had once told him—had seemed to shrink. Now it was full to the point of bursting. Erica and Tristan had intended on making only a brief visit on their way from London to Hawesdale Chase, Tristan's family estate, which they had not seen for more than a year. Paris's parents and Daphne and Bell had been traveling northward with them, planning to return to Dublin. No one could have predicted the heavy snow. The same weather that had stranded the lot of them in Berkshire had also forced Cami and Gabriel and their daughters to take refuge before they could reach London, where they had been expected at an important event being hosted by Cami's publisher in her honor.

"I'm sorry we all just descended on you like this," Cami said, "especially at Christmas."

"I'm not," Paris insisted. Frankly, he welcomed the distraction. The new year would usher in two of the most momentous events in his life: the birth of his first child and the first parliamentary session of the new United Kingdom, at which he would take his seat in the House of Commons. Two awesome responsibilities for which he would have sworn he was unfit, if not for the strength and assurances of his wife.

As if his thoughts had summoned her, Rosamund appeared in the doorway with Eileen, now a sleek cat, curling sinuously about her ankles. "There's such a thing as too much quiet," she said, echoing the words he had once spoken to her in this very room.

Before any reply could be made, a deep *woof!* reverberated through the house, followed by a clatter of dishes from the direction of the kitchen and a girlish shriek. Eileen's back arched and her tail puffed to twice its normal size before she scooted off—running towards the fray, rather than away from it. "Too much quiet?" Cami sighed and heaved herself from the chair. "That's one problem we've got sorted, at least."

Paris took Rosamund's hand and led her to the window nook, her favorite spot in the house. Whatever changes the next weeks would bring, he knew that her cleverness and her genuine concern for others would show her to be both an excellent mother and an ideal politician's wife—no, *partner*.

"You've been helping in the kitchen, haven't you?" he chided as he brushed his thumb through the smudge of flour on her cheek. She looked radiantly lovely, though if he'd told her as much, she would have tried to make him see her mussed hair and calico work dress and most of all her ungainly belly, swollen with his child. So he simply took in every inch of her with greedy eyes, plumped the cushions before she sat, and counted his blessings. "You're not supposed to be on your feet, you know."

"I wasn't," she insisted. "Much. Your mother is helping Mrs. Riggs with the baking. I was only observing."

Once she was settled as comfortably as she could be, he knelt on the floor beside her, one hand resting lightly on the curve of her belly, the other hand still holding hers. Silence settled over the house, humming in his ears. He broke it only to whisper, "I love you, dear Roisín."

He told her every chance he got. But if he spoke those words a hundred times a day, every day for the rest of his life, it still would not be enough.

And no matter how many times he said it, it still elicited the sweetest gasp from her. "Oh." She laid her hand atop his where it cradled her abdomen. "Paris, I—"

A door slammed in the entry hall, followed by the stomping of boots. His father and brother-in-law returning from their expedition into the village, no doubt.

Gabriel's voice rang out: "You'll never guess what I found in the snow."

"Hold that thought, my dear," Paris murmured, brushing a kiss across her lips as he rose.

When he reached the threshold of the study, he stopped short, not quite believing his eyes.

"Galen?"

His brother turned and hurried toward him, his gait stiff, but no longer requiring the aid of a walking stick. "Paris! I thought to surprise you. But I'm the one who got the surprise. How came everyone to be here?"

After Paris had explained, he said, "I thought you and your Christ Church friends were celebrating the holiday in Bath?"

"Oh, well. Don't I see enough of Lambert during the term?" Galen shrugged, indicating that the change in plans was of little consequence, though the slight rise and fall of his shoulders wasn't entirely convincing. "Hugh Pritchard declared there was bound to be better sport in London and managed to find a sleigh, of all things. I persuaded him to drop me off along the way."

"Your decision to come away from Bath wouldn't have anything to do with Mr. Lambert's sister, would it?" asked Rosamund, slipping her hand into Paris's.

"Rosamund," cried Galen, ignoring her question but coming forward to kiss her cheek. "Are you well?"

Her blue eyes twinkled. "I'm—"

"Did I hear Galen's voice?" Erica raced down the stairs, Tristan following at a more sedate pace with Arthur in his arms. The middle Burke siblings wrapped one another in a hug, Erica's brilliant copper curls tangling with her younger brother's mop of darker red-brown ones.

As Cami had predicted, there were no more quiet hours to be had that day. Daphne and Bell were the next to discover Galen's arrival, quickly claiming him for their side in the great snowball war. Then an hour or so later, not perfectly thawed and still replaying the highs and lows of battle, all but the very youngest members of the party seated themselves around a groaning table. Their appetites whetted by the exercise, they fell quickly on the repast, though full mouths did little to mute the constant hum—no, roar—of conversation.

When Paris at last pushed his plate away, marveling over the fact that the true feast was not until tomorrow, Galen leaned toward him. "I have something for you."

He'd kept his voice low, but not low enough to prevent a number of heads from swiveling in their direction as he reached beneath the table and brought out a small wrapped package.

"What's this?" said Paris, taking it from him. "A book?"

"Open it."

He peeled away the heavy paper to reveal a slim duodecimo volume, neatly bound in tooled green leather. Flipping to the title page, he read aloud, "*Poems, from the Pen of a Gentleman and a Patriot, inspired by a Celtic Muse*."

"Yours, Galen?" demanded Cami, craning her neck to see.

Their brother blushed. "It's not much, compared to what Cami's accomplished. Or Erica, getting to name her discovery and present her findings to the Royal Society," he demurred. "But the early reviews are heartening." Proud siblings and prouder parents gathered around, dismissing his attempt at modesty and offering congratulatory hugs and back slaps and shouts. "I've got copies for all of you in my bag," he explained. "But I wanted Paris to have the first, because he—"

Doubted. Complained. Criticized. Reflexively, Paris shook his head. He'd been too hard on Galen when they were younger, too caught up in his own troubles to be all that an elder brother should.

"Because he makes me proud to be an Irishman," Galen finished.

Something like quiet fell for just a moment, as Paris tried and failed to get words around the lump in his throat. *Proud?* Cami, whose novels were busily reshaping English opinion of their homeland, nodded her agreement with their brother's claim.

Perhaps there were many ways of being a patriot.

While the book of poetry was being handed around the table, Erica wandered to the window and looked out. "It's snowing again." Though it would delay their homeward journey even longer, he fancied she didn't sound disappointed.

Their mother, however, sighed. "Oh, dear. I was looking forward to attending the midnight service at that charming little church in the village."

"It isn't far," insisted Gabriel. "After this marvelous dinner, I daresay a brisk walk would do us all good."

Murmurs rose and fell as everyone debated the matter, the depth of the snow, the length of the vicar's sermons. For himself, Paris could not imagine a more fitting celebration of the season's deeper meaning than this moment, this place, shared with everyone he held dear. His eyes sought and found Rosamund at the foot of the table. "Well, Mrs. Burke. Will we brave it?"

She laid aside her napkin. For the first time, he saw that her plate had hardly been touched. "No, I don't think so. You may go if you wish, of course, Mr. Burke. But as I've been trying to tell you all for hours…" Her gaze was clear, steady. "I'm going to have a baby."

* * * *

Paris had no idea how much time had passed when he was finally allowed to enter his own bedchamber. The local midwife had been trapped in a neighboring village by the storm, and Tavisham hadn't so much as an apothecary. But his mother and Cami, with their usual calm, matter-of-fact manner, had managed the situation admirably, while the rest of the family had taken it in turns to keep him from wearing a path through the rug on the study floor.

The large window overlooking the back of the house glowed with the luminous darkness of a snowy night. By that curious light, he could just make out Rosamund's shape in the bed, and the tiny bundle in her arms. For a long moment, he did not speak, not wishing to disturb them if they slept.

"What's that in your hand?" Rosamund's voice sounded tired, but not weak.

He managed to tear his eyes from her long enough to glance down at the crumpled sheet of paper he held. Laughter tickled in his chest. "Daphne and Bell's list of names." Slowly he moved toward her. The paper drifted to the floor. "But I confess I'm more interested in what you've got in your hands. Are you going to keep me in suspense?" Cam had told him only that mother and baby were well.

At this distance, he could see Rosamund more clearly, a long golden braid hanging over one shoulder, stray hairs curling damply around her face. A soft smile curved her lips. "Your daughter." He would have sworn that his heart flipped in his chest. She nodded for him to sit on the edge of the bed, then reached out to lay the baby in his arms. Not a moment's hesitation, not a hint of doubt. His wife's unwavering faith in him would never cease to amaze.

When her own hands were free, she gently arranged the blanket around the tiny, wrinkled face. "Holly, meet your papa." The baby stirred but did not wake, content to sleep in the safety of her father's arms.

"Holly," he repeated. A fitting name for the newest addition to the botanically-inclined Burke family, certainly. And a fitting name for the daughter of his Rosamund: strong and beautiful and just a little bit prickly.

"It's perfect," he whispered, carefully leaning forward to press his lips to Rosamund's forehead. "She's perfect. Our perfect Christmas gift."

Author's Note

The hero of this story was inspired by a single line in the "history" section of the Bar of Ireland's website. In the late eighteenth century, "A good barrister was considered a major catch – and many women attended the Four Courts hoping to catch a glimpse of their heroes in action." It wasn't difficult to picture the sort of man who would have attracted those ladies' attention. Because the leaders of the United Irishmen and the bloody and doomed 1798 Rebellion were drawn from the ranks of the Irish Bar (Theobald Wolfe Tone among them), I knew such a man would likely have had strong political opinions, as well as intimate knowledge of violence, trauma, disappointment, and condemnation. Thus, Paris Burke was born.

He's introduced in his sister Camellia's book, *The Companion's Secret.* Paris disapproves of the conciliatory politics in the novel his sister has written, which I modeled after Sydney Owenson's *The Wild Irish Girl* (1806), a so-called "national tale." These stories used the metaphor of marriage to explore the limits and possibilities of the 1800 Act of Union between Ireland and Great Britain. Typically, an Irish heroine teaches an English hero about her homeland, and he comes to love her (and Ireland) in the process of getting his education. Paris, of course, finds himself in the inverse plot: an Irishman who falls in love with an Englishwoman. (Such a variation was rare; sometimes heroes don't know what's good for them.) I borrowed the notion of the heroine keeping a "pet Irishman" from another Owenson novel, *O'Donnel.*

Oh, and if you, like Rosamund, wondered about the botanical meaning of his name, you shouldn't be surprised to learn that it refers most commonly to the *Paris quadrifolia*, or "true lover's knot," frequently incorporated into Celtic symbolism.

Don’t miss the rest of the adventures of

The Burke Family in

THE COMPANION’S SECRET

and

THE DUKE’S SUSPICION

Available now from

Susanna Craig

and

Lyrical Books

About the Author

Photo credit: Vicky Lea Hueit Photography

A love affair with historical romances led **Susanna Craig** to a degree (okay, three degrees) in literature and a career as an English professor. When she's not teaching or writing academic essays about Jane Austen and her contemporaries, she enjoys putting her fascination with words and knowledge of the period to better use: writing Regency-era romances she hopes readers will find both smart and sexy. She makes her home among the rolling hills of Kentucky horse country, along with her historian husband, their unstoppable little girl, and a genuinely grumpy cat. Find her online at www.susannacraig.com.

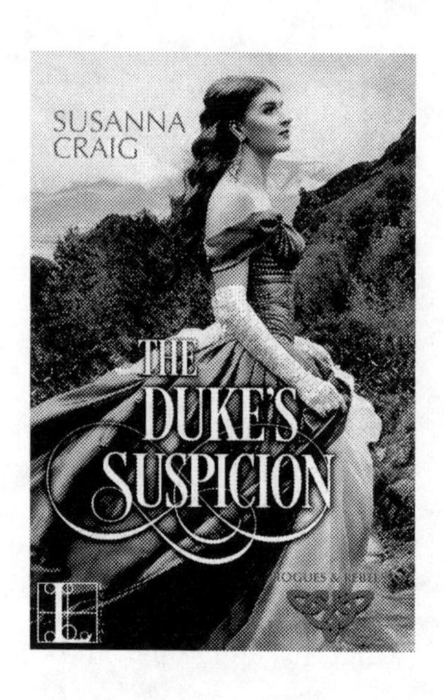

An English war hero must unlock the secrets of an Irish beauty's heart…

Named for the heather in her native Ireland, botanist Erica Burke dreams of travel—somewhere she won't be scorned for her scientific interests. Instead, a storm strands her with cool and commanding Major Tristan Laurens, the Duke of Raynham.

An unexpected heir, Tristan is torn between his duties as an intelligence officer and his responsibilities as a duke. A brief return to England to set his affairs in order is extended by bad weather and worse news—someone is after the military secrets he keeps. Could the culprit be his unconventional Irish guest? He needs to see her journal to be sure, and he'll do what he must to get his hands on it… even indulge in a dangerous intimacy with a woman he has no business wanting.

Erica guards her journal as fiercely as she guards her heart, fearing to reveal a side of herself a man like Tristan could never understand. But though she makes Tristan's task infernally difficult, falling in love may be all too easy…

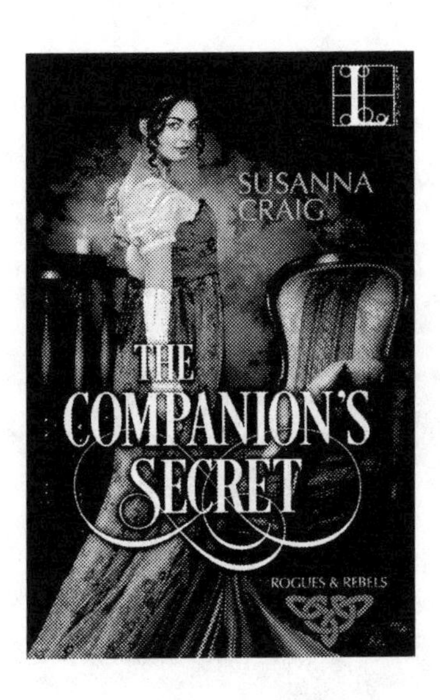

In this tempestuous new series, rebellious hearts prove hard to tame—but can England's most dangerous rake be captured by a wild Irish rose?

They call him Lord Ash, for his desires burn hot and leave devastation in their wake. But Gabriel Finch, Marquess of Ashborough, knows the fortune he's made at the card table won't be enough to save his family estate. For that he needs a bride with a sterling reputation to distract from his tarnished past, a woman who'll be proof against the fires of his dark passion. Fate deals him the perfect lady. So why can't Gabriel keep his eyes from wandering to her outspoken, infuriatingly independent Irish cousin?

Camellia Burke came to London as her aunt's companion, and she's brought a secret with her: she's written a scandalous novel. Now, her publisher demands that she make her fictional villain more realistic. Who better than the notorious Lord Ash as a model? Though Cami feels duty-bound to prevent her cousin from making a disastrous match, she never meant to gamble her own heart away. But when she's called home, Ash follows. And though they're surrounded by the flames of Rebellion, the sparks between them may be the most dangerous of all…

In this captivating new series set in Georgian England, a disgraced woman hides from her marriage—for better or worse…

Sarah Pevensey had hoped her arranged marriage to St. John Sutliffe, Viscount Fairfax, could become something more. But almost before it began, it ended in a scandal that shocked London society. Accused of being a jewel thief, Sarah fled to a small fishing village to rebuild her life.

The last time St. John saw his new wife, she was nestled in the lap of a soldier, disheveled, and no longer in possession of his family's heirloom sapphire necklace. Now, three years later, he has located Sarah and is determined she pay for her crimes. But the woman he finds is far from what he expected. Humble and hardworking, Sarah has nothing to hide from her husband—or so it appears. Yet as he attempts to woo her to uncover her secrets, St. John soon realizes that if he's not careful, she'll steal his heart…

Susanna Craig's dazzling series set in Georgian England sails to the Caribbean—where a willful young woman and a worldly man do their best to run every which way but towards each other…

After her beloved father dies, Tempest Holderin wants nothing more than to fulfill his wish to free the slaves on their Antiguan sugar plantation. But the now wealthy woman finds herself pursued by a pack of unsavory suitors with other plans for her inheritance. To keep her from danger, her dearest friend arranges a most unconventional solution: have Tempest kidnapped and taken to safety.

Captain Andrew Corrvan has an unseemly reputation as a ruthless, money-hungry blackguard—but those on his ship know differently. He is driven by only one thing: the quest to avenge his father's death on the high seas. Until he agrees to abduct a headstrong heiress…

If traveling for weeks—without a chaperone—isn't enough to ruin Tempest, the desire she feels for her dark and dangerously attractive captor will do the rest. The storm brewing between them will only gather strength when they reach England, where past and present perils threaten to tear them apart—even more so than their own stubborn hearts…

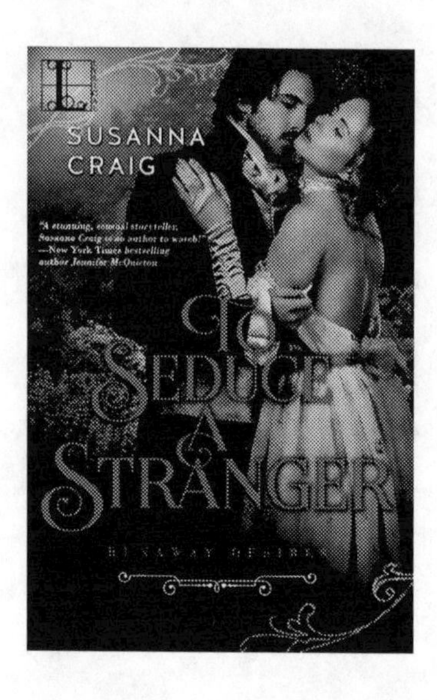

Desire waylays the plans of a man with a mysterious past and a woman with an uncertain future, in Susanna Craig's unforgettable series set in Georgian England.

After her much older husband dies—leaving her his fortune—Charlotte Blakemore finds herself at the mercy of her stepson, who vows to contest the will and destroy her life. With nowhere to turn and no one to help her, she embarks on an elaborate ruse—only to find herself stranded on the way to London…

More than twenty years in the West Indies have hardened Edward Cary, but not enough to abandon a helpless woman at a roadside inn—especially one as disarmingly beautiful as Charlotte. He takes her with him to the Gloucestershire estate he is determined to restore, though he is suspicious of every word that falls from her distractingly lush lips.

As far as Charlotte knows, Edward is nothing more than a steward, and there's no reason to reveal his noble birth until he can right his father's wrongs. Acting as husband and wife will keep people in the village from asking questions that neither Charlotte nor Edward are willing to answer. But the game they're each determined to play has rules that beg to be broken, when the passion between them threatens to uncover the truth—for better or worse…